After digging about two  something scr

I lifted the shovel to clear away the dirt. The blade zinged against something hard underneath the blue plastic tarp, a sound that made me sick at heart. I tossed aside the shovel, fished out my folding knife, straddled the blue cocoon on my knees, and slitted the plastic from the near end. The frozen gray face that stared up at me when I spread the material might have belonged to a marble statue, but it wasn't lifelike enough for that. It was just dead, with one eye shut and the other not seeing. It seemed to be including me in a private joke.

I picked up the shovel again, and used it to lever myself up out of the grave. I felt the chill again now, like clammy chain mail against my slick skin, and put on my suit coat before I went into the inside breast pocket and unfolded the church circular I'd taken from Starzek's supply inside the house trailer. I looked from the face in the picture to the dead face in the ground, with the edges of the tarp framing it like a monk's hood. That seemed appropriate. I was 90 percent sure they were the same. I knew more than I should have about what happens to a human face when the muscles that operate it stop working.

It had the petrified look of something that had been in the earth for ages. I'd spoken to the owner only a little more than twenty-four hours ago. Or someone who'd said he was Paul Starzek over the telephone.

Turn the page to see raves for *Nicotine Kiss* and the Amos Walker series. . . .

NICOTINE KISS

An Amos Walker Novel

Loren D. Estleman

A TOM DOHERTY ASSOCIATES BOOK
NEW YORK

NICOTINE KISS: AN AMOS WALKER NOVEL

Copyright © 2006 by Loren D. Estleman

Edited by James Frenkel

A Forge Book
Published by Tom Doherty Associates, LLC
175 Fifth Avenue
New York, NY 10010

www.tor-forge.com

Forge® is a registered trademark of Tom Doherty Associates, LLC.

The Library of Congress has cataloged the hardcover edition as follows:

Estleman, Loren D.
    Nicotine kiss : an Amos Walker novel / Loren D. Estleman.—1st ed.
        p. cm.
    "A Tom Doherty Associates book."
    ISBN 978-0-7653-1223-5
    1. Walker, Amos (Fictitious character)—Fiction. 2. Private investigators—
Michigan—Fiction. 3. Missing persons—Fiction. 4. Counterfeiters—Fiction.
5. Michigan—Fiction. I. Title.

PS03555.084 N53 2006
813'.54—dc22

                                                                          2005057454

ISBN 978-0-7653-2845-8 (trade paperback)

First Edition: April 2006
First Trade Paperback Edition: March 2011

Printed in the United States of America

0 9 8 7 6 5 4 3 2 1

For John and Mary Ann Verdi-Huss:
patrons of the arts, with the patience of saints

ONE

Someone had disinterred "Big John" from the back of the vintage Rock-Ola. Jimmy Dean's bass struck bedrock on the big, bad refrain, buzzing the speakers and rippling the surface of my Carling Black Label, the muscatel of bottled beer. The neon tubing behind the bar cast rose-petal light over everything.

Spike's Keg o' Nails smelled of beer and cedar and mothballs, the last from the blaze-orange and red-and-black-check coats that had hung in upstairs closets from January to November. Two hunters with sooty eleven o'clock shadows taught body English to the shuffleboard table and some smoke-cured campers from outside town trumped one another at euchre with loud oaths every time a card smacked their table. A graying couple danced, dressed identically in jeans and flannel, and a waitress built like Johnny Bravo fox-trotted between crowded tables hoisting a cityscape of longnecks on a round tray. It was opening day of firearms deer season in Grayling, Michigan, where they close the schools as if it's the Fourth of July, and I was the only relatively sober customer on the premises. Even the ninety-year-old moose head on the wall was listing slightly to the left.

Spike's hadn't changed a tick since I was fourteen and hunting with my father and his friends, and he'd said then it hadn't changed in twenty years. He'd pointed out the corner where he'd once seen Cesar Romero, grinning dazzlingly in his three-day whiskers and ordering rounds for his rumpled party. What might have been the same rickety table and captain's chairs were now occupied by a heavyset blonde with a map of every motel in the northern Lower Peninsula on her face and three National Guardsmen in fatigues from Camp Grayling, plying her with beers. She was older than any two of them combined and looked as if she could drink off a case with one hand and arm-wrestle all three of them with the other. She'd practiced on Cesar and his friends.

I wasn't hunting deer, although I'd dressed for the part in a woolen shirt and lace-up boots and let my beard grow for two days to fit in. A lawyer in Royal Oak had hired my agency of one to find a man named Hegelund and keep him in sight until an officer could arrest him on a warrant for nonpayment of child support. He'd quit his job, canceled his credit cards, and left town, and his ex-wife was at the top of the list of people who hadn't heard from him since June. But he hadn't missed an opening day in Grayling in seven years. Going after deadbeats is a lot like deer hunting: You pick your spot, sit tight, and wait for your trophy to come along. Sooner or later everyone passed through Spike's on his way to the woods.

My heart wasn't in it. The lawyer's client had gotten the house, the car, and the dog, and the sixteen-year-old daughter had moved in with her thirty-seven-year-old boyfriend in Clarkston. Hegelund had walked away from the marriage after years of stagnant counseling, giving up grounds, and hadn't contested a single claim. The picture in my pocket showed a tired face with white flags all over it. Hunting him was like cutting the weak and aged from the herd. But I had winter taxes to pay and deadbeat dads are 15 percent of my income.

An hour before closing, the hardcore sportsmen who got up at 5:00 A.M. started evaporating, the juke ran out of dead country singers and sausage tycoons, and the clinking bottles and loud card tournament became the only ambient noises in the room. Then the piano began to tinkle.

I hadn't even known the place had one, but there it was, a basic upright no one had tuned since the moose had reached the age of consent. The party seated on the bench was built close to the ground and wide across the back, like the concrete stop at the end of a railroad. He had a full head of chestnut-colored hair, razored carefully at the nape, and wore a brown leather Windbreaker too thin for the North Country and tan cords rubbed shiny in patches, scuffed white high-tops on his feet. He wasn't my man, but I recognized him from behind. I got up and carried my beer over.

"I wouldn't wear that outfit into the woods." I parked the bottle next to his glass on top of the piano. "You could wind up on the buck pole downtown."

Jeff Starzek didn't look up. His glass wasn't for drinking. It was filled with clear liquid, probably water, and reflected most of the room like a convex mirror. That wasn't any more an accident than his fingering. He was playing Rachmaninoff. I could tell, because there were too many notes and they were batting away at one another like hockey players. "They better shoot fast. I can do eighty on those sand trails."

"Still driving that Charger?"

"Challenger." His stubby fingers scampered across the bridge. "Not anymore. I cracked the block in Kentucky. It's hard to read a 'Water Over the Road' sign when you're topping a hill at a hundred and five."

"You must've been running hot for some time."

"Still am. How about you, Amos? Still climbing trellises?"

"I'm climbing one now."

"Not mine. I wouldn't have seen you coming."

"You're federal game," I said. "I can't meet their dress code."

"I can outrun the feds okay. These days they're spread pretty thin. It's the troopers I have to watch out for. That new tax hike's got them all angling for commander."

I asked him what he was driving. He smiled at the keys. He had a moon face and a delicately curved mouth with hard muscles at the corners. A lock of hair broke over his left eyebrow. No face or body looked less like Ben Affleck's, yet women responded to him. It wasn't the danger, because he didn't tell them what he did for a living. He didn't talk much at all, in fact, which may have been the secret. People who don't have a lot to say get the reputation of being good listeners. In his case it was true. But he could always talk about cars.

"Hurst Olds," he said. "Sixty-nine."

"Four fifty-five. I've got that in my Cutlass."

"I bought it for the trunk. I can squeeze in a dozen more cartons than I could in the Dodge." He screwed up his face. "You think you could blow that somewhere else?"

I'd lit a cigarette. I laid it in a tray on an empty table. "What are you hauling?"

"Kiddie cigs. Marlboros."

"You smuggle 'em, but you don't smoke 'em?"

"Ever hear of Larry Fay?"

"Old-time song-and-dance man."

"That's Eddie Foy. Fay was a big-time bootlegger in New York during Prohibition. Never touched a drop."

"Rumrunners are a lot more popular now than Big Tobacco."

"Better PR. And I'm not big."

I'd met Jeff Starzek when he was running interference for truckloads of cargo hijacked from Detroit Metropolitan Airport. He'd painted his 1970 Dodge Challenger a shade of orange you could see from outer space and averaged thirty miles over the speed limit all the way to Chicago, drawing cops, like Buster Keaton, toward him and away from the big rigs and their contraband. He had more license suspensions than a drunken congressman and no convictions for anything more serious than reckless driving. At the time I'd been tracing a teenage runaway who'd mixed himself up with the operation. If Starzek hadn't broken precedent and told me what I'd needed to know, the kid might have gone on jumping from one felony to another until he wound up behind chain-link and razor wire. He might have anyway, for all I knew, but I returned him to his parents for however long he stayed.

The next time I'd seen Starzek, he'd gone into business for himself, hauling much smaller shipments of cigarettes bought in lower-tax states and on Indian reservations where no taxes were paid and selling them to wholesalers and party stores at a profit. The merchants sold the cigarettes over the counter and pocketed the amount that would have gone to Lansing. That time, the smuggler was a client; someone had sold a store in Eastpointe a case of menthols laced with pesticide, Starzek had been arrested on a tip, and although charges were dropped for lack of evidence, the family of a customer who'd died of poisoning had brought civil suit against Starzek, who claimed he'd never done business in Eastpointe. Everything I turned pointed to the store manager's son-in-law, who'd stolen the case from a shipment targeted for destruction after a crop-dusting blunder in Virginia.

By then, of course, Starzek was known to the Bureau of Alcohol, Tobacco, and Firearms, and just repainting his Challenger an unassuming brown wasn't enough to keep agents from hauling him over and running him through the system.

"I thought you'd retired," I said.

"Diversified is the word." He trilled a finger down the keyboard

Jerry Lee Lewis style. "I'm carrying something else back down the coast."

"I won't ask what."

"Honestly, who cares?"

I gave him the point. It wasn't anything to me whether he smuggled Lucky Strikes or fake Beanie Babies. The tax just went into the bail fund for state senators.

I swigged beer. It was warm already. The bar was overheated, like every other place up there in late fall. "Well, good luck. That lake effect from Chicago's a bitch when it snows."

"Wrong coast. I like the little towns on Huron. Everybody minds his own business and the feds stick out like ears on a frog."

"In nineteen-fifty, maybe. They're as suspicious as in the city."

"Cynic."

"Pirate."

The square-shouldered waitress box-stepped our way to announce last call. Starzek, who hadn't touched his water, shook his head. I was looking at my watch and wondering if waiting twenty more minutes would make any difference when Hegelund came in.

His face looked sadder and more tired under an orange cap with a buck silhouetted on the front. He wore a camouflage coat with splashes of orange on it and insulated boots that flapped about his ankles. I ordered another beer and started back to my table, not making eye contact.

Maybe I was too conscientious about it. You try to make your mind blank, just in case there's something to telepathy, but prey always has the advantage. Hegelund didn't know me from J.D. Salinger, but he stopped when he saw me, turned around, and trotted back out. I gave him fifteen seconds, then left cash for the beers including the one I had coming and followed, casual as a picnic.

I'd parked in the dirt lot next to the building, pale under the phantom glow of a mercury bulb with a light dusting of snow. My breath curled. There among the campers, pickups, and RVs was Starzek's Hurst/Olsmobile, painted light blue—that year's version of plain brown—and built along the lines of my Cutlass, but with twin scoops punched into the hood. He'd have reinforced the springs to keep the rear end from sagging under its load and bolted the bumpers with angle irons to the frame, in order to run roadblocks and sustain ramming from behind. I didn't get down to look. It would have a new transmission and a rebuilt engine. Everything else that might have slowed him down—radio, heater, rear seat, spare tire—would have been stripped away. It was a power plant on wheels, with space for cargo and an operator.

Hegelund was driving an eight-year-old Jeep Cherokee, parked on the edge of the lot near the street. The lawyers hadn't left him enough to buy anything younger. Rust had nibbled at the wheel wells and someone had taped thick plastic over a missing window in back. He'd had luck; a shaggy spikehorn buck lay on the roof, lashed in place with clothesline around its hooves fore and aft. Shaking loose my keys, I watched Hegelund out of the corner of my eye as he bent to reach into the backseat. I was walking down a rutted aisle between rows of cars.

I heard the crash and felt the jolt when my shoulder hit the ground. My leg never felt the impact and for an instant I thought I'd slipped on a patch of ice. Then I felt the numbness below my waist and knew I'd taken a lead slug big enough to change my life. I began to float away from the light. The second crash belonged to something that had no connection with me.

TWO

missed the second half of November, which in Michigan is no great loss, but I was out of the hospital in time for Christmas, which was. Herds of fat busted cops in gamey security uniforms prowled the malls, and everyone who had ever been rejected by *American Idol* seemed to have released a holiday album. My little monastic cell on the third floor of an office building as old as gunpowder looked like a heap of boiled rice after all the colored lights.

I was getting around with a cane, which an emergency room nurse told me would have been a plastic leg if a "short fat guy" hadn't scooped me up off the parking lot and delivered me to the Grayling hospital in less time than it took to put an ambulance on the scene. He hadn't stayed long enough to give his name, but I knew Jeff Starzek from the description, even if it wasn't strictly accurate; his bulk was mostly muscle and he was taller than he looked. I didn't mind his not checking in later to find out my condition. Cops swarm thick around hospitals and some of the incoming calls are recorded. He could have left me there to bleed out and avoided all risk.

An ambulance with twice the horsepower of his Hurst/Olds

couldn't have done anything for Hegelund. The way the police worked it out, he'd put a .30–30 round through his head from the same deer rifle he'd used on me while I was still trying to figure out what had happened. I was his last defiant act, and maybe his only one. He had long arms, a carbon test on his hands and clothing indicated his wound was self-inflicted, and none of the patrons and employees of Spike's reported seeing anyone else in the lot when they piled out after the shots. No one knows anyone, not well enough to predict what he'll do in a corner, fight or surrender. He'd done both. Maybe his blood had been up from the deer kill. In any case, it didn't last. I said he'd looked tired.

Cranked up in bed in ICU I told the cops who I was working for and why. They didn't believe me when I said I didn't know who the short fat guy was and that I'd only struck up a conversation with him in the bar because I liked the way he played piano, but they didn't lean too hard. They don't get many shootings up there except the accidental kind in the woods, and when they get one all sealed in shrink-wrap they don't poke at it. Also I'd just been upgraded from critical.

I never found out how Hegelund knew I was looking for him, or even if he did. Putting aside metaphysics, I guessed he was suspicious of everyone, and I fit the mold. You don't do what I do for as many years as I've done it without taking on some of the physical characteristics of a rat terrier. Whoever had represented him in the divorce might have had an informant in his ex-wife's legal firm, who'd seen me in the office and had a gift for description. It's screwy to give a lawyer the benefit of the doubt when it comes to ethics. None of this was as certain as the throbbing in my leg when it rains, or the limp when I'm tired or forget myself.

The bullet had gone clean through, missing the bone but taking away enough meat and muscle to stuff a softball, and the surgeon who cleaned and dressed the canal told me I'd owe whatever mobility I regained to muscles designed for another purpose. The client paid me for my time and took care of the medical expenses, including six weeks on the parallel bars at Henry Ford Hospital. All in all, it was the most I'd ever made from one case, even if it had all been spent on probes and painkillers. I hadn't been armed that night; it didn't seem to be that kind of job, and anyway I wouldn't have gotten the chance to fire anything but a distress signal into the air from a prone position. It had happened that fast.

Barry Stackpole, an old friend, drove the six-hour round trip to bring me home after my release from Grayling, and drove it again a month later to retrieve my Cutlass when I had enough strength in my leg to work the pedal. Since one of his legs was man-made and he had a steel plate in his skull, I didn't complain about my infirmity, just the loss of work. He offered a loan, which I declined. One of the advantages of living so close to the poverty level is you're never paralyzed worrying about money. It's just like being rich, only without the good Scotch and cigars.

"I can swing something your way," he said when we were cruising between two solid banks of motels with vacancies along the strip outside town; one month earlier they'd been booked to the roofs. "I'm negotiating a ghost job on the memoirs of a Korean mobster currently in the witness-protection program. He says. I want his background checked."

Barry's a freelance crime reporter, the author of several books on the Mafia and all its franchises, and a long-standing speed bump in the road to ill-gotten gains. That's how he got the leg and the hubcap in his head.

I said, "I didn't know there were Korean mobsters."

"These days they come in all colors. This one says he swung asylum from the Justice Department after he ratted out some fellow racket guys in Seoul. He could be a mob plant to find out what I know about a couple of parties I steered into witness protection.

They're all pretty much scum, but I'm not going to turn finger for a six-figure deal and a spot on the Book Channel."

"Check him with Justice."

"That would be awkward. They don't know I know what I know. If they suspect, I might have to join the program myself. The government boys play for blood since nine-one-one."

I plucked out a cigarette. Before I got it lit, he had the window down on my side. Barry was on a health kick: no liquor, no secondhand smoke, fresh box of condoms first of every month even if he hadn't used up last month's supply. I threw the match into the slipstream. It froze my fingers on contact. "I don't know how you keep it all straight."

"That's because you keep company with a different class of crook." He buzzed the window back up partway.

I'd told him about Starzek. We hadn't any secrets from each other except when one of us was working. "There are crooks and crooks," I said. "This one never stole a dollar or an election."

"I'd keep my distance. Cigarette smugglers have terrorist ties. I read it in *USA Today*."

"That's just a dodge to shame people into paying the tax."

"Either way it's heat. Where's the impound?"

He'd stopped for a light at the main four corners. There were sporting-goods stores in both blocks with survival gear in the windows and a concrete movie house playing one feature three days each week. Everything had the trod-on look of a neglected dog. Strip malls are called strip malls for a reason.

I got out the paper with directions and read them off. We went there and I paid my fee and found him still sitting behind the wheel when I came out of the office. He was driving a brand-new maroon Lincoln that year, shaped like a cough drop. It would be registered to someone else. He was a professional sociopath, never left a paper trail.

When he opened his window I leaned on the sill. "Thanks for waiting. Also the ride. Can I let you know about the godfather of Seoul?"

"Sure. I can always stall him by demanding an 'As Told To' credit. If he's legit he'll never agree to it."

"In that case, you might not need the background check."

He gave me his slow easy smile. "Well, once you've been blown up, you tend to double-team."

I gave him back a wave and limped around to the garage side. Behind me I heard his engine start and when it didn't explode this time he drove off.

Nothing came of the Korean job. I was still thinking about it when Barry called and said his would-be collaborator had turned out to be a Hyundai dealer from Phoenix who'd made up the story to impress a girlfriend and hadn't known when to bail out. The confession had come under pressure from Barry; the man knew too much about the details of zero-percent financing for an ordinary thief.

By then I had an employee-fraud job, nothing too strenuous, just a couple of hours in the evening parked behind the Troy K-Mart, videotaping stockroom clerks stashing new DVD players in a Dumpster. My leg interrupted my concentration when I'd been sitting too long, but changing positions took care of that. By the time I'd gathered enough evidence to prosecute, I'd found new uses for the cane, such as flipping the telephone receiver out of its cradle into my hand when I didn't feel like tipping my office chair forward. I was getting to be as good with it as Charlie Chaplin.

The nightmares took longer to get used to. You hear a lot about wound trauma in the physical sense, but no matter where you get shot it always ends up in your head. I woke up plenty of times with my sheets soaked through with sweat, sure it was blood. I wished the Hyundai dealer hadn't let Barry down. I needed the work more than my bank account did.

Christmas came and went, as it will despite Marshall Field's best efforts to keep it alive through Super Sunday. The all-purpose, no-offense holiday display in front of the City-County Building came down, spruces and Scotch pines turned orange in the gutters. Most of the toys were broken and the kittens had all outgrown their red ribbons and started in on the furniture. I made a host of calls, but I couldn't even land a security job until I could outrun an old-lady shoplifter in a slick parking lot.

Dick Clark doddered in the new year, and I reminded myself to use it when I postdated my checks. I stayed home on the holiday to look in on the multimillionaires in pads and helmets, woke up the next dawn lying in a pool of blood behind Spike's Keg o' Nails, and instead of going back to sleep got dressed and made coffee. Twenty minutes later I let myself into the office from a street swept bare of life. Behind the desk I dozed until the first spasm of the day sent me into the water closet for Vicodin.

While I was washing it down with water from the tap, I heard the door from the hall open and close. The buzzer had been out of service since September. I hadn't bothered to have it fixed because there is little off-the-street trade in the investigation business, and none at all on my street. I stumped to the connecting door and opened it on the first knock.

"Are you Walker?"

I confessed to that condition and hooked the cane over my left wrist to shake the man's hand. He gave mine a brief squeeze that would have bunched my fingers like copper wire if I hadn't shoved them deep into his fist from instinct. He was my height, with the sloped shoulders of a tired grizzly and a head the size of a soup kettle and just about as easy to dent. He was completely bald—not even a fringe—wore no hat on the coldest January day in recent memory, and burned cranberry red from his crown to the coarse black hairs twisting out of his open collar. I placed him at forty; he could have been fifty-five and cured in the barrel. He had on a blue Detroit Edison uniform and tractor-tread boots with the toes worn down to the steel caps.

"I'm Oral Canon," he said. "It's pronounced like the artillery piece, only you spell it with two *n*'s, not three."

"Like the camera. Any relation?"

"Not the money side."

He had a deep, burring voice, like a circular saw on idle. I said I had the same arrangement with my cousin Hiram and pointed the cane at the customer's chair. He used two inches of the seat, bracing his hands on his thighs. They were big-veined hands, the kind that were comfortable in work gloves, and wore a class ring and a plain gold wedding band on the usual fingers. "I'm a splicing technician. I'm supposed to be on the job now."

"What's a splicing technician?" I sat down behind the desk.

"A guy that climbs poles in a blizzard so's you can make popcorn in the microwave."

"A lineman."

He swiveled his eyes. "Sure, if you're Glen Campbell."

That explained his coloring. The sun bounces hard off the snow when you're thirty feet up.

"What can I do for you, Mr. Canon-with-two-*n*'s?"

"You can pay your phone bill for starters. I tried to call twice, in case I dialed wrong first time. You're disconnected. That's why I had to take off work and come downtown."

I lifted the handset. I got a dial tone and hung up. "What number did you call?"

He unbuttoned the flap over a breast pocket, drew out a narrow pasteboard slip, and handed it across to me between two fingers. The business card was soiled and fuzzy around the edges and the corners were dogeared. I read A. WALKER INVESTIGATIONS, the office number and building address, and the telephone number.

"I haven't had this number in two years," I said. "It was one digit off from the Venus Escort Service. I had to keep turning away calls from the mayor." I held out the card.

He didn't take it. "It was all I had. My wife's brother sent it to her in a Christmas card. It came the day after Christmas. He never has been on time for anything except his damn drop-offs."

"Who's your brother-in-law?"

"Jeff Starzek. I figure you must know him or he wouldn't have sent the card."

I fingered the worn edges. Jeff must have been carrying it around in his wallet for years. I didn't remember giving it to him. "He say why he sent it?"

"I don't even know for sure it was him sent it, except Rose recognized the writing. There wasn't a return address and the postmark just said 'U.S. Postal Service.' He didn't even sign the Christmas card. All he wrote's there on the back."

I turned over the business card. I'd never seen a sample of Starzek's handwriting, but the pencil script looked like him, no frills and impossible to misunderstand:

Rose—if you don't hear from me by the first of the year, hire this man.

THREE

My leg twinged. I let it. The Vicodin had blunted the sharp point. I made a meaningless little cricket noise on the desktop with the edge of the card. Oral Canon watched me. If he'd blinked since he came in I'd missed it.

"When was the last time you heard from him before he sent the card?" I asked.

"First week of November. Rose invited him for Thanksgiving and he called to say he was making a run up north and probably wouldn't be back in time. You know he's a smuggler."

I nodded. "I ran into him in Grayling on the fifteenth. He said he had a load of Marlboros and another delivery to make down the Huron shoreline afterwards."

"Well, that's more than he told his sister. I guess you're an accomplice." He got everything you can out of the word, and there's plenty to get.

"I just smoke 'em. Did you file a missing-persons?"

"I wanted to, but Rose said no. She don't want to have to go down to Milan once a month just to see him. It didn't do any good to tell her she'd be seeing him more often than she does now. It sure wouldn't make her any more miserable. She's soft on him, always has been. That's why he went bad. She as good as raised him after their mother walked out. The old man was a drunk."

"She didn't do as bad a job as you think. That day in Grayling he saved my life."

"That how you got crippled?"

I gave that one a pass. I'd been tested enough for one season. "I can find him, if he wants to be found. It won't be easy. He doesn't file flight plans."

He unbuttoned the other flap and smacked a roll down on the desk. Ben Franklin's face looks swollen on the new currency.

"I'm not angling for cash," I said. "Your wife should know it will take time."

"I just came off five solid days on duty after that blow in Oakland County last week, with double time for the holiday. It's either this or a plasma TV. I don't watch that much."

I separated three C-notes from the bale and parked them under the stapler. "Expenses. I figure I owe Jeff the rest."

"This ain't for him, it's for Rose. We never took a penny from that damn crook. I pay you or I pay somebody else that ain't so shy."

I blew air. I didn't know if I wanted to shake his paw again or break my cane over that head.

"Twelve hundred more for the retainer," I said. "I refund the time I don't use. Have you got a recent photo? I know what he looks like, but the people I'll be showing it to won't."

He peeled off a dozen more bills, got a wallet-size out of the same pocket, and laid it on top. Starzek had a smile on his face I'd never seen and one arm around a good-looking brunette in her middle thirties. "Rose?"

He nodded, and the expression on his big face when he looked down at the picture made me dislike him a little less. "You know how you see the prettiest women hanging all over the asshole-ugliest apes? I figure I had the brother-in-law coming."

"Where can I reach you?"

He made another trip to his portable office and planted a DTE Energy card—what they're calling it now—on the pile. It contained his name, the company's business number, and the number of a cell phone. "Home's on the back. Don't call it over any old thing. The baby might be sleeping."

I reeled it all in. "I don't guess you or Rose would know if he was in trouble."

"No, and that's the only good thing I can think to say about him. This is the first flare he ever sent up." He looked at a watch strapped to his wrist; not pointedly, but no sneaking either. You can tell a lot about a man by the way he looks at his watch. This one only wanted to know what time it was. He stood up.

"I'll be in touch when I have something," I said; and he was gone. The outer door closed on him as quietly as drifting snow.

I was putting the cash in the safe, minus a few hundred for gas and desk clerks, when the telephone rang.

"I wasn't sure I'd get you this early," said the voice in my ear. "I thought all you plastic badges staggered in two hours late the day after New Year's."

Lieutenant Mary Ann Thaler doesn't sound half as sexy as she looks, and the way she sounds turns 911 into 900. She's with Felony Homicide, which is the closest thing the Detroit Police Department has to a detective without portfolio. Every crime in the city falls under her jurisdiction as long as it includes a citizen at room temperature.

"I staggered in at seven," I said. "What's the body count so far this year?"

"I missed the box scores. How long are you there?"

"About six feet, same as at home."

She closed the curtain on the act. "Company manners. I'm bringing a guest."

I said I'd clear my calendar. She said she'd be there in thirty minutes.

Welcome to the new year.

The twinge in my leg didn't qualify as a twinge anymore. It felt like a root canal starting at the knee. I went into the water closet and studied the little folding program that came with the bottle of Vicodin. I wasn't to take it with alcohol under any circumstances; but it had been twenty minutes since I took it.

That was the loophole I'd been looking for. I went back to the desk and poured an inch and a half from the bottle of single malt I'd bought myself for Christmas. I wanted a healthy glow, not the three days in Tijuana I get from the radiator wash I drink the rest of the year. When the glass was empty the pain was still there, but I had paying work, an appointment with a cop, and a mysterious visitor. Liquor was mandatory.

The outer door opened at thirty minutes on the point. I'd left the connecting door open. She found me standing behind the desk without the support of the cane: male vanity, and trouble for nothing. She spotted the stick leaning against the windowsill.

"Where's your straw hat?"

"Where are your glasses?"

"Lasik. I only need them for reading now."

"Put them on. Only plain women are safe on this street."

That irked her in a way it only does women who would never be described as plain. "So what happened?"

"I got shot. And how was your holiday?"

She had her brown hair pulled back, but it only called attention to the long smooth line of her neck. She'd wrapped herself in one of those knee-length glossy black all-weather coats, with a tall collar and a belt around the waist. Fur-topped boots and a shoulder bag big enough to hold a SIG-Sauer automatic, three clips, and the usual feminine bric-a-brac. She looked like a Midwestern version of Marlene Dietrich. A pretty woman, and a cop who liked her job just a little too much.

"Amos Walker, this is Herbert Clemson. Clemson's with Homeland Security."

I gave her companion some attention then. He was thirtyish, slim, dark, and curly-haired, in a long charcoal coat trimmed with fur grown in some lab. He had chilly gray eyes and a carefully tended five o'clock shadow, the kind you see in men's cologne ads. His chin was deeply cleft. I hated him with all the healthy instincts of the alpha male.

He showed me a gold badge and his picture in a pigskin folder. Of course I shook his hand. Here was another healthy grip, but he wasn't too generous with it. I asked him who was winning the war on terror.

He smiled. "We are, at the moment. It's still early innings."

We all stayed standing. There was only one chair for visitors, and most of the time I could have hired it out to the rare coin dealer down the hall. I propped my hip against the desk. I felt hot from my belt to my pant cuff and cold everywhere else.

"Agent Clemson's territory covers Michigan, Ohio, Indiana, and the eastern portion of Illinois," Thaler said. "Today he's in Detroit. Tomorrow, Chicago. You and I could live in Tahiti on what Uncle pays him by the mile."

I said, "I knew an encyclopedia salesman who covered all that and Canada. But the worst he had to deal with was a housewife with sewing shears. Find any new sleeper cells in Dearborn?"

Dearborn is the cradle of the American automobile industry, and incidentally the largest concentration of Arabs outside the Middle East. There are some Cold War leftovers who want to surround it with reinforced concrete and razor wire, but then there would be nobody left to sell liquor and gasoline.

Clemson's face went flat. "That's racial profiling."

A sweaty little silence followed. Thaler broke up then, laughing like a drunken teenage girl. I gaped at her.

"He's pulling your leg," she said. "Feds have changed since Melvin Purvis. Some of them can even tell a joke."

Clemson smiled.

I realized the bottle was still standing on the desk. "Do they drink?"

The agent's eyes prowled the walls, searching for a clock. There wasn't one. I measured time by the whiskers on my chin.

"It's early for me, but help yourself."

"That would be detective profiling." I put the bottle back in the cellar.

"Give it up," Thaler said. "He won't prod. We went through all that when he came to my office. Agent Clemson wants to consult with you."

"I always suspected I had a file in Washington. I didn't know anyone ever checked it out."

"He never heard of you before this morning. I fed him your name."

Clemson said, "It's about contraband traffic."

"Pirate DVDs?"

"They're a serious problem—in Hollywood," he said. "Personally and professionally, I don't care. I'm interested in cigarettes."

A carpet shark clamped down on my leg. I sat, fighting the urge to flop. I'd had a bugging incident recently, and still had some residual paranoia. Cigarette smuggling doesn't come up twice in one morning, even in Detroit. Drugs are the common coin.

"Sorry," I said. "Sometimes it feels like all one hundred and seventy grains are still in there."

Agent Clemson looked interested. "Thirty-thirty?"

I hesitated. "Ballistics?"

"Six months in Quantico. It's standard training now for field agents."

I expected him to ask about details, but he'd finished talking. He was the least curious G-man I'd ever met. I asked him to sit down.

"Lieutenant?" he said.

"I'm no lady." Thaler was looking at me. "The reason for this field trip is a name came up in conversation in my office. When I opened that file on the computer, yours popped up, just like a Viagra ad. Let's just cut the comic relief and say you and Jeff Starzek go way back."

"Way back is right. I haven't had any business with him in five years." Which was true enough.

"Glad to hear it. The people he's doing business with these days are nobody's choice for Good Neighbor of the Year. Not this side of the Persian Gulf," she added.

"Terrorists?"

"At this point we're calling them 'persons of concern.' " Clemson kept his face as flat as paint.

"He *can* tell a joke," I told Thaler.

"We need to talk to Starzek before we upgrade them," he said. "It's possible he isn't aware of the full extent of what he's involved in. One way he can convince us of that is to tell us what he does know. But no one seems to have seen him in weeks. Even his former associates can't get in touch with him, and we've offered them plenty of incentive."

"Did you talk to his family?"

"He's never been married."

"I didn't think he had. I meant a brother or sister."

"He has a brother twenty years older, who's some kind of a preacher in Port Huron. They haven't spoken since the Eighties. After meeting him, I believe him. No sister."

I broke open a fresh pack, to give me something safe to frown at. I let him see the tax stamp.

"I buy at places like Seven-Eleven," I said, "or cross into Ohio when the state ups the ante. All I know about the tobacco business is how much I burn by the day or week."

"I'm not talking about cigarettes now. That's ATF, and if you think Home Security has issues, you've never dealt with that bureau. Starzek's branched out in a whole new direction."

I met his chilly gray gaze and tried to make my mind blank. I succeeded just the way I had in business. *Diversified is the word.* Starzek's word, accompanied by himself on piano. He'd said he was carrying something else back down the coast.

Jeff Starzek, who had no sister named Rose and therefore no brother-in-law named Oral Canon.

"The specific nature of his cargo is classified." Nothing in Clemson's expression said he'd read anything in mine. "It always will be, if we can get to him before he makes delivery. If he's been duped, as we think, he may just walk."

"Is that on the table?"

"I said 'may.' I'm not authorized to speak for the attorney general. At least he'll keep his citizenship."

He produced another pigskin folder from a side pocket and dealt me a card with the usual eagle on it, armed to the beak and carrying a box lunch. "The cell and pager's in the lower left-hand corner," he said. "If you hear from Starzek, or remember anything helpful, I'd appreciate the call." He stuck out his hand again before I could get up. I shook it.

"Lieutenant?" he said.

"Wait for me."

She watched me light up a cigarette while the office door closed and then the one to the hall.

I dropped the match in the ashtray and poked Clemson's card

under the wooden base. "How you getting along with the new chief?"

"What's not to like? She's a woman." She wasn't smiling.

" 'Duped,' " I said. "He said it. You heard him say it."

"It's in the dictionary."

"So's 'brigand,' but he didn't hang around long enough to use it. I guess you checked his credentials."

"They checked." She pointed her eyebrows toward the cane. "It's my business to ask. Don't read anything into it like I care."

"Hunting accident up north. Somebody mistook me for a buck."

"Try again. You don't resemble Bambi even a little bit."

I gave it to her then, all except Starzek. He lifted right out. "I think it got a paragraph in the *News* or *Free Press*. Probably not both."

"Doesn't matter. I was on jury duty all last month. It eats into keeping up with current events."

"What defense attorney would put you on a jury?"

"Is it permanent?"

"Just about everything is this side of forty. But I plan to donate the stick to the Lion's Club before Easter. They can paint it white and give it to an umpire." I sat back, smoking and stretching out the leg. "I'm considering retirement."

"Seriously?"

"No. I anticipated the suggestion."

"I wasn't even thinking it. Someone else would just creep into the empty space and I'd have to get used to a whole new set of misdemeanors."

"I'd miss you too. I was just waiting for you to say it first."

She flashed me a signal that was not the universal sign of affection and left me alone with my thoughts.

I chewed another pill and almost washed it down with Scotch

before I remembered what happened to Judy Garland. I went back to the sink for water and when I came out I was surprised not to find another visitor in the slot.

Two walk-ins in one morning. If this kept up, I'd have to put in another chair.

FOUR

thought for a while and when I got tired of thinking I dug out Oral Canon's card and picked up the telephone. His cell wasn't answering. I broke the connection and tried the number he'd written on the back, which he'd said went to his home. If there was no Rose Starzek Canon there probably was no baby either. An annoying female bray came on after five rings and offered to let me record a message for a dollar six bits. I cradled the receiver for free.

There were no Canons in the metropolitan directory, but when I called an operator she told me there was a number in Belleville but I couldn't have it. She wouldn't confirm it was the one I had. Next I got a dispatcher at DTE Energy and asked if Oral Canon worked there. I tried to sound like a worried homeowner with a stranger at his door. The worried part wasn't hard. The dispatcher put me on hold for thirty seconds and said they had a splicing technician by that name and that he was on the road.

I dialed Barry Stackpole and gave up six rings in. Most of the people who tried to reach him didn't like to leave voice prints behind, so he'd never bothered with a machine. Anyway he was a long shot. If Canon wasn't mobbed up, Barry wouldn't know him from Paris Hilton.

I sat there listening to traffic stumbling over potholes on West Grand and felt like the old man on the rock. I had no wisdom to impart and none coming. I called another operator and asked for the number of a Starzek in Port Huron, where Agent Clemson had said Jeff's brother was some kind of preacher. She found a Paul Starzek on something called Old Carriage Lane and tripped the switch on a recording with the number. I let Ma Bell dial it for me; I was getting a case of tennis elbow.

"Church of the Freshwater Sea," blatted a voice on the second ring. It seemed to have come with its own built-in amplifier. I held the receiver out from my ear.

"Paul Starzek?"

"This is Dr. Starzek. The church is closed for the season. Call me in April."

"I'm good for now," I said. "My name's Walker, Dr. Starzek. I'm a Michigan State licensed investigator calling from Detroit. I'm trying to locate your brother Jeff."

"Why do you people keep bothering me?" he blared. "I withheld myself from that foul trafficker fifteen years ago. I'm not his keeper."

"My motives are different. I'm not with the federal government."

"That's what the last one said."

"What last one was that?" But I was talking to an empty line.

I listened to the dial tone and unplugged myself from the system. I sat back and played with the cane, twirling the crook. My leg felt better but my head was starting to hurt. Herbert Clemson was a fast man with his credentials. He didn't seem the type to claim he was a private citizen even if it would get him what he wanted. Being a private citizen myself, I didn't know just when that would be. And if there had been a "last one" coming to him with questions, that was one more than I knew about.

Finally, if fifteen years had passed since the Starzek brothers had had any contact, Jeff had been a teenager, with all his foul trafficking days far ahead of him. The Reverend Dr. Starzek lied as well as any sinner in his flock.

There was no reason to take the thing further, especially when I had an appointment with my physical therapist that afternoon. No reason at all, except if it weren't for a ten-cent smuggler in thousand-dollar trouble the only appointment on my calendar would be with the embalmer. The therapist had warmer hands.

I hadn't been to Port Huron in years. I wondered if they'd cleaned up the beach.

Michigan has two industries, automaking and tourism. When either of them catches cold, the state catches pneumonia, and the EMS team has to break out the paddles to jump-start Port Huron's heart.

When the logging business ran out of trees under President Cleveland, the sawmills shut down, and with them the railroads connecting them to Flint, Saginaw, and Ludington, clear across the state on Lake Michigan. Port Huron sold pencils for a while from a tin cup. When the foundries in Detroit couldn't keep up with the production lines at Ford and General Motors, steelmaking plants sprang up on the mouth of the St. Clair River where Lake Huron emptied into Lake St. Clair. Then miles of white beach opened for business, and for a little while, until the black flies came and the superhighway system discovered Miami, the place was a little northern Riviera three months out of the year, complete with freshwater clam restaurants propped up on piers and "Rhapsody in Blue" drifting out from a bandshell. On a hot Sunday in July or August, striped umbrellas still crowd the shoreline, and the sails of the Port Huron–to-Mackinac Race blot out the blue water in midsummer, but most of the time it's the sanitation crews shoveling up dead fish and old condoms who get the best tans. On the first iron-scraped workday of the year, the place was Moscow, with a view of Ontario.

Downtown's an hour's drive north of Detroit when you obey the speed limit. I made it in forty minutes, and two state troopers passed me without their flashers on. Throttling down from the off-ramp, I drove past the county courthouse and a row of sidewalk cafes, closed for the season with snow skirting the ornamental fencework, and then followed the wide river north, where gray empty sky seemed to be reflecting the surface of the big lake rather than the other way around. A couple of disgruntled-looking gulls picked at something frozen in the crags of boulders left by ancient oceans and polished by waves as tall as watchtowers. Kelp lay in loose black coils on the sand with empty Coke cans winking among them in the diffused light like giant squid eyes. But they say even Beale Street looks desolate after Mardi Gras.

I had a book of county maps open to St. Clair County on the seat beside me, with the secondary roads marked out in blue ball-point. I almost missed Old Carriage Lane at that, and had to back up to read the sign, marked PRIVATE ROAD and pitted all over with rust and .22 slugs. I followed broken pavement between Grim Reaper trees and metal-sided bungalows that had started out as tarpaper shacks, most of them shuttered until spring, with here and there a boat trailer sunk up to its hubs in snow and chained to a post in the front yard. You can still buy property up there by the acre instead of the foot, as long as it doesn't touch the lake. From there it's all high six-figure log mansions and Frank Lloyd Wright knockoffs with pontoons and cabin cruisers tied up to sheltered docks like four-car garages.

The road angled down from the highway, bootjacked, and

ended in an egg-shaped turnaround, with plenty of pine and brush separating it from the beach. I parked in front of a 1950s house trailer on concrete blocks with no footprints in the snow around it and backtracked on foot. I had no address for Paul Starzek, but a 1979 Dodge Club Cab was parked in front of a no-longer-mobile home of the same vintage with a magnetic sign on the cab:

CHURCH OF THE FRESHWATER SEA
P. Starzek, Pastor

Behind the house rose a pole barn of dull aluminum with icicles drooling from its green roof. It didn't look much like a place of worship, but then Pastor Starzek had not sounded much like Bing Crosby over the telephone.

I had to be careful where I placed the tip of my cane. There were patches of ice, and drifting snow had filled in the potholes, smoothing them over like tiger traps. Private roads are only as well kept as the people who live on them, and from the look of it, Old Carriage Lane hadn't seen a snowplow or a fresh coat of asphalt since tubeless tires.

Starzek's driveway, at least, was open, and his steps swept. My hands came away from the painted metal railing with a peeling sound and the two-by-eights were frozen hard as iron; there was no give under my feet. I used the doorbell, sheltered in a bell-shaped depression plated in dirty brass. I couldn't hear if it worked. I rapped on the metal frame of the storm door. When nothing came of that I let myself back down the steps and hobbled around behind.

The door to the pole barn was sealed with a combination padlock on a hasp. I'm no good with combinations and hadn't the equipment with me to get around it the blue-collar way, and in any case I wasn't curious enough to damage property. The door hadn't been opened since the last snow; it was drifted up over the sill. I went around, cupped my hands, and peered through a storm window. I saw rows of folding metal chairs, a woodstove, a trestle table with a lectern set on it as at a Friars Club roast. It was all pretty dim. Sheeted shapes suggested the building doubled as storage in the absence of the faithful.

I shifted my angle—and flinched when I saw a human face staring back at me. It belonged to an armless naked male store mannequin standing on a platform behind the trestle table with a couple of dozen fletched arrows sticking out of its torso at all angles like quills. Whatever denomination the Church of the Freshwater Sea belonged to, it went beyond a cross and a handful of nails. Maybe the pope had canonized Custer while I was under anesthesia.

A cord of wood was stacked against an outside wall in a pile of snow where a section had slid from the metal roof. A six-foot oil pig fueled the house. No gas lines yet in that country.

Nothing seemed to be stirring inside the house. Some snow was tented around the tires of the pickup truck, which meant nothing; in those areas, the year-rounders often buy their supplies in bulk and only venture forth once or twice a month to restock. You never know when that lake effect will close the roads for a week.

The front and back doors were dead-bolted; those communities where folks don't lock their doors are a rural myth. Someone had weather-stripped the windows and sealed them in clear plastic. All except one, facing the pines lakeside, where wind had worried the plastic to shreds. I parted them and had a look. There didn't seem to be a catch, but the sash was sealed to the sill with old cracked paint.

Of course there wasn't anything in sight that could be used as a pry. My leg was aching merrily by the time I got back from the car with a screwdriver concealed under my coat. I don't know why I bothered with stealth. The neighbors were all in Florida.

A bit of scraping, the heel of a hand against the butt, and a little leverage broke the seal with a gasp. When the gap was wide enough I inserted my cane and used it the same way. Then I curled my fingers underneath the sash and slid it high enough to crawl underneath. Inside, I sat on the sill with my hands on my thighs and panted a little. I was out of shape from the hospital and as a housebreaker out of practice.

There wasn't much more to the house than there had been to the makeshift church: in the bedroom a rumpled bed and dresser that didn't match, shirts and sweaters and slacks and socks and underwear folded neatly in the drawers, some change scattered on top; sink and toilet and shower stall in the little bathroom, nothing more powerful in the cabinet than blood-pressure medication prescribed by a doctor in Port Huron; a pair of cheap new platform rockers and a fairly old sofa in the living room; a two-burner stove in a papered kitchen and sheet-metal table where Pastor Starzek took his meals. No dining room. The place was heated by an olive-colored oil stove in the living room, thermostatically adjusted somewhere between *The Bridge on the River Kwai* and the temperature at which blood comes to a boil. I wanted to open more windows.

I found a handful of wiry gray hairs in a brush, a pile of printed circulars advertising the Church of the Freshwater Sea, with a picture of a burly, bland-faced party in his fifties wearing a hairpiece that looked like a rasher of bacon. He bore a slight resemblance to what Jeff Starzek might look like in twenty years. The wide mouth seemed a fair vessel for the blaring voice over the telephone. It would ring off the metal walls of the church out back like a cherry bomb.

I folded one of the circulars and put it in my pocket for a souvenir. I didn't think he'd miss it.

There was a cheaply bound copy of the New Testament in every room, bathroom too; and on the wall above the sofa a framed print of a Renaissance-style painting showing a nearly naked man bound to a pillar and pierced from forehead to calf with a quiverful of arrows. "St. Sebastian, by Andrea Mantegna" was engraved in italics on a narrow strip of brass screwed to the bottom of the frame. Just looking at the picture made my leg throb.

The telephone was an old black rotary perched on a spindly table with a paper doily on top; no Caller ID, and no Star 69 to retrieve the last number dialed, either. A private, pious man, Dr. Starzek, as old-fashioned as a double broiler. D.D. followed his name on the circulars. Doctor of Divinity. I hadn't come across a diploma.

A chest freezer in a little pantry off the kitchen was packed with chickens frozen as hard as bowling balls, broccoli and Brussels sprouts in Ziploc bags, bundles wrapped in white paper marked VENISON in black felt-tip, and dated. Nothing store-bought. The reverend appeared to have a lively barter system going with his congregation. No room there for a body to have been stored recently. I hadn't really expected one, but I have a bad track record with empty houses.

What was missing, apart from a radio or television—not uncommon among those who spend their evenings with Mark, Matthew, Luke, and John—was the personal touch: family photos, letters from friends and relatives, the odd piece of memorabilia that didn't go with anything else in the house, suggesting a gift kept for sentimental reasons. No sign of a spouse or close association from either sex. A monastic life—or one lived by someone who took pains to give that impression.

I let myself back out the way I'd come in, seating the window sash securely against the sill. Only a hairline crack showed where the paint had parted, and a few shavings from the screwdriver. I blew them away and went back to my car, leaning on the cane and chewing Vicodin. I had more investigating to do in the neighborhood.

FIVE

alf a mile up the highway from where Old Carriage Lane branched off, a low, flat-roofed construction of glass and reinforced concrete with pumps out front advertised convenience items for sale inside. VIC'S SUPER SENTER, announced a professionally painted sign on the roof.

Inside were the usual displays of chips, cookies, and sandwich spreads in little cans among the motor oil and antifreeze. A glass-doored cooler filled with pop and bottled water pumped and wheezed, and there was a smell of smoked fish and ammonia from a horizontal refrigerated glass case where fresh catch was sold in season. The white head of the woman behind the computerized cash register was just high enough to read the LED. She blinked at me from behind black-rimmed trifocals as big as cafeteria trays.

"Vic in?" I asked.

"Right in front of you, mister. I'm Vicki outside the store. Painter charged by the letter."

She had a cigarette bass that would have silenced a bullfrog.

"I'm looking at some property down Old Carriage Lane," I said. "Couldn't help noticing there's a church in the neighborhood. What can you tell me about it?"

"Who's selling?"

There didn't seem to be any suspicion in the question, just curiosity. She would know most of the locals. That's what I was counting on.

"I haven't spoken to any of the owners. I'm trying to get out of Detroit. The road caught my eye and I took a drive down it. I knocked at the house in front of the church, but there wasn't anyone home."

"His truck there?"

I nodded. "I don't think he's had it out in a while."

"Huh."

"My wife's undecided about moving," I tried. "She's a born-again Christian. Church nearby could be just the thing to win her over."

"Mister, I don't believe there's been a soul under sixty inside Doc Paul's place in years. Most of 'em'll never see seventy again, and every spring there's less than there was the year before. For all I know, he uses it to store rock salt in the winter. He's about the only one on that road don't fly south with the robins. He almost never leaves the place except to fill his freezer, and when he does he always takes the truck. Most likely he was asleep when you knocked on his door."

"He must sleep sound. I knocked loud."

"Well, I wouldn't know how he sleeps. I gave up my interest in men when my Al died. A bit before, if you catch my meaning." She stuck her tongue out between her teeth like a naughty little girl. The teeth were small and even and white as Junior Mints.

"He sounds lonely. Not much family, I suppose."

"I never heard him mention any, but don't take anything from that. I only see him when he gets a taste for smoked coho, when they're running, and even then he's not what you'd call a gossip. I guess that comes with being a preaching man. He's a hermit is what he is."

"No visitors."

"Huh."

I waited. Vickie wasn't the type to tell any secrets—if you didn't keep your mouth shut long enough for her to talk.

"Normally, I'd say yes," she said. "Only you're the third one to stop here asking about him since Christmas."

I didn't fall off my cane. I'd been expecting something on that order since I'd talked to the preacher.

"What makes him so popular all of a sudden?"

She leaned her chin across the counter and dropped her voice to foghorn level. "Federal trouble. Fifth Column stuff. Spying for the A-rabs."

"Terrorists?" I almost whispered the word. Talking to her it was hard not to sound like old-time radio.

She showed her teeth again and nudged her glasses farther up her nose. "Hang on." She rattled some keys with scarlet nails at the end of mummy's fingers. The drawer of the register licked out and she rummaged among the checks and food stamps under the tray inside. She showed me a card I'd seen before, decorated with an eagle.

" 'Herbert Clemson,' " I read aloud. "Was he genuine, do you think?"

"I seen a badge, all gold and blue enamel. A polite young man. He asked me the same questions you did. Only he didn't pretend he was checking out property to buy."

I grinned. It had been pretty thin to begin with, but I was off my game. I showed her my license with the discontinued Wayne County deputy's badge pinned to the bottom of the folder. It didn't have any gold or enamel. "I know Agent Clemson," I said. "He came to my office this morning to ask for my cooperation.

There's always some duplication in these cases; can't be helped."
I put away the folder and gave her a card.

She held it next to Clemson's, comparing them. There was no
comparison. My jobber did a two-year bit in Jackson for faking
birth certificates and driver's licenses; Clemson's engraved invi-
tations to the White House. "It don't say here you're with the
government."

"Homeland Security's understaffed. It fills the spaces from the
private sector." I showed her the card Clemson had given me. It
was identical to hers.

It worked. It does, often, although I don't know why. Anyone
can get hold of a card or have one printed up. "You get that bum
leg in the line of duty?"

"Terrorists shoot first and don't ask questions. What about the
other man?"

"Who said it was a man?" She put my card and the agent's under the tray and bumped shut the drawer.

That put me back a little. Then she stuck her tongue out again.

"An old woman's got to take her fun where it comes," she said.
"It was a man. Bald as a coot and red as a radish. I thought he was
an Indian till he opened his mouth. The Chippewas that fish these
parts grunt like Tonto. It don't matter if they went to Harvard;
they all go native once they come back here."

"Was he wearing a uniform?"

"Uniform?" That troubled her. She squinted, as if he were still
standing in front of the counter. When she did that, her face
wadded up like a candy wrapper. She was nearly as old as the
lake. "Red-and-black Mackinaw, I remember that. I guess you
might call it a uniform in this part of the country."

I hadn't really expected him to dress like Detroit Edison on an
errand like that. I was pretty sure it was the man I knew as Oral
Canon.

"When was he here?"

"After the government man. New Year's Eve day, I want to say. Yes, I'm sure of it. Young Tommy Flint just finished clearing seventeen inches of partly cloudy from the lot, just in time for the holiday rush. 'Partly cloudy,' that's what the TV weatherman predicted. The bald man was the first customer I had since it finished piling up the night before. Not that he bought anything or gave me a dime for the information."

That was the big blow Canon had mentioned, that had had him working overtime in Oakland County. If he really was a lineman, it wouldn't be hard for him to wander a few more miles north without having to account for his movements.

"What kind of questions did he ask?"

"Just directions to Doc Paul's. Old Carriage is hard to find even with a map, and I don't think he had one. Then too, snow covers signs."

I thanked her by buying ten dollars' worth of gas and a carton of cigarettes. She rang up one of Canon's C-notes and gave me change. "Economy must be looking up."

"I'd appreciate your not telling Dr. Starzek I was asking about him. We don't really figure him for a spy, but he might start talk among the flock. It's just routine. These little church congregations are getting a closer look."

"Don't you worry about it, young man. Vicki's a vault."

A little squall blew up before I got clear of the lake country, hurling snow across I-94 and slowing traffic to a shadowy crawl. By the time I got out of it I'd missed lunch and high tea. I stopped at a drive-through in Warren and bought a burger and a cup of coffee. The kid in the window looked at me closely as he made change. My leg was hurting and I guessed it showed on my face.

A state trooper's car followed me down the off-ramp in Detroit. I didn't think anything of it until his flashers came on. I pulled over.

He was a young left tackle in a fur hat, zipped to the neck in a leather coat trimmed with pile. He unbuttoned the strap on his sidearm and asked to see my license, registration, and proof of insurance. When he was through reading he asked me to step out of the car. He stepped back when he saw me struggling with the cane, but he didn't kick it out from under me. He frisked me with his eyes. My coat hung open. I wasn't armed.

"Mind telling me what your business was in Warren?" His tone had nothing in it. His hand rested on his holster.

I thought. "I stopped for lunch. Did I forget to pay?"

"That's a city complaint." He unzipped his jacket with his off hand and took out a crumpled twenty-dollar bill. "You paid with this. Counterfeiting's federal, but they're tied up just now. Care to tell me where you got it?"

SIX

For a window jockey, the kid in Warren had had a good eye; or rather sense of touch. The old-style twenty, which is still in circulation, looked genuine as to color and engraving, and was convincingly stained and crumpled by what appeared to be passage through many hands. It was printed on very good paper. But it had been printed on paper.

I popped it a couple of times, stroked it between thumb and forefinger, held it up to the light, and gave it back to the trooper. I'd milked things a little, but then I'm a born ham.

"I'm poor," I said. "I don't handle the stuff often enough to know the difference."

"Not good. Not even funny. What else you got?"

We were sitting in the front seat of his cruiser with a console separating us, bumped out all over with equipment and coiled black cords and wee colored lights. He had a two-way radio, an onboard computer with a printer, GPS, and something that looked too much like a professional doughnut maker for comfort; if I didn't stop looking at it I was going to say something unfortunate and lose whatever chance I had at freedom. Every now and then a call came gurgling over the radio that had nothing to do with us, and from the lack of tone in the dispatcher's voice, not much more to do with her. They recruit them from Thorazine-testing laboratories.

"Okay." I got a cigarette out, to keep my fingers busy; nothing more than an electrical fire had ever been lit in that car. "So long as it's understood knowing a bit about counterfeit money doesn't make me a counterfeiter."

"No free passes," he said, flat as a paddle. "I tore the last one off the pad. Go."

"Paper money isn't paper, really. Mostly it's cloth. That's why it doesn't fall apart when it goes through the wash in your jeans pocket. That bill's mostly paper with some threads running through it. Bed-and-breakfast stationery is good as a rule, but it isn't Treasury stock. The kid who called in my license plate must've kept his fingers off the griddle."

"The new bills are harder to fake, and the old ones are starting to thin out. Some business owners train their people to give the discontinued series more attention. These others are fine." He put back the bills he'd taken from my wallet and held it out.

I took it and returned it to my hip pocket without counting. He looked too spit-shined to palm anything less than a hundred, and maybe not even that. Anyway he hadn't the palms for it.

"This kid ought to get a raise," I said. "As it is, his boss will probably take the twenty out of his time."

"It's always the little guy gets it in the neck. But not on my beat. Go home."

"You're kicking me loose?"

"If I were passing bad bills, I'd drive a better car. Someone slipped it to you, I'm pretty sure. Whether you didn't notice or decided to slip it to someone else is between you and Andy Jackson. I'm not your spiritual counselor."

"The car's a classic," I said. "Punks kept choosing me at stoplights so I went over it with a baseball bat."

"You wouldn't remember who gave you the bill." I didn't see any faith in his expression. They leave it in the locker with their civvies at the start of the shift.

I made my face thoughtful. I'd driven straight to Port Huron from Detroit with nothing in my wallet but a few of the C-notes Oral Canon had paid me to find Jeff Starzek. The only place I'd broken one was at Vic's Super Senter, around the corner from Paul Starzek's house and church. The old lady making change behind the counter had even made a crack about the economy looking up.

I said, "I could give you a list of possibles, but you'd have to shake loose every police station in this part of the state. I've been on the road all day."

"That's the trouble with money. Everybody squawks about it, but nobody looks at it when he's getting it or spending it. Chances are whoever slipped it to you had it slipped to him and he passed it on all unawares."

"All unawares," I said. "Landagoshen."

The cop's face got as hard as quartz. It hadn't been puff pastry to begin with. "Go home. Pay more attention to your cash from now on. It's only what drives the whole system."

I limped back to my car. The cruiser kicked gravel and pieces of broken pavement U-turning back the way it had come. I threw away the cigarette I'd been playing with, tapped out a fresh one, and fired it up from the dash lighter. I felt a little bad about ragging the cop, but it had taken my mind off my leg. I figured he'd pass it on to the driver of the next sports car he saw topping seventy, just like a counterfeit bill.

It was cold in the car, but I didn't start it. I smoked and thought and rode the shockwaves from the traffic slapping past, trying to beat the rush.

Funny money's like food poisoning. Everyone's had it at one time or another without really knowing it. Since laser printing had eliminated the need for bulky photo-engraving plates and big cumbersome printing presses, fake twenties had become as common as northern black squirrels; worth looking at when you noticed them, but not worth getting excited over. Washington disagreed, and in response had redesigned its bills for the first time since the Depression to make counterfeiting more of a challenge. That would hold until the last of the old bills went to the furnace and the paperhangers returned to the drawing board. The only sure way to stop a crime is to make it legal.

That was someone else's problem. Just because a scrap of false currency had found its way into my hands while I was looking for Jeff Starzek didn't mean it had anything to do with the job. It was just curious that he'd spent most of his adult life ducking the Bureau of Alcohol, Tobacco, and Firearms, and that ATF is a division of the Department of the Treasury. Same old enemy he knew by type if not always by name. Agent Clemson of Homeland Security had said Starzek had branched out in a whole new direction, and Starzek had hinted he'd thrown over cigarettes for another kind of cargo, just before he'd driven off the edge of the map.

If there was anything to it, God help him. You can murder a federal agent and Uncle Sam will track you down with no more than his usual resources and prosecute you according to the book. You might even get off with life, or nothing at all if the lawyers and investigators blundered the way they so often do where national security is involved. But print and pass one dirty dollar and he'll come down on you like frogs on Egypt. They'll bury you inside.

It might have been the Vicodin talking. Anyway I didn't know what to do with it. It was too big a subject—IMAX times ten—

and I was sitting too close to the screen, where I couldn't see around the wings of the eagle. I got better results in a neighborhood theater, with a simpler script and a smaller cast of characters. Someone who'd said his name was Oral Canon had paid me in cash to find his wife's kid brother. Except Jeff Starzek never had a sister and so far all the client's contact numbers had given me was a sleigh ride through the chilly winter wonderland of fiber optics.

I'd sat too long. Cold lay on my ears and nose and pierced my femur like an ice pick. I twisted the key and pumped the pedal, grinding at the starter until it caught. A glacial gust blew from the heater. I switched off the blower. A bank thermometer changed from eight to seven as I passed it.

The four and five o'clock rush hours had melded into one lump of slow-moving steel downtown. Windows lighted against the early dusk and hung like the last leaves of autumn among the abandoned offices and apartments next door and on the floors above and below. The city had emptied into the suburbs when I got back to the office and climbed back aboard the sleigh.

A voice with plenty of bottom welcomed me to Verizon Wireless and told me the cell number Oral Canon had given me was unavailable. I broke the connection and tried his home once again. Three stories down in the street, someone's car alarm started hooting. It sounded like one of those goofy birds in a Tarzan movie with no room in the budget for elephants. On the fifth ring I took the receiver away from my ear.

"Hello?" A woman's voice, sounding farther away than the alarm-bird. I put her back to my ear.

"I'm trying to reach the Canon residence." I'd probably dialed wrong. No one had picked up all day.

"This is Mrs. Canon. Who's calling, please?"

SEVEN

Rose Canon," I said.

"Yes."

"Mrs. Oral Canon." I couldn't think of any other conjugations. The woman on the other end of the line prevented me from going back and starting over.

"Is this Amos Walker?"

Her voice had dropped like the temperature outside. She sounded as if she were talking through a paper tube. You can usually tell when someone's cupping the mouthpiece with her hand. In spite of that I heard a male voice in the background, the hand-rubbed baritone of a TV anchorman reading the results of a presidential poll.

"Oral's there, isn't he?" I asked.

"Yes."

"You don't want him to know you're talking to me."

"No."

"Stop saying yes and no. When's he leave for work in the morning?"

"Eight."

"I'll call back then. Tell him you just lost a radio quiz."

"Thank you, anyway." Something plopped in my ear.

I'd poured a finger of Scotch and let it come up to room temperature. The bottom drawer where I kept it caught the draft from the floor. I swirled it like brandy and threw it back like a movie cowboy. It hit my stomach like a bass drum and crawled through my limbs, driving out the chill. Alcohol thins the blood, they say, making you more vulnerable to hypothermia, not less. Five generations of alpine St. Bernards had labored under an illusion.

Her voice was a little husky in the low registers, the way I like trombone music and women's voices. Maybe she had a cold. I got out the snapshot Canon had given me, of the woman he'd said was his wife and Jeff Starzek, the man he'd said was her brother. The face went with the voice: pretty, lightly seasoned. I had a hunch cameras didn't do her justice.

I wondered what was this fascination for other men's wives.

The card Oral Canon had given me had come out with the picture by accident. I looked at my name and the old telephone number, then turned it over and read the handwriting Canon had said was Starzek's: *Rose—If you don't hear from me by the first of the year, hire this man.* No signature or initial.

No vibes either, but that was okay. Preternatural communication exists, all right, but it's wrong just as often as the regular kind. I put the card and picture back in my pocket, stuck the bottle out of temptation's path, and took a pill instead. Then I drove home through empty polar streets with houses on both sides still wearing Christmas lights and opened a can of soup.

My leg woke me the next morning ten minutes ahead of the alarm, but I was lying in my own bed and not a frozen parking lot, which was progress of a kind. I had coffee and painkillers for breakfast. At eight o'clock I called the Canons' home. A baby with steel lungs wailed in the background. That was another suspected lie laid to rest, and I resolved to give Oral the benefit of some doubt until I could question Rose in detail. She couldn't talk right then, so I got the address and said I'd be there at nine.

The house was a two-story frame in Oak Park with a hip roof, one of several built on a tree-lined street in the second generation after VJ Day and something of an improvement over the G.I. Bill ranches that had preceded them. A pair of mature cedars towered in the front yard, their upper branches hollowed out in a U by Detroit Edison crews to keep them from taking down wires during windstorms. Oral Canon might have done the job himself, if he was with DTE as he said and splicing technicians weren't above that sort of work. I still had some reservations about him.

A hand-lettered three-by-five card inserted in one of the small panes in the front door asked visitors not to use the bell. I rapped gently and waited. My breath smoked and the iron air frosted the hairs inside my nostrils. It was like breathing through fiberglass.

"Thank you for coming, Mr. Walker. Come in and take off your coat. It must be zero." Her husky voice was almost a whisper.

She had blue eyes and the blackest hair I'd ever seen on an Occidental, a color combination that always puts blondes in the second rank. A crumpled red face and a full head of coarse black hair showed above a blue blanket wound into a coccoon in the crook of her left arm. The kid seemed to have his father's complexion; but I had one more point to clear up before I stepped inside.

"It was two below when I left the house." I kept my voice low. "Could you describe your husband for me, Mrs. Canon?"

Her face showed no surprise. It was oval, pale as milk, with a strong straight nose and a dimpled upper lip with edges as delicate as a ski track in fresh powder. It looked as if it would collapse if you touched it with a finger.

"He's a big man, like you, only heavier. Bald and sunburned. I can't get him to wear block. My father died of melanoma."

"I heard he drank."

Her eyebrows went up, black contrails against her fair skin. "Oral? Not—"

"Your father. Oral said he drank and your mother walked out on you."

"You get personal right on the doorstep, don't you?" The whisper was harsh. The bundle in her arm stirred and opened its eyes a crack. They were blue like the mother's, but they say that's true of all babies. I'd never paid them that much attention. They can't answer questions and don't hit very hard.

"The answers could save us both time and you money. Your husband hired me to look for a brother it turns out you don't have."

"He didn't lie." She jiggled the baby, pulled the edge of the blanket up around its ears. "Please come inside. The doctor said a little cold air isn't really bad, but Jeffie doesn't know that."

I stepped in past her. It was the *Jeffie* that did it. She closed and locked the door.

A heavy oaken hall tree stood to one side with a variety of outerwear hanging from it. I shrugged out of my overcoat and used a vacant hook. "You named him after Jeff Starzek?"

"I've always liked the name. It has strength and tradition. You'd never believe how many babies in the maternity ward were named Joshua and Jason."

"Why not Oral, Junior?"

She made a face; whether at Oral or Junior I couldn't tell. It didn't make her any less pretty. She wore a blue-and-white-checked flannel blouse with the tails out over black stirrup pants with her bare feet in blue fleece slippers. She had a trim waist, athletic legs, nice ankles. She was five-four but looked taller. She wore her hair in bangs with a ponytail; two minutes from shower to fixed. Motherhood breeds efficiency. "I'll hold onto him for a little, if you don't mind. He'll fuss if he isn't asleep before I put him in his crib."

I said I didn't mind. I was pretty sure it wouldn't have changed anything if I had.

The living room took up the front half of the ground floor. A rug with Oriental borders covered the hardwood floor to within eight inches of the walls. It was the most expensive thing in the room. A cheap new sofa with two matching platform rockers, an old green naugahyde recliner for the buttocks of the master of the house, a glass-topped coffee table stacked with books on infant care, and an electric fireplace answered for the rest. Family pictures in plastic cubes crowded the mantel, above which hung a Thomas Kincaide print of a medieval-looking lighthouse where the Seven Dwarfs spent their summers. TV, VCR-DVD combo, a speaker telephone to free both hands for diapering. There was the usual truckload of baby stuff testifying to the reign of the little tyrant in the blue blanket. A comfortable room, sprinkled with potpourri, faint cooking odors, and scented Lysol.

I consented to an offer of coffee and sat down in one of the padded rockers to stretch my leg, hooking my cane over the arm, while she carried the baby through an arch into a kitchen the size of my living room. I heard the disheartening sound of a jar opening and boiling water pouring into two mugs: The coffee was instant. She came back thirty seconds after she left, juggling the baby and both mugs with the fingers of one hand twined through the handles. I struggled to get up and help.

"I've got it," she said. "After three months, I could join the circus."

I leaned forward far enough to unburden her of one of the mugs and sat back to warm my hands around it. "He seems small for three months."

"He's a triplet. His brothers didn't make it out of the incubator." She lowered herself and Jeffie into the other rocker without spilling a drop, from mug or baby. She smiled down at it and planted a kiss on the crown of its coarse black head. "We tried for years. 'Patience,' a word we both came to despise, along with doctors and nurses and snippy receptionists and the magazines in waiting rooms: *Sports Illustrated, U.S. News and World Report—Runner's World,* for God's sake. You know how fast-food restaurants purposely design their seats to be uncomfortable, to keep the traffic moving?"

"I wouldn't know. I drive by the window."

"I think doctors' office managers choose the magazines they subscribe to for the same reason, to discourage you from taking too much of their time. It turned out there was nothing medically wrong with either of us, but I finally took fertility pills. At the clinic they suggested artificial insemination—AI, they call it. Oral was willing, but I set myself against it. Too much like mixing martinis. Anyway we conceived finally, and after twelve hours in labor I agreed to a C-section. Jeffie was stronger than either of his brothers. He's a special child, and that's why I named him after Jeff. What happened to your leg?"

"I fell on the ice. Tell me about Jeff. He isn't your brother."

"Oral doesn't know that. He didn't lie to you. I'm the liar in this marriage."

She sounded proud of it. I said nothing and sipped from my mug. What was inside bore a closer resemblance to a lemon Fizzie dissolved in radiator water than it did to coffee, but I didn't comment or gag. I'd had worse, much worse. In order to get the answers you need, you have to put up with the ritual of hospitality. I groped for my pack of cigarettes.

"No one's smoked in this house for ten years. I made Oral give it up after we married."

I apologized and put it back. I hadn't paid attention to what my fingers were doing.

"If you need it, you need it. I was just making an observation. I want visitors to be comfortable in our home. I don't have any use for people who make you take off your shoes before they let you walk on their rug. You can always clean up after they leave." She looked down at Jeffie. "He's asleep now. I'll put him down. Please feel free to smoke. I'll open a window later."

It was an order, the "please" notwithstanding, and I complied while she went out of the room, toward a hallway and a set of stairs that creaked under the combined weight of mother and child. I parked the cup of reconstituted cardboard, found a dish on the coffee table with a lone Jolly Roger inside, and used it for an ashtray. When she came back, she inhaled the secondhand smoke with the dreamy erotic grace of a connoisseur.

"I've always liked the smell of tobacco. The taste, too; though I've never smoked." She sat down and curled her hands around her mug. She hadn't drunk from it yet. "I miss that nicotine kiss. I only made Oral give it up because I want him to be around to attend Jeffie's graduation. That's the point, isn't it? Not how the drapes smell."

"My ex-wife told me it was like licking an ashtray." I blew a plume of smoke into an uninhabited corner.

"That's just stupid."

"I asked you to tell me about Jeff. So far all you've told me is you named Jeffie after him because he's a special child."

"Jeff's a child of tragedy. I thought you might have known

something about that. Oral said you were friends."

"It's more complicated than friendship," I said. "I helped get him out of a jam once. He more than canceled that out the last time I saw him."

"Do you like him?"

"I don't know if he prefers football to basketball or collects redheads or eighteenth-century chamber pots. I didn't know he played piano before that night. We had the longest conversation we'd ever had and all I found out was the brand of cigarettes he was smuggling." I took another drag and snuffed the butt in the candy dish. "Yeah, I like him."

"Oral hates him. Not just because of what he does. He's seen what worrying about Jeff does to me." She drank from her mug, grimaced. I was beginning to like her too. "If Jeff told you what he was doing, it's more than he told me. You read the note he sent."

I drew out the card and put it on the coffee table. "I just borrowed it. You're sure he wrote it?"

"I know his hand as well as I know my own. I taught him to read and write. I'm also the one who taught him to play the piano."

"You knew him when he was a boy?"

"He's my brother," she said. "But he's not. That's something you can never tell Oral."

EIGHT

Rose Canon cocked her head suddenly, excused herself, and scampered upstairs. I hadn't heard anything, but I'm nobody's mother. In a little while she came back down and curled back up in her chair.

"He was just restless," she said. "Do you think a three-month-old baby can have nightmares?"

"They're born naked, in a room full of people wearing masks. I don't see how they can have anything but."

She didn't seem to be listening. She'd left her instant coffee to grow cold on the glass-topped table. I took another sip, purely for the caffeine, and let mine grow cold along with it. My leg felt better than it had in days. Doubts about the story Oral Canon had told me had made it worse, but relief seemed to be within my reach.

"My maiden name's Aseltine," she said. "Oral thinks Jeff took Starzek from some accomplice to keep anything from coming back to me. I may have said something to give him that impression. Anyway it makes him less intolerant toward Jeff, so there's no point in setting him straight. His parents, the Starzeks, were overage flower children: stupid people who left him with friends

while they chartered a plane to Cuba to cut cane with the prole-
tariats. The plane went down in the Caribbean. Jeff was three."

"The friends were your parents?"

She nodded. "The Starzeks were responsible enough to draw
up a will naming a guardian in case they never came back from
Cuba, and irresponsible enough to name my dear mother."

"This is the mother who left you?"

"That happened later. I said they were stupid and irresponsible.
I didn't say they were criminally neglectful."

"Why'd she agree to it?"

"I can only assume that when they approached her she thought
it was a remote possibility at best. When the worst happened, I
suppose she had some idea raising a second child would save her
marriage. Everyone knows what a positive effect that has on a
husband who sleeps on a barstool more often than his bed at
home."

"It's been known to happen," I said. "But only at the turning
point."

"All it did was turn him deeper into the bottle. A lot of men in
those circumstances just leave, but he was too weak even for that.
In the end he was too weak and afraid to see a doctor when a mole
on his neck started changing shape. But Mother wasn't weak. One
morning she gave me lunch money, put me on the school bus,
dropped Jeff off at day care, and kept on driving. My father was
passed out in his chair as usual when I came home, and when the
day-care people called to find out why no one had come for Jeff, I
was the one who answered.

"That was twenty-seven years ago last September," she said.
"We were living in South Lyon. The police tracked her to a hotel
in Chicago, but she'd checked out before they got there. She may
still be alive. Then again, she may have driven straight from the
hotel into Lake Michigan."

"Oral said you practically raised Jeff."

"It was a little more than practically. Dad tried to dry out several times, but he wasn't much more help sober. I was just five years older than Jeff. He was in and out of trouble all though junior high and dropped out at sixteen to park cars at Carl's Chop House. One night he forgot to bring one back. He did six months at the Boys Training School in Whitmore Lake, but all he learned there was how to jump wires and take a car apart in under an hour. He was crazy about cars."

"Still is. I didn't know about the stretch in juvie." I wondered if Homeland Security did. They'd know his rap sheet as an adult, and Agent Clemson knew his blood relations were extinct. That was as much as he'd told me, apart from the fact Starzek had outgrown the cigarette trade into something of more interest to his bureau.

"You wouldn't," she said, "unless Jeff wanted you to know. They seal records under age eighteen."

"And you think your husband wouldn't understand if he found out Jeff isn't really your brother."

"I know he wouldn't."

"Not very charitable to Oral. He might be more open-minded than you think."

"Open-minded," she said. "Not stupid. Can I count on your confidence, Mr. Walker?"

Her face was polished alabaster, the delicate mouth less fragile than it looked. A jackhammer couldn't chip it into an expression I could read.

I said, "I know who Deep Throat is. I've known for thirty years. You didn't see it in the tabloids."

"I only have the vaguest idea what you're talking about, but I'll trust you. Jeff trusts you or he wouldn't have told me to hire you. I love him, Mr. Walker. I love him more than Oral and, God help me, more than little Jeffie. And not as a brother."

This time I heard the baby cry, but not before she did. While she was upstairs, and to take my mind off the Deep Throat guff, I got up to look at the photographs sealed in Lucite on the mantel: a wedding shot of Oral and Rose, she in a tailored eggshell suit, he boiling like a lobster out of a tight collar and gray pinstripe, orchids pinned to their breasts; a studio pose of a couple hard on eighty who had contributed in equal parts to Oral's big bald head and sloping shoulders; Rose pregnant; Rose holding Jeffie; Jeffie; an underexposed Polaroid of a grave-faced boy of about six, taken in someone's backyard; a five-by-seven version of the wallet-size Oral had given me of Rose and Jeff Starzek. No shots of them together as children, or of Rose as a young girl. A spare, sad album—if Rose hadn't lied to me the way she had to her husband.

I smelled her at my side. The scent or soap she used was slightly almond. It might have been baby oil.

"That's Oral's mother and father at their golden," she said. "He died last year. They wouldn't let me hold Jeffie or his brothers in the hospital. We took these pictures the day we brought him home. That's Jeff. He was a skinny little kid. He filled out later. I guess you can tell we weren't a big picture-taking family."

"There's one missing."

"I had one of my father, but I haven't seen it since we moved in. I tore up all the pictures of my mother the day I turned sixteen."

"I meant there's no picture of Jeff's brother."

She hesitated. "He doesn't have a brother. I'm his only family."

"Paul Starzek runs a do-it-yourself church up in Port Huron. He's twenty years older than Jeff."

She went back to her chair and curled up in it, hugging herself as if she were chilled. The electric fire kept the room an even seventy. "You waited long enough to toss that in my lap. Any other surprises?"

"What surprised you, that he has a brother or that I knew about him?"

"What do you think?"

"You didn't hire me to think. Pound for pound it's a bad deal."

"I didn't know. I don't care whether you believe me. I don't know what the advantage would be if I did and pretended I didn't. As a matter of fact, I don't know now. It's possible. Jeff's parents were in their forties when their plane went down. I never heard my mother and father say anything about their having a grown son; but then they hardly talked to each other. Who told you?"

I hung on to that surprise, to find out if it was one. "Paul wouldn't give me the time of day over the telephone, so I paid him a visit. He wasn't home. His church doesn't seem to be doing too well. What do you know about St. Sebastian?"

"Nothing. I wasn't raised Catholic."

"Episcopalian here. I'll have to look him up. He seems to be the patron saint of Paul's faith. Anyway the church is shut up for the winter, and maybe for good. It looks like he's using it for storage."

"Jeff's never mentioned him. Maybe he doesn't know he even has a brother."

"He knows. Someone told me they broke off communication right around the time you say Jeff went wild. Paul confirmed it over the telephone. Maybe he tried to tap his big brother for a get-away stake."

"I'd have lent him whatever he needed. I've offered many times. He always turns me down."

"Maybe he thinks you don't owe him anything and Paul does."

"He hasn't needed money in some time. He tried to give us some when I was in the hospital, but Oral wouldn't take it."

"It's not money. He's driving thirty thousand dollars' worth of Detroit muscle. Whatever he's after, he talked to Paul about it recently. Paul damned him for a smuggler, but he didn't get into smuggling until he was in his twenties. How else would Paul know?"

"You said you weren't paid to think."

"It's an expensive hobby."

"Since you aren't charging for it, do you think Paul knows where Jeff's gone?"

"Someone else thinks so, or did. One of them is Oral."

I watched her closely, but she'd been too long in the cold war. I needed a court order just to take her pulse.

"Oral doesn't know about Paul," she said. "*I* didn't know, and I know my husband."

"That's a common mistake. He was up there New Year's Eve, asking about Paul."

"He was with me New Year's Eve."

"It was during the day, when he told you and his supervisor he was busy climbing poles after a storm up north."

"He was. He came home exhausted. Why would he hire you if he already knew where to look?"

"That was before he came to my office. Maybe he ran into the same wall I did."

"But how would he even know about Paul?"

"Those tree-toppers get around. Paul had flyers printed advertising his church, and Starzek isn't a common name. Maybe Oral went up there on a hunch and when it didn't pan out he didn't think it was worth sharing."

"If he knows Starzek is Jeff's real name, he knows I've been lying to him all these years."

"Another good reason to keep his mouth shut."

"That's why he agreed to hire you. My God," she whispered. "He's looking for grounds."

"Could be he's waiting for you to say something."

She cocked her ear toward a small whimper, decided to stay put. Her eyes were Arctic blue and just as dry. "You said someone else thinks Jeff's brother knows where he is, or did. Who?"

"A man named Herbert Clemson. He's the one who told me about Paul. He's been up there asking around, like me. He told me there wasn't anything in it, but those federal types lie to their parakeets just to stay in practice. He's with Homeland Security."

She might have paled a shade. I saw a spread of blue veins under the skin, like sea grass in the shallows. It was the first real reaction I'd gotten from her.

"I was pretty sure he hadn't been here," I said, nodding. "So far his information is strictly basic, the stuff of public record. He'll come around when he gets the rest. You'll like him. For a government sneak he's got a well-developed sense of humor."

She looked away. "It must be the cigarettes. They think everyone who doesn't pay the tax sends the difference straight to terrorists. It wouldn't occur to them people just like a bargain."

"Cigarette smuggling puts him to sleep. He's more interested in what Jeff's carrying now."

"How do you know he's carrying anything?" She was looking at me again. "You just said Clemson's a liar on principle."

"Jeff told me that night in Grayling he was switching loads. Not long after that, you got a Christmas card from him as much as telling you he was about to disappear. I'd tell you to figure out the rest, but you're the client. Turns out there's some thinking to the job after all."

"Is Jeff dead?"

"It's a theory."

The house got as quiet as a house in a bedroom community ever gets. Even the baby had stopped fussing.

I shifted my cane to the other side and my weight with it. "I doubt it," I said. "He's fast and smart, and he's lasted this long. I'm more concerned about the people who are looking for him."

"Not Oral."

"Not Oral. He's big, but he's got a high center of gravity."

"Clemson."

"What he represents. Some people's idea of chess is to clear the board to take the king. Pretty tough on all the other pieces. And if Clemson's right, Jeff's running out of his class."

"You said you fell on the ice."

She was looking at my leg. I hadn't realized I was rubbing it. That was a habit I'd have for a long time, like stroking a phantom beard.

"I didn't say why. It was Jeff who picked me up."

"Does that mean you're not quitting?"

"Who said I was? Everyone lies in this house. I can't concentrate on the questions I need to ask if I can't trust the answers I've got. Let me know when you and Oral get your collar and cuffs to match. You can leave a message with my service. I'm going north."

"You just got back from there."

"I left something behind."

"Find Jeff, Mr. Walker. Whatever happens to Oral and me."

She went up to look in on Jeffie. I drove back to my house, got a pair of long-handled bolt cutters out of the garage, and put them in the trunk. Churches ought never to lock their doors. You never know when someone might need enlightenment.

NINE

The Web site was called Martyrs R Us. You can't make this stuff up.

It belonged to a small Catholic press in some inexplicable place like Bayonne or Newport News. Its feature that month was a life of St. Thomas More, available in either trade paper or a deluxe limited edition bound in cardinal-red calfskin with a CD laid in of Gregorian chants, recorded by the brothers of Our Lady of Perpetual Dolour in Kirkwall, Scotland. You could also buy silver-and-enamel cuff links fashioned in the shape of John the Baptist's severed head.

Barry Stackpole had found it by typing in "St. Sebastian" and patiently nursing the entry through sites on cities of that name, church-sponsored pie-eating contests, the late actor Sebastian Cabot, and—mysteriously—Benito Mussolini. There appeared to be no Christian sects registered online that paid any more than lip service to the arrow-riddled martyr of Paul Starzek's Church of the Freshwater Sea. I hadn't really expected there to be: Starzek hadn't appeared to own a television, much less a computer.

At the last minute I'd postponed my return junket to Port Huron to find out what I could about the pole-barn parish. Barry had moved again, from the suburbs into the belly of the beast. With the kill fee a satellite network had paid him not to air a six-part series on the history of organized crime in America, he'd bought a condo on the fourth floor of a former steam radiator factory in the shrinking warehouse district off East Jefferson, within pistol range of the Renaissance Center. Bullet-resistant windows provided a view of Windsor, Ontario, across the river and also of cranes picking apart what remained of industrial-age Detroit.

He'd paid enough for it to build a small mansion of six thousand or so square feet but, typically, had furnished it out of someone's garage. The scattered sticks preserved the integrity of the loft's bulk-storage origins, with steel utility shelves packed with commercial books on the mob arranged by geographical location and rows of transcripts of wiretapped conversations bound in paper covers stamped FBI PROPERTY—DO NOT REMOVE FROM LIBRARY. The only decoration was a battered eight-by-ten photograph in a brass document frame of Al Capone shaking hands with Babe Ruth, putatively signed by Scarface and the Bambino themselves. I don't know how he came by it, but it was the only thing he'd taken with him through all his midnight moves. If I knew Barry at all—and I'd known him for thirty years and ten thousand miles— there was a working fire escape out back and a speedboat tied up to a dock for a fast exit. He wasn't paranoid, just practical.

I sat on a plywood potato-chip chair salvaged from some failed high school next to the sheet-metal kitchen table Barry used for a workstation and watched him riffle the keys on the most expensive fixture in the house. He was dexterous for a man with only eight fingers. Joe Zerilli's street soldiers had blown off the rest, along with a leg and a piece of his cranium, but you wouldn't know it by the way he got around on his prosthesis and combed his fair hair across the steel patch.

The audio sample that came up with the Gregorians sounded like an overworked compressor in a refrigerator car. He turned down the volume on the speakers, tapped his mouse. His eyes never wandered from the seventeen-inch screen.

"What's that you're whistling?" I asked.

He stopped, then whistled the last couple of bars again. He hadn't been paying attention. " 'The Thieving Magpie.' Rossini."

"Oh."

"Theme from *Prizzi's Honor.*"

"Oh." Different emphasis.

"Fun flick. Inaccurate as hell. The Mafia doesn't employ lady hitmen. Never has, never will. Even if they look like Kathleen Turner."

"Nicholson was good, though."

"Nicholson's good even when he's bad. Ah!"

"What?" I never know where to look when I'm looking at a computer screen.

He played an arpeggio. Suddenly the monitor was filled with postage-stamp images in full color of what looked at first like freeze-frames from a slasher film. A score of images displayed every manner of agony possible of a nearly naked man perced from hairline to ankle with arrows. Some were as green as amateur Polaroids, others so lifelike they made me bleed from pure osmosis. Evidently the fate of St. Sebastian had inspired Renaissance artists who had gotten all they could out of Christ on the cross. Winged angels appeared in flocks. They could fly, but as to intercepting arrows they were as useless as hairdressers at the Battle of the Bulge.

"Fourth century," he read. "Maybe earlier. Whenever the date's unknown, it starts to read like pulp fiction. At one time I was studied up enough to take the veil. Not that they call it that when it's the priesthood. Went to confession regular as the dentist. You'd be surprised how fast those made guys turn back into altar boys when you sprinkle the conversation with ecclesiastical Latin. I'm talking about guys that put other guys' heads inside drill presses when their notes came past due. Not bad for a Dutch Reformed kid from Grand Rapids."

"Still go to confession?"

"No point. The *paisani* are on the run. Now it's Jews, Russians, Irish Protestants, blacks, and Asians. The Mexicans still attend, but they don't believe. Damn shame. Like what happened to rock after the Beatles landed."

"I can't figure out whether you hate the mob or love it."

"I wonder myself sometimes. Then bedtime comes around and I take off my leg with my pants."

He clicked on one of the postage-stamp images. A screen-size picture shot down from the top like a shaft of light. He was always upgrading his servers and equipment, supercharging the circuit boards and bundles of wire inside the computer tower like a kid tinkering with a hot rod. He had the hardware to manipulate the stock market in his favor, but he chose to use it for good, and the occasional exclusive.

I looked at the same pathetic punctured figure I'd seen on Paul Starzek's living-room wall. This was a cleaner reproduction from a plate generations closer to the original painting. The carving on the pillar he was bound to was wedding-cake sharp and the blood streaming from his multiple wounds was bright arterial red. The picture dated back to the middle of the fifteenth century and the paint still looked wet.

I read the artist's credit line. "Andrea Mantegna. Wonder who she was."

"She was a he, you lowbrow flatfoot. The Renaissance didn't begin and end with the *Mona Lisa*."

"Tell me about him, smart guy."

"What's to tell? Look at the picture."

"What I thought. You don't know any more about him than I do."

"You didn't know he was a him until two seconds ago. I thought it was Sebastian you wanted to know about."

"I know how he died."

"You don't even know that. It takes more than a shitload of arrows to kill these Mediterraneans." He turned the page, or whatever they call it. Anyway a paragraph of text came up. I leaned over to read.

Sebastian, of Gallic birth, was an officer in the imperial guard under Diocletian. Someone ratted him out as a Christian and he was strung up and used for archery practice. The widow of another martyr, St. Castulus, cut him down, patched up his wounds, and nursed him back to health. Diocletian found out and brought in more muscle, who beat him to death with cudgels.

"His emblem's the arrow," Barry said, as if I couldn't read. "It ought to be the blackjack, but you can't expect scripture to make sense."

"Arrows take better pictures. A battered corpse is just side meat."

He sat back. His eyes reflected the cursor blinking on-screen.

"What's the attraction, Amos? Most of the stiffs you bring me are still warm. Anything in it for an out-of-work muckraker?"

"I thought you were busy ghosting for fake gangsters."

"That's cold. I thought we were good."

"I can't make promises, Barry. There's federal interest. You know where that always leads."

"Tell me. My FBI file has sequels. Is it them?"

"Higher."

He rotated his chair, an ergonomic item he'd smuggled out of Rockefeller Center when NBC gave him his walking papers. "Attorney general? Don't tell me you've got me in bad cess with the Pentecostals."

"Not that high."

"Homeland Security. Son of a bitch."

"I was impressed myself."

"This have anything to do with what happened in Grayling?"

I wanted to smoke. I didn't know what it might do to his equipment. "That's a personal debt. If I can help you out I will. I can count the friends who'd drive six hours to take me home from the hospital on the fingers of a leper. If it turns out I can't, it'll have to be a favor to be named later. Right now I'm walking backwards in the dark."

"Well, if it's as bad as what happened to this poor bastard, CNN will get it before I do." He drummed a tattoo on the keys. The text vanished and his screensaver popped up. He'd traded his montage of classic gangster movies for a still life of Frank Nitti sprawled dead in an alley.

He had two emotions he shared with the world, flippant and petulant. He was as high maintenance as a prom queen.

"What do you know about the Church of the Freshwater Sea?"

"Sounds like a brand of canned tuna." He went back online. I couldn't read the response, but no flags went up. "Just a lot of crap on the history of the Great Lakes. Is it a terrorist cell?"

"I'd hate to think my tax dollars were being spent fighting a pole barn in Port Huron." I told him what I knew about Paul Starzek.

He typed in the name, waited. "Nothing. Which means it's something. It's much harder to stay off the Net than get on it. It sucks up everything."

"Not if you never go near it. This guy's just a little bit right of Amish. Bill Gates couldn't find him without a two-dollar map of Michigan counties."

"So Jeff Starzek's the job?"

"I didn't say that. But yeah. He's in a hole of some kind. I may not be the rope, but since I didn't bleed to death on a patch of frozen dirt, I can't not try."

"Yeah. If I ever disappear, I know someone will look. It's a comfort, like knowing where you'll be buried. The family plot's in Grand Rapids, by the way. Call my sister. She's in the book."

"You did disappear, and I went looking. Our friendship hasn't been the same since."

"I like to think the patch job held."

"November went a long way in that direction. Thanks, Barry. If they don't slam the lid too tight I'll let you in." I levered myself off the stiff chair and tried not to suck in air through my teeth. I'd sat too long. He leaned back in his trick chair, watching me with eyes as clear and untroubled as a boy's. He'd stopped aging twenty years ago.

"I can float Paul Starzek and his church among the boys on the street," he said. "It's probably not his street."

"I wouldn't risk it. If we all wind up in the same hole, who'll throw us the rope?"

"Good point. Back to Port Huron?"

"I might cut a hole in the ice and drop in a line."

"Put an anvil in your lap. The big ones pull back."

Clouds sagged a few feet above the Huron channel as if they were filled with lead shot. Out on the white ice, some fishermen were hiding from their families in shanties built of scrapwood and galvanized iron; the smoke sliding out of their stovepipes was no darker than the overcast. The iron-nuts diehards sat exposed to the elements on fish buckets, holding short brightly painted rods above the holes they'd punched in the surface and getting up occasionally to swish away the rapidly re-forming ice with their bare hands. You have to really like the sport, or need the fish, to pursue it under those circumstances. I'd tried it just once, a long time ago, and hadn't gotten the chill out yet. I don't even care for fish.

The tension of the coming snow pressed at my temples like a carpenter's clamp. I had my blower on full blast against the icy air sucking at spaces where the rubber had checked away from the glass. When I adjusted its direction my forehead prickled with sweat and my feet turned into flat stones. When I turned it back, my socks soaked through and my ears stung. The weatherman on the radio advised listeners to give up any hope of a January thaw before February. He sounded giddy about it, as if he had all his money in flannel. I switched to an oldies station in search of the Beach Boys and got Dean Martin crooning, "Baby, It's Cold Outside." The knob came loose in my hand as usual when I turned it off. I put it in the ashtray next to the cigarette lighter that had stopped working that morning.

The lights inside Vic's Super Senter glimmered sullenly under the cloud ceiling, which was growing blacker by the minute. I turned off before it, slewed and spun my wheels on the glazed surface of Old Carriage Lane, and jerked down the decline, gently pumping my brakes, until it leveled out. It was coming on noon but looked like twilight. The tangle of trees and underbrush that separated the neighborhood from the money property on the lake was primordial black, and as I rolled past a thousand-square-foot crackerbox sided with yellow tile, all the lamps in all the windows sprang on in response to a light-sensitive switch. Most of the other houses, hooked up to twelve-hour timers or nothing at all, were telltale dark. Out of season, break-ins would keep the local law busier than anything else.

Just as the thought occurred to me, a low-slung, wide-bodied St. Clair County sheriff's cruiser came drifting up at crawl speed from the lake end. As we passed within inches of each other, the deputy in the driver's seat glowered at me from behind walrus whiskers, but he kept rolling. I watched in my rearview mirror as the cruiser topped the hill and flared its brake lights. I got out for their entertainment, mounted the porch of a converted house trailer two doors down from Paul Starzek's, tapped on the door, waited, then went back to the car. I did a little acting with the cane, as if it were the only thing holding me up. Anyway it seemed to work. By the time I turned around and got back to the highway, the cruiser had disappeared.

I picked it up again on the other side of Vic's, where it boated out from the other side of an orange tanker blocking the pumps and hung three car lengths behind me for the next mile and a quarter. I drove just below the limit with my shoulders tensed, just as if I were guilty of something. I had a pair of bolt cutters in my trunk.

A side road led inland between an empty-looking farmhouse and a sign announcing the site of a future subdivision. Dry snow swirled and settled in its wake. I relaxed my shoulders. I had a sore spot between them that felt as if an ice pick were sticking out of it.

I turned around again in a gravel clearing belonging to a fruit and vegetable stand and went back the way I'd come. There was no sign of the cruiser on the side road. It ran straight as a knife for a mile and ducked over a hill.

Time seemed to have stood still around Paul Starzek's old trailer. Windblown snow half covered the steps and nothing larger than a squirrel had made tracks in it. Snow fleas speckled the bread-colored stuff frozen around the Dodge Club Cab's tires, which were dusted with fresh powder from the lake. I drove around the truck and parked behind the trailer, out of sight from the private road. I got out, snicked the door shut, and stood looking and listening. The Cutlass' motor ticked as it cooled, then fell silent.

The icicles hanging from the roof of the metal building behind the house hadn't grown any longer; you need a thaw for that, and the last sluggish drip at the end of the longest bayonet had frozen into a glassy knob the size of a marble. Wind soughed in the pines, a haunted sound. My ears numbed. My nose dripped. My leg hurt. I got the bolt cutters out of the trunk and went to work.

TEN

Right away I knew I wasn't going to need them.

It wasn't premonition, but detective's instinct; the kind judges throw out but everyone in real law enforcement from the prosecutor's office on down takes to the bank, with manacles and Miranda and a cautiously worded statement to the press—and, with some artful exaggeration, to a request for a search warrant for the judge who issued it to throw out in open court.

The basis was the chevron tread of a tire belonging to a tractor or some other piece of heavy equipment, clearly visible in the flat, recently swept surface of the hard frost coating the drive leading from Old Carriage Lane to the Church of the Freshwater Sea. I hadn't seen it from the car, but when I started across the no-man's-land between the house trailer and the pole barn behind it, the long-handled bolt cutters swinging from my right hand in time with the cane in my left, I felt something crunch beneath my foot and looked down at the intaglio engraving left by the space between two rectangles of rubber set at right angles and knew the movers had been at work. When I got to the door, the combination padlock that had barred me on my last visit lay, sheared through and crooked, in the fan-shaped depression left by the door when someone had opened it against the snow that had drifted to the sill. The lock had been pressed into the snow by a boot with a tread not unlike the tire's. The door was secured only by the hasp, swung by an afterthought into place with the naked loop poking through the slot.

I placed my foot inside the bootprint. I felt like a tourist at Grauman's Chinese Theater. The depression stuck out a full two inches all around. I don't take ballet shoes myself. If the rest of him ran true to his shoe size, he was an animal, and probably no one's ideal partner for the science fair. He would be paid in cash, with a bonus to forget what he didn't know in the first place: a state senator in the making.

Not wanting to make any more noise than I already had, I leaned down and laid the bolt cutters gently on the ground. The cane was a better weapon, and as usual I'd left my gun in the car when I most needed it. Breaking and entering and armed invasion were mutually exclusive crimes in my view. It was a definite flaw.

But I was pretty sure a gun wasn't needed, or the equipment would still be there. I knew when I pulled open the door, the hinges grating against days of regular disuse, that I was as alone as an igloo on a floe in the Arctic Sea. The interior of the metal barn, open to the rafters where birds' nests waited glumly for tenants, yawned at me, dank and cold and deserted. Anyone waiting for me, crouched behind the trestle-table altar or under the blue plastic tarp that lay in a crumple in the aisle between the rows of folding metal chairs, was frozen as stiff as—well, something frozen and stiff. I'd run out of brute poetry.

The naked store mannequin maintained its vigil behind the wooden lectern, its vinyl smile stuck in its sartorial smirk. It re-minded me a little of Barry Stackpole, aged and ageless and cynical to the end. The arrows sticking out from it at all angles were props after all. The two wood burners that kept Paul Starzek from shivering through his fire-breathing sermons and his parishioners from blowing on their hands instead of clasping them in prayer were gray and cold, the coarse ash in their bellies like the remains of sacrifices in a pagan temple as old as Emperor Diocletian, whoever he may have been. Just another profile on a coin.

Twenty-four hours ago, I'd peered through cupped hands at the window at a bulked tarp covering all manner of storage of no interest to me—bags of rock salt, maybe, as ancient Vicki of Vic's Super Senter had suggested. The tarp was still there, but the bulk had gone. I reached down, took hold of a corner, and threw it into a heap. I looked at a snow shovel, a long-handled spade, a leaf rake with twigs and pieces of calcined leaves caught in the tines.

There was a tented corner in the tarp opposite the one I'd tossed aside, nearly my own height. It might have been covering a string trimmer or some other upright implement. I stepped across the abandoned tools, gathering up folds of plastic as I went, and twitched it aside. I jumped back, fisting the cane. I stood face to face with a naked man.

It was a face twisted in anguish, with mouth agape and eyes turned upward, as if anticipating reinforcements from the rafters. It was as gray as frozen liver, but uncannily alive. Two arrows pierced it from opposite angles, one through the brow, the other the tender skin beneath the corner of its jaw; they were perfectly in line, and at first I thought it was one long shaft transfixing the brain. A dozen or more arrows stuck out randomly from its chest, the rib cage on both sides, its sternum, left thigh, and right calf, the one in the thigh having tunneled clear through the fascia muscle and stuck out on both sides. The figure's arms were clasped behind its back, as if fastened with manacles or a rope. It wasn't quite naked. A twist of plain cloth encircled the pelvic area in the modest tradition of the otherwise bold Renaissance. The statue appeared to be a faithful copy of the figure in the Andrea Mantegna print framed on the wall above Paul Starzek's sofa, with one or two interpretations added. The expression on the face reflected a good deal more of the agony of the situation. Whoever had fashioned it understood pain, and not by rumor.

I reached out and touched the figure's right pectoral. It was smooth as glass and cold, but not quite as cold as ice. Marble has its own source of heat, as the sculptors claim. It was beautiful work, more lifelike than a cadaver, yet somehow just as corporeal. You don't find that kind of craftsmanship at Pottery Barn.

What a cheap plastic dummy was doing standing in for St. Sebastian while the real thing stood under wraps joined the long list of questions I needed to ask Dr. Starzek.

I cleared more floor space and walked around in a circle. The floor was a concrete slab, treated and coated with a polyurethane finish in a honey shade with a satin sheen. It wore a fine coat of dust everywhere but where feet had tracked through and a vaguely rectangular expanse of clean floor. Something large and square had lain there until recently. The shape corresponded roughly to what I'd seen through the window the first time. Whatever it was, it held more value for whoever had removed it than the marble statue. I don't know much about art, but I know about money. Someone had paid thousands to carve that slab into a saint. Even the arrows and loincloth had been shaped from the stone.

A mouse scampered the length of a rafter overhead. It was the owner of the only other heartbeat in the place.

The house of worship held nothing more for me. I'd fallen out of the fold years ago, in a jungle God had rented out, and just regarding the figure Starzek's congregation had chosen for its conduit reminded me of all the places I'd been poked and punctured in the course of my work. I had the stigmata without the beatification. Starzek was the man I wanted to see, and the pastor had left the building. Also the house. Nothing had disturbed the snow around it since I'd been there last.

I went outside where the cold settled a little less close to the bone and leaned on my cane and smoked. A snowmobile whined like an asthmatic mosquito from the direction of the lake, oblivious to the fishermen and the fish it was scaring away. Fortunately for the murder statistics, winter anglers are a gentle lot. The noise Dopplered away. It was just me and the pines and the first translucent flake from the heavy black udders of the clouds, turning and sailing on the currents like a moth that refused to land.

My gaze settled on the firewood stacked against the barn's outside wall. It was a standard cord, eight feet long and four high, frosted like a cake on top with a heap of snow that had slid off the edge of the roof. The impact had dislodged several chunks from one end, sending them rolling into a pile. I went over and pushed at the stack with one hand. It swayed and another chunk came loose atop the collapsed end and tumbled down among the others.

I didn't like that by half. People who are practiced at stacking wood make a better job of it, to get the most into the least space and keep it from falling apart before the first gust. They have competitions where you need a half stick of dynamite to break loose the runners-up. Paul Starzek didn't seem the type to compete, but he'd been through too many northern winters to slap the dash. I ground the tip of my cane through to the frozen earth, braced myself, and pushed the end of the pile high up with the heel of my good leg. It was an amateur job, all right. The stack canted toward the other end, twisted in the middle, and spilled most of its top three layers into a heap. A three-quarter round of hickory wobbled drunkenly on its square edges and bumped my cane. If I hadn't been leaning all my weight on it the collision would have swept it out from under me.

When the avalanche stopped I went over, cleared away the bottom layers to the dirt beneath, brown and flecked with black bark but no snow, and tested it with the cane. The original stack had been erected before the first frost, insulating it from the cold. It was the only patch on the property you could penetrate without a jackhammer.

I went back inside the church, traded my cane for the long-handled spade, and used it as an alpenstock on my way back to the demolished stack of firewood, the blade ringing every time it struck hard earth. During the next twenty minutes I forgot the cold. Just clearing away the fallen wood had me sweating, my leg throbbing like a flashing red bulb precisely where the bullet had gone in. The dirt was unfrozen but packed hard, compressed by the weight of the firewood, and I hadn't the leverage to shove the blade in deep with my foot. I took shallow scoops and made slow progress. After five minutes of digging I climbed out of my overcoat and suit coat and flung them down on the ragged pyramid of hickory and chestnut and white birch.

They hadn't gone very deep. About two feet down something scraped and a patch of electric blue showed for just a second before the loosened earth slid back down to cover it. I bent over and brushed it away with my hand. The place was rotten with blue plastic tarp. I lifted the shovel to clear away the rest. The blade zinged against something hard underneath the tarp, a sound that made me sick at heart. I tossed aside the shovel, fished out my folding knife, straddled the blue cocoon on my knees, and slitted the plastic from the near end to eight inches. The frozen gray face that stared up at me when I spread the material might have belonged to another marble statue, but it wasn't lifelike enough for that. It was just dead, with one eye shut and the other not seeing. It seemed to be including me in a private joke.

I groped at my chest, realized I was in my shirtsleeves, picked up the shovel again, and used it to lever myself up out of the grave. I felt the chill again now, like clammy chain mail against my slick skin, and put on my suit coat before I went into the inside breast pocket and unfolded the church circular I'd taken from Starzek's supply inside the house trailer. I looked from the face in the picture to the dead face in the ground, with the edges of the tarp framing it like a monk's hood. That seemed appropriate. I was 90 percent sure they were the same. I knew more than I should have about what happens to a human face when the muscles that operate it stop working.

It had the petrified look of something that had been in the earth for ages. I'd spoken to the owner only a little more than twenty-four hours ago. Or someone who'd said he was Paul Starzek over the telephone.

"Police! Drop the shovel and put your hands on top of your head!"

I jumped, the circular fluttering out of my hand. I hadn't heard the cruiser coasting to a stop behind Starzek's pickup or the two deputies approaching on foot on either side of the truck. Both had their pistols thrust toward me in the two-handed clasp, their feet spread and four yards separating them, a firing perimeter. I let the shovel fall with a clank and put my hands where they said.

ELEVEN

The command officer was a sheriff's sergeant named Finlander. He had clay-red hair chopped off straight across his forehead in little-boy bangs, but his face was ancient, pleated longitudinally from brow to jowl like vertical blinds. His eyes were glittering black slits, his nose broad and flat, his mouth a parenthesis turned on its side with the corners curved down and just enough lip to prevent fraying. His uniform shirt was ironed as flat as posterboard. Finns are Huns by ancestry. Give this one a fur hat and a tough little monkey of a steppe pony and he looked as if he could sack Rome on twenty dollars a day.

The substation was a brick box no larger than a caretaker's shed in a cemetery and bore evidence of having been used as a community library sometime in the past. The musty perfume of disintegrating paper was still apparent and the remaining shelves held a complete run of red-bound copies of the *Michigan Penal Code* up to 1974, a four-drawer steel index-card file box filled with juvenile offenders, and a couple of hundred yards of loosely coiled yellow extension cord. That left just room for Sergeant Finlander and me to sit on either side of a gray sheet-metal desk with a scarred composition top and for Walrus Whiskers to stand. The deputy's name was Yardley, for the record. The spare tire pressing at his belt of torture tools was as hard as the rest of him.

"You should smile when they take your picture. I've seen happier faces in maximum security." Finlander had my ID folder in his hands. My wallet and its contents, car keys, cigarettes and matchbook, Paul Starzek's church circular, and my cane decorated the desktop, the cane across the corner nearest the sergeant and farthest from me. Yardley and his partner had found the gun in my car, but it was nowhere in sight. My carry permit lay openfaced among the money and receipts from my wallet.

"That's my game face," I said. "It cracks peepholes and destroys alibis."

"Let's process him, Sarge," Yardley said. "He had the shovel in his hands, for chrissake."

Finlander fixed his slits on me. "Unlawful disposal of a corpse is a misdemeanor punishable by jail time. Then there's breaking and entering; we've got the bolt cutters and the busted lock. I haven't mentioned suspicion of homicide, but only because we don't know yet what killed Starzek. Have you visited our fine modern facility?"

"It's an empty spot in my collection," I said. "I think you know I didn't kill Starzek or bury him. I came prepared to cut off the lock, but someone already took care of that. We've been over it."

"Go again."

I sighed and went again: the job Oral Canon had hired me for, Homeland Security's interest in the person of Agent Herbert Clemson, my first visit to Paul Starzek's house, and the second one that had landed me where I was. I'd told him about Grayling because he'd asked about the cane, but left Jeff Starzek out of that part, also both Canons and what Rose had told me about her real relationship with Jeff. I didn't mention I'd broken into Paul's house on my first visit. I said I'd found the circular in the pole barn.

"You're sure it was Starzek you talked to on the phone?" Finlander had listened as closely as he had all the other times, and let the same length of silence stand while he turned the details over in his mind, or seemed to; he might have been thinking about what Mrs. Finlander was making for supper, if there was a Mrs. Finlander. There wasn't a personal photo, family or otherwise, anywhere in the little room. It was just as much a monk's cell as Paul Starzek's house trailer, without the religious gimcrack.

"I'm not sure at all," I said. "I never spoke to him before in my life."

"So this is just a job to you. Your past association with his brother doesn't figure in."

"I know Jeff only a little bit better than I knew Paul."

"Blood's blood, but money's money. If you didn't kill him—which I'm not considering—I'll bet you whatever you're making on this job it was baby brother. There was a shitload of cigarettes in that church before it got moved out. Money to burn, you might say."

"You don't know it was cigarettes. If it was, they were overequipped for the cargo. Cigarette cartons are mostly air. A stack the size of what was taken out of that barn wouldn't weigh more than a crate of oranges. A station wagon would've done the job."

"You're going by floor space, from the clear spot in the dust. Those cartons might have been stacked to the rafters. Unless you know different." His slits narrowed to seams.

"I saw it through the window before. I told you that."

"I forgot." He squeaked his chair twice, rocking. "Someone tampered with a back window of the trailer. I don't guess you noticed that, Mr. Big City Detective."

I decided to get mad. It was the only thing I hadn't tried short of diving out a window. "Your hick-sheriff gag needs work. You don't have the accent. If you can't rig it so I broke into the church—and you can't—and you can't rig it so I broke into the house—and you can't—how can you tag me for murder?"

Squeak. Squeak. "People say liars can't look you in the eye. I figure they've never been lied to by a professional."

"I guess that's still an insult up here. Let's not fight." I shifted positions to put out the fire in my thigh. "You've only got cigarettes on the brain because of Jeff Starzek's record and crooks don't usually change their lay. But experienced smugglers don't kill each other over a six-month supply of butts. Whatever came out of that church was a lot more compact and a hell of a lot more valuable pound for pound."

"Such as what?"

"Such as that's your headache. I was hired to find Starzek, not break up Murder, Incorporated."

Deputy Yardley smacked his lips and redistributed his weight from one foot to the other. There's one in every department. It was too bad for him the place didn't have a basement. That's where they keep the rubber hoses.

Finlander stopped rocking. "Who's paying your freight?"

"That's confidential."

"Is it a lawyer?"

I said nothing. Hoping he'd run with it.

He didn't. "If you're not a lawyer, or representing one, you can't suppress so much as a fart without obstructing justice in a criminal investigation. Not under the law. And you sure don't look like a priest."

"I've already told you a lot more than Deputy Yardley's partner said I have to."

"Keppler's studying for the bar. He's got a fine clear voice. Put his bracelets back on," he told Yardley. "You're in luck, Walker. You get to fill out your jail collection."

Walrus Whiskers stepped forward, jingling his manacles. I'd

had them on before, but this time I'd feel them every time I shot my cuffs for a month.

"Do I get a telephone call up here?"

Finlander raised a hand, stopping Yardley in midcharge. "Lawyer?"

"Client. I need to clear it before I give up the name."

He was less imposing when he stood. He had short legs and they bowed slightly. It wasn't a comfort. The lower the center of gravity, the harder they are to tip over.

"Use line two," he said. "Line one goes directly to headquarters in Port Huron. Let's step out, Deputy."

"We going to just leave him here alone?"

"That window looks in just as well as out." The sergeant picked up my cane and looked down at me. "I'd stay in the chair. If you get up, you may need two of these."

He left by the only door, carrying the cane like a baton. Yardley jingled out after him. There was a window in the door and he filled it with his big fish-eating face. He would spend his weekends on the ice, bullying the bass out of the water.

I punched the second button on a black conference telephone the size of a window planter and dialed the Canons' home number. While it rang I fiddled with some of my effects on the desk, steering clear of the cigarettes and matches; Yardley might have thought I was getting set to torch the place. I stroked one of the small bills I'd broken out of one of Canon's C-notes. It had a velvety texture you can't duplicate no matter how much you pay for paper stock. That was where Honest Abe got his smug expression. I hadn't said anything to Finlander about last night's comedy with the state trooper, but only because I'd forgotten all about it. In the cold light of a cold day, counterfeiting seemed a long way to reach. Jeff was a small-time smuggler when all was said and done, working just a little less hard than the average stiff for the same blue-collar wages. His brave new cargo was probably stolen pantyhose.

"Hello?" Rose Canon's husky voice. No baby crying in the background today.

"Walker here. Talk to your husband?" I snapped away the five-spot, picked up my keys, and counted them. There was one I'd been carrying so long I forgot what lock it opened. I didn't want to throw it away in case I came across the lock. That was the investigating business all over.

"Yes. He knew someone had been smoking in the house the minute he walked in. When he started asking questions, the speech I had ready went right out of my head. I—made a clumsy job of it."

She sounded on the edge of hysteria. I talked her off the ledge, or tried to. "Speeches don't work. The truth sounds better when you shake it straight off the tree. What did he say?"

"Nothing."

"Nothing?" I laid down the keys and unfolded the circular Paul Starzek had had printed to advertise the Church of the Freshwater Sea. I couldn't keep my hands still.

"He sat in the same chair you did all the time I talked, staring at the floor and crackling his knuckles. I've asked him not to do that; it's like chewing tinfoil. Then he got up and went out.

"I thought he was coming right back," she went on. "He left the door open, something he never does. He says he isn't paying Michcon to heat the whole neighborhood. When I heard the car start I went to the door to call him back, but he was already gone. That was two hours ago, Mr. Walker. I think he's left me."

"It's never that clean." I drew a deep breath. "The ball took a nasty hop, Mrs. Canon. Someone killed Jeff's brother and buried him next to his church. The police want to talk to Jeff."

Air stirred on the other end.

"Jeff's no killer," she said. "He certainly wouldn't kill his own brother."

"We don't know yet what kind of brother he was."

I was barely listening to myself. I'd been smoothing the circular flat on the desk, idly pressing out the creases with my thumbs. Now I picked it up and rubbed one corner between my fingertips.

"Mr. Walker?"

She'd been talking, but for me it had been just so much buzzing on the wire. I apologized and asked her to repeat what she'd said.

"I asked if you were quitting. I need you to find Jeff now more than ever. He's all I have except little Jeffie."

"That's the job. It doesn't change until I find him or you fire me. Maybe not even then."

"Did you tell the police about me?"

"Not yet. That's why I called."

"What will they do to you if you don't?"

"That doesn't have to be your problem. I can tie my shoes and I'm pretty good at staying out of jail. I get plenty of practice."

"I just don't think I could face the police. Not until I know if Oral's coming back."

"Chances are he's out looking for me. I have one of those faces guys want to push in when they feel like pushing in a face. That doesn't have to be your problem either. I push back."

"You won't hurt him."

"I'll try not to. And thanks for the compliment."

I said good-bye, but I didn't hang up. That would be Deputy Yardley's cue to enter. After an empty silence, the dial tone kicked in. I nodded a couple of times as if I were listening and fiddled again with the five-dollar bill, rubbing it between my fingers the way I had Paul Starzek's circular. I put it back where I'd found it and cradled the receiver. Three seconds later the room was full of law, bringing the cold in with it.

Sergeant Finlander made himself comfortable behind the desk. Snow dusted his shoulders, but he didn't brush it off. The flakes, finer now, blinked as they melted into his uniform shirt, like fairy lights going out. "What's the verdict?"

"I couldn't reach my client."

"Horseshit," Yardley said. "You were talking to somebody."

"I had to leave a message with someone. They'll call back."

Finlander said, "I'll be sure and put them through to headquarters. You might have noticed we don't have any holding facilities here. We could lock you in the can, but then we'd have to go over to the White Castle to pee."

"I'm not worth that kind of trouble. Yardley saw me pull into Paul Starzek's place. There wasn't time for me to kill Starzek and put him in that hole. He was frozen as hard as cinder block."

"You could have killed him anytime and stashed him in the church, then come back to clean up." The sergeant played with a corner of the circular. I watched his hand like a dog. I couldn't help it.

I was holding my breath. I let it out. "I may have a lead. There's someone else I need to discuss it with."

"You had your call. You may think murder's instant overtime up here in Hooterville, but it's just one more thing on the blotter. We got vacation cabin break-ins, domestic shit, a meth lab we've had our eye on six weeks. You've used up our discretionary time."

"You can listen in. Or you can make the call yourself."

Yardley said horseshit again and took out his cuffs. He stood straining at the leash.

Finlander rested his hand on the circular. His face looked like a woodcut. "Who am I calling?"

I put one finger on a card he'd taken from my wallet and slid it across the desk. It had Herbert Clemson's name and number on it in raised glittering black letters.

TWELVE

Treasury paper." Clemson stroked both top corners of Paul Starzek's circular between the balls of his thumb and forefinger. "When you said you had two words for me I was afraid they were 'Fuck you.'"

"I wouldn't have brought you up here for that," I said. "I didn't think you'd want me to be specific with the local cops listening in."

Sergeant Finlander had caught him on his cell, half an hour west of Ann Arbor on his way to the FBI field office in Chicago. He'd been intrigued enough to turn back without pressing for details. I knew then the thing was no coincidence. The case was too important to discuss any way but in person.

We were sitting away from customer traffic in a White Castle, the one whose bathroom the deputies and command officer used when the one in the substation was occupied. I'd suggested it because I was hungry. Clemson had agreed because the late-afternoon rush hour was in full cry and most of the diners were lined up at the drive-in window and on foot at the counter for take-out; the sit-down crowd wouldn't start gathering for another couple of hours. We had a table without neighbors by a window overlooking a four-lane highway that never went empty, and whenever an employee wandered by to wipe off a table or sweep under a chair, Clemson stared at him until he went away.

"Better give me a bill, just to make sure." The agent let go of one corner to snap his fingers.

I munched on a greaseburger. "Use one of your own. I paid my taxes already."

He clicked his tongue against his teeth and got out a wallet made from the same pigskin as his badge and ID folder. There were at least two more John Doe warrants folded inside it, separated from the bills by a suede partition. He'd used one of them to remove me from county custody. Finlander had taken his signature on a sheaf of forms as thick as *National Geographic* and let me go without a squawk. Deputy Yardley had chewed off the ends of his walrus moustache and gnashed most of the way through his second set of teeth.

Clemson selected a crisp ten-spot, rubbed it and the circular simultaneously using both hands. He turned his back to the room, shielding himself while he held first one, then the other, then both side by side up to the light coming through the window. It gleamed red through his curly hair and made a shadow in the deep cleft in his chin. He hadn't stood any closer to his razor today than yesterday. I'd probably been on stakeout somewhere when that became a fashion statement.

"Watermark's genuine, and at a glance I'd say the thread count checks. The Bureau pays someone else to count them." He put away the bill and the wallet and looked at the circular, as if reading it for the first time. "We get anonymous tips about these shirttail churches every day. We try to check them all out. Most of the time, one of them built its porch too close to someone's property line, or some career atheist is afraid his kid will catch a dose of piety. It was the name Starzek that got us interested in this one.

Some of these Christian organizations are blinds to funnel donations to Islamist causes."

"What's the difference between Islamist and Islamic?" I slurped syrup and water through a straw. It tasted like cough medicine.

"Islamics pray to Allah. Islamists only get on their knees to blow an arms dealer. Not the official definition, but accurate."

"What's that got to do with funny money?"

"Same thing as cigarette·smuggling. Anything that generates a steady flow of untraceable cash is potential funding for weapons."

"Most smugglers are grifters. They wouldn't know how to find Iran on a map."

"I'll give Jeff Starzek a geography test. Why didn't you tell me yesterday you were looking for him too?"

"You didn't ask."

"That's so twentieth century. Now the burden's on the citizen to come forward and tell what he knows."

"You carry the burden. My leg hurts."

"Who hired you?"

"I hired myself."

"That isn't what you told Finlander."

"I didn't like Finlander. He looks like a cigar-store chief."

"You only tell the truth to people you like?"

"Sometimes not even them." I pulled a shred of soggy coleslaw out of my burger and laid it on my plate. I prefer my side dishes on the side.

"I don't like to snap people in the ass with the flag," he said. "Ever do a stretch in Milan?"

"I came close once. I understand the food's better in those federal pens."

"It's a shithole. Worse when you're being held on an open-ended charge of being a reluctant material witness in a national-security investigation."

"It's all tied up with my getting shot," I said.

"I wondered about that."

"Everyone does. You're the only one who didn't ask about it." I told him about Grayling, all of it, including Jeff Starzek. He listened with his arms folded on his side of the table. He hadn't ordered anything.

"You helped out a friend because he saved your life," he said when I finished. "What makes your hide worth more than your country's?"

"I just learned how to program my VCR." I wiped my hands on a napkin the size of a lens wiper. "How long would you have gone on wandering all over your sales territory if I hadn't given you that circular?"

"How long would you have hung onto it if you hadn't jammed yourself up with the law?"

"It's a chronic condition. Don't tell me you didn't pull my file."

"It reads a little like Victor Hugo. What's a vet with a bachelor's degree in sociology doing crawling over transoms and walking exercise yards?"

"The Peace Corps wasn't hiring. What's a hipster like you doing chasing guys in skirts and sandals and talking into his shoe?"

"How are the fries here?"

"Help yourself."

He plucked one off my plate, scooped up some ketchup, and ate it in two bites. "Could be crispier. Okay."

"Okay what?"

"Okay, you've made more progress on this case in twenty-four hours than my people have in three months. Your last contact with Jeff Starzek is more recent than anyone's I've talked to, and without a little thing like due process to slow you down, you've found something that's been missing almost a year."

"The circular? Paul Starzek had a whole stack."

"More than just a stack. Did you know Treasury paper isn't paper?"

"Don't tell me it really *is* lettuce."

"Okay, so you know." He frowned. We seemed to be saying *okay* a lot. "All those holograms and infrared ink in the new bills are basically bullshit. It'll slow down the counterfeiters, but only as long as it takes the old bills to wear out and stop being passed from hand to hand. The printing stock's our only real defense. No one's figured out a way to duplicate it in a couple of hundred years of trying, and hijacking's out because it has better security than the president. A single blank sheet is worth as much as the biggest denomination you can print on it. With modern methods and the right material—" He unfolded his arms and sat back.

"It might as well be genuine."

"It *is* genuine. The printing image can be copied within a gnat's whisker of the original. Even the authentic article varies microscopically. No two fifty-dollar bills are exactly alike."

"Like snowflakes."

"It's a lot less obvious than that. You need a couple hundred thousand dollars' worth of optical equipment to track the generations." He refolded his arms and leaned on them. "Civilian technology caught the District with its pants down, big time. We should've introduced the new bills twenty years ago, when we had the hardware and no one else did. It would have bought us some time to stay ahead. There are still billions of the old-style in circ, and one percent is fake."

"That's still just a few million, printed on toilet paper." I looked at the circular. I couldn't believe I'd forgotten it. "Oh."

"We've given the counterfeiters time to catch up with the new design, and now we've given them the stock to go on duplicating the old one and finance the research."

He stopped talking. A middle-aged couple and a boy of about

ten, dressing out to six hundred pounds total in bulky quilted over-coats, had begun to transfer sacks, paper cups, and a twenty-piece set of plastic utensils from a tray onto the next table. We stared at them hard until they became aware of us, packed up, and de-camped to another part of the restaurant. I felt like a bully in a ju-nior-high cafeteria.

"You can't steal Treasury paper," Clemson said. "It's not like knocking over a bank or an armored car. It isn't transported the conventional way, and the guards are troops in tanks. Direct as-sault is out; if it looks like an attack will succeed, the sentries have orders to destroy the shipment. There's more, but I can't tell you about it, because I don't know myself. My clearance only goes up to the attorney general."

"So how'd they steal it?"

"They had an accomplice named Uncle Sam. Same lazy bu-reaucracy that let five hundred tons of fissionable material drain out of the federal stockpile over ten years."

"My mother wanted me to take the civil-service exam," I said. "I kept putting it off."

"No one's ever failed it. Eleven months ago, someone too new to know how things are done in Washington decided to do an in-ventory in San Francisco and Denver. He lost his job, naturally. But not before it was discovered a ton of stock had disappeared from the United States Treasury."

"That's a lot."

"Not so much, in volume. You know how much paper weighs?"

"My old man drove a truck. He made regular deliveries of bound copies of newspapers to University Microfilms in Ann Ar-bor. Dock boss blew his whistle when the trailer was still three-quarters empty. The truck was already overweight. But that was paper."

"Cheap newsprint at that. Linen stock like they use for currency would've tipped those scales much earlier. Can you give me an idea how big that stack was you saw in Paul Starzek's church?"

"I'd say about the size of a double bed."

He nodded. I heard his brain ticking. He'd said he wasn't an accountant, but intelligence is a right-brain operation.

"That'd be a day's run in Denver," he said. "At a guess, fifty billion dollars."

"That's plenty of attrition. Who was minding the store?"

"Some foreman, just like your old man's. A bunch of them over who knows how many years. Sheet at a time, say, like Johnny Cash's Cadillac. At the end, enough to bankroll every paperhanging operation in North America."

A yellow schoolbus snorted to a stop outside the window. The black legend along the side branded it the property of a Baptist Bible study school in Monroe. The door cranked open, spilling out a matron in a fleece-lined coat and the first of half a hundred children in bright-colored snowsuits. The place was about to get noisy.

"What's their game plan?" I asked. "Flood the economy with phony scrip and bring it to its knees?"

"Some of my superiors think so. The Germans tried it once. You can't fault their reasoning; they saw what happened between the wars, when you needed a wheelbarrow full of deutschemarks to buy a stick of gum. It didn't work here. Our economic system's pretty sound, no matter what you hear during elections. A ton of paper won't push it over. But it'll buy enough weapons and sabotage to keep the jihad going for decades."

THIRTEEN

The church kids trundled in, with the matron shouting above the din for silence. I dumped my debris in a chrome bullet trash can and we left.

Young Deputy Keppler had driven my Cutlass from Old Carriage Lane to the restricted zone in front of the substation. The oyster-colored Chrysler parked behind it was invisible except when the sun pierced the overcast. That would be Clemson's. We stood waiting in blowing snow for a break in the traffic before crossing.

It would be a while. The community was a church, an extinct movie theater advertising Red Wing shoes on the marquee, and a row of brick two-stories joined by common walls on either side of a state highway. The traffic lights were timed to burn as much fossil fuel and run over as many impatient pedestrians as possible. Bitter little flakes swarmed in the high-beams coming from both directions.

"I can buy Paul Starzek's little church fronting for terrorists," I said. "The martyr they chose for their symbol is just the sort of overripe set piece those gibbering types go for. Now tell me why he printed his circulars on Treasury stock."

Clemson didn't seem to be in a hurry. His leather-clad fingers squeaked as he worked them deeper into the gloves, a sound that never failed to make my fingernails shrink back into the cuticles. "He must have gotten it mixed up with his everyday stock. Did you find a printer?"

I shook my head.

"Whoever took away the paper probably took that too. No professional shop would ever take credit for that circular."

"Amateur's one thing, stupid something else. That's a whale of a mix-up."

"The one time I interviewed Paul I didn't get the impression his ski lift went all the way to the peak. His name didn't cross with any of the legitimate schools of divinity in the FBI database, by the way."

"Phony preachers are as common as funny money. The old lady in the convenience store around the corner from Starzek changed a bill for me yesterday with a fake twenty, printed on common stock. It had to be part of the same mistake. But he did okay for a dope. He didn't buy that marble statue with Camel Cash."

"Recent purchase, or he'd have dumped the store mannequin by now. We'll trace it. There can't be many sculptors in the country doing that kind of work, if it's as good as you say."

"Maybe he signed it. I didn't look that close."

He didn't seem to be listening. "Of course Starzek was paid to store the stock until they came for it. He couldn't resist printing a little on the side. He had the equipment, for his circulars. That's why they killed him."

"Why didn't you haul him in as a material witness when you talked to him?"

"Same reason he screwed up. He was too dumb to trust with covert information, anyone could see that. The professionals may talk like fanatics, but they don't mix rhetoric with work. The rest—the five hundred virgins and the rotten poetry—is theater. They just underestimated his greed."

"That's kind of encouraging."

"Not really. They learn from their mistakes." He flicked a snowflake off an eyelash. "Paul was routine when I interviewed him, a family contact for a man who had no other family. We knew counterfeiting was involved. I wanted Jeff and his cargo. They were probably still on the road then."

"You better hope. It won't look good if that stuff was out behind the house the whole time you were grilling him about his brother."

"I forgot my bolt cutters," he said. "Also a warrant for probable cause to search the place. We go through channels, no matter what the civil libertarians say."

It was the first time he'd sounded less than ironic. I wondered if he really thought Jeff had no family apart from Paul. I was starting to feel like a cricket on a fishhook.

I said, "Paul wasn't so dumb he couldn't lie to you and make it stick. On the telephone he called Jeff a foul trafficker. He might call him anything else after fifteen years with no contact, but not that. The trafficking came later. Unless you told him."

"You know I didn't."

"Actually I don't."

He looked at me with the cold gray lines of the Milan Federal Correctional Facility in his expression. Then the cars thinned out and we started across, Clemson on the trot, me propelling myself with the cane in broken hops. I was getting better at locomotion. Give me six more months and I'd be outracing ice-cream trucks.

"I should've put Paul's place under surveillance," he said. "We'd have rounded up the whole ring and the Treasury paper when they tried to move it out. We're still a small agency; you need more than a hunch to tie up a detail twenty-four-seven indefinitely. Now we have to start pumping our informants all over again."

"You might also have prevented a murder. As long as we're dreaming."

"Speaking personally, I mourn a life lost. Professionally speaking, he can go to the part of hell where they keep the rich evangelists. My agency deals in whole populations."

A flatbed pickup hauling a pair of snowmobiles shushed between us, stranding me in the center lane with my shoes full of slush. I waited for it to pass, then gunned the cane to catch up. It was like skiing with one pole. "You think Jeff killed him?"

"Someone was bound to, a liability like Paul. Right now I don't know anyone killed him. Tomorrow I'll fly in a team of pathologists from Quantico and open him up. I'm sure these local medical examiners are competent, but the best is the best."

"He ought to be thawed out by then."

"You should've come to Finlander and let him do the digging. What are you, some kind of ghoul?"

"My physical therapist said I needed exercise." I was panting.

"Well, the crime scene is federal property now. There's no higher authority to bail you out if you set foot on it."

"And you feds have such a good track record in court."

We reached the opposite sidewalk. Little gray jets shot out of his mouth like water rockets. I was leaking steam all over like Old Number Nine. I hobbled over to a parking meter and leaned on it. Up there they put them against the buildings to clear the snow lane. "Which of your informants tipped you Jeff was involved?"

"That was fieldwork. I've been tracking that stolen stock all over my territory. That false twenty the old lady slipped you had relatives, all in this area. It might have been a trial batch before they committed the genuine paper. Who better to spread it around than the local cowboys?"

"Too thin. In my office you came on like you had him dead to rights."

"What, you never ran a bluff into day money?"

"You're bluffing now. Who's your man inside?"

"I couldn't answer that even if I had one. Why ask?"

"Was it Paul?"

Snow grizzled his dark curls. His expression didn't change. It was still filled with bars sliding on tracks like theater flats. "If it was, he'd be alive now. We look after our people better than that."

"I didn't mean that. Maybe he doubled back on you and your people downsized him."

"You must buy your fiction off remaindering tables. We retired all the death squads under Gerald Ford."

"And reinstated them under George W. Bush."

"You're just a goddamn lone rider, aren't you?"

"By default. Most of the time I can't get anyone to ride with me."

"Paul wasn't one of ours," he said. "Our recruiting pool's a bit less polluted than the enemy's."

"I'll run with that for now. I've only got two shoulders to look over."

"You don't have to look over either of them. You can go back to Detroit and work the private sector." He got out his keys and pressed a button. The Chrysler's lock opened with a falling note. "If I tell you how we got onto Jeff Starzek, will you do that, or do I have to take two hours away from defending America processing the paperwork on your arrest?"

"No."

He blinked. "No to what? You won't give it up, or I won't have to take you into custody?"

"The first. Two hours or two years. Four weeks ago I didn't have two minutes." I tapped my leg with the cane.

I didn't hear his response. He spoke under his breath and a car was passing behind him ten miles above the limit, spraying fantails of snot. But I saw the plume of vapor escape between his teeth and knew it was one syllable. He crossed the sidewalk and leaned in close. For a man who didn't shave every day he used expensive cologne.

"Jeff's our informant," he said. "Tell that to anyone—anyone, and I include your lieutenant lady friend in Detroit—and the FBI will open you up right next to Paul Starzek."

FOURTEEN

Most physical therapists are built like Bluto. Mine was a scrawny-looking five-eleven, 140, with Barton Fink hair combed straight up from the scalp and glasses with old-fashioned two-tone frames, black over transparent plastic, Buddy Holly–type metal inlays in the upper corners. Sometimes he reported to work in sweats, others in scrubs. Today it was hospital whites, with a blouse that buttoned at one shoulder, and navy deck shoes with thick white soles. He looked like a mad scientist and could bench-press a BMW.

He examined my thigh, first without touching, then pressing the muscles with his wiry fingers and bending and straightening the leg, cocking his head to one side as if listening for hemorrhages beneath the skin. I'd changed into my college boxing trunks and a Detroit Police Department T-shirt for the session. The thigh was bruised eggplant purple with mustard-colored streaks, and the pink new skin that had grown over the wound glistened like spackle. The suture tracks looked like teeth marks.

At length he lowered my foot gently to the floor and sat back on his low stool, resting his hands on his knees. "No session today," he said. "I can see you didn't sit out yesterday's appointment in a Barcalounger. I advised short walks, not racing city buses."

"I took a hike in the country." I was sweating a little from the pain of the manipulation. I was sitting on the end of a padded table that doubled as examination platform and exercise bench. We had the therapy room in Henry Ford Hospital to ourselves at that hour.

"You can't rush recovery. It takes as long as it takes."

"Says you. I'm going for the record."

"You're a police officer?"

"I'm a sleuth."

"What's a slooth?"

"A cop without a badge or authority or a pension plan. I'm a licensed private investigator."

"Oh. A sleuth. You might try doing your investigating from a sofa for a couple of days. No one knows for sure just how much a ligament can take before it goes out on strike, but I'd say you're getting close."

"What's the worst that can happen?"

"Worst?" He pursed his lips; not a flattering expression when you already look like a carp's cousin. "A handicapped card on your rearview mirror for the rest of your life."

"What's the next worst?"

"A year in a steel brace. This isn't a sprained ankle. A piece of metal tore a path as big around as a drainpipe through one of God's most magnificent designs, carrying away flesh and muscle and missing a major artery by a sixteenth of an inch. The human system can't replace those things, only stuff the hole with scar tissue. You're not the man you were before you were shot. You never will be. But you can live a normal life if you follow the program."

"I wouldn't know what to do with a normal life."

He drew a weary breath. He thought I was kidding. "You're in excellent physical condition otherwise. If you don't push it, you can throw away the cane in two or three months."

"Pushing it is my job description. What can I do short of stretching out in my pajamas and finishing *Jane Eyre*?"

"Are you haggling with me?"

"Just measuring my limitations. I'm not talking about paying holiday bills. Someone who never asked for help before is convinced I'm his only hope."

"That's one I never heard," he said. "Usually it's, 'I have tickets to Stanley Cup.' What are you taking, Vicodin?"

"Should I cut back?"

"Definitely not. If anything slows you down short of a rupture, it will be the pain. The addiction you'll have to deal with later. I didn't tell you that. My opinions aren't the hospital's. They're not even mine."

"What else?"

"Elevate the leg when you rest. If it swells, apply cold compresses. If it gives out on you entirely, call nine-one-one. What the paramedics do for you in the EMT will make the difference between a permanent limp and amputation."

"Thanks."

"If I hadn't seen interns push themselves past all human endurance, we wouldn't be having this conversation. Which of course we're not," he added. "Is this person you're helping a relative?"

"No."

"I never had a friend like that. Not one I'd give my life or my leg for."

"I don't know him well enough to call him a friend."

"Well, remember what I said. And that I didn't say it." He got up to see to his towels and things, abruptly enough to set the stool spinning.

———

So after all those years of carefree piracy, sailing the asphalt seas for treasure, adventure, and the pure joy of sticking his face into the slipstream, Jeff Starzek had become a spook.

Maybe he always had been. Maybe he'd been a mole from the start, not a lone wolf. Maybe the whole sordid chain of moonlit loading docks, flyblown motel rooms, and Benzedrine-fueled hours rocketing along gravel roads, two-lane blacktops, and heartless, hypnotic stretches of superhighway had all been part of the cover.

Pancho Villa. Jean LaFitte. Robin Hood. The line between bandit and freedom fighter has never been more than a smudge, a pencil line erased by the stroke of a dollar bill, a letter of amnesty, the Declaration of Independence—all, curiously, made of paper, good for rolling cigarettes and printing money, two things Jeff knew a lot about. Claire Chennault. Cole Younger. Chuck Barris, host of *The Gong Show.* Stirring stuff, and also the stuff of high comedy.

I drove downtown from the hospital, letting my reflexes do the reacting while I turned my thoughts to other things. The street was Teflon, generations of frozen slush with a fresh layer of soup on top. The gutters were flooded. I hydroplaned over black ponds and flinched when passing SUVs slung brown rooster tails across the windshield. Snow fell with sullen determination. It heaped the sills of boarded-up windows and capped the rusty banks rucked up by the plows from the last big fall. The winter was shaping up to be one of those where the first snow of November is still there in April, covered by layers like lasagna, each dyed a different color by the soot and oxidized iron that has bled into it in varying amounts. Ugly doesn't begin to describe it. Squalid is too kind.

I didn't think Jeff had started out as an informant. I knew relative strangers better than I knew him, but I'd known his type, in the twilit streets best crossed at forty miles an hour and in the

Cambodian jungle and in the locker room at Detroit Police Headquarters. You can always spot the one unbroken horse in the pad-
dock. If he's wearing a harness, you can bet it's his idea, and that
he won't be wearing it a minute longer than he has to. He's wearing it for himself, not for you.

After all those years working closely with hijackers, venal
store clerks, pliant cops, and his own wild breed, the first time Jeff
had asked for help from outside his circle had been Christmas.
That was just weeks after he'd scooped me up off that parking lot
in Grayling. If he was in a crunch that only a jobber like me could
get him out of, it was something new in his history. He knew how
to handle crooks, and a lawyer could free him from any legal tangle he couldn't bribe his way out of. I was sure it wasn't terrorists.
You knew you were in trouble with them only when the bomb
went off or the sack fell over your head. They didn't let you send
greeting cards. That left pressure from above. That was something
I knew a little about.

Chaos and order, black and white, the rock and the hard place.
I'd built my business square between them. That makes me the
only police force some people can turn to when they have a complaint. It's a definite niche. The pay stinks, but the hours are long,
and the benefits include county food, a cot, and free burial by the
state.

My building is a brownstone slab with Gothic ambitions, on a
block lodged halfway between small success and urban blight,
like a scraggly bush clinging by one root to an eroding cliff. An
ageless gnome named Rosecranz prowls its stairs and corridors,
downgrading the wattage of the lightbulbs, letting his telephone
ring, and pushing around the same cigar bands and Black Jack
gum wrappers with a broom nearly as old and bent as he. The
nine-inch Admiral TV in his office/apartment has been tuned to
the same station since the Mutual Broadcast Network went bust,

and he hasn't switched it off or turned the volume up above a mur-
mur in all the years I've been doing business two stories above his
head. Pigeons winter on the sills in their muted gang colors, and
once every couple of years a woodpecker in from the sticks blunts
its beak trying to pluck a caterpillar out of the solid stone face. My
neighbors make false teeth for patients who can't afford for them
to fit, set up budget vacations in North Platte, and teach the fox-
trot to customers who check their walkers at the door. Occasionally someone moves in for three months, monitoring auctions on
eBay and offering the losers a better deal on the items they
missed, then clears out before the FCC investigates the complaints. The tenant longest in residence is a deaf old man in a
straw porkpie hat and a beautifully pressed suit, out at the elbows,
who paints fiberglass fish and duck decoys for a mail-order firm in
Toledo that donates 20 percent of its profits to lobby for the aboli-
tion of fishing and duck hunting in the United States. The rumor is
he spent twelve years in prison in the state of Washington for
painting and selling fake Vermeers, and that his old cell was covered wall to wall with a mural depicting the third and fourth books
of the Old Testament. (Michelangelo held title to Genesis and Ex-
odus.) Acrylic paint crusted his nails and he let himself down the
stairs a step at a time, leaning on the rail, carrying a bundle under
one arm for the post office, and humming "Rag Mop"; every time
I passed him the song stayed in my head the rest of the day.

It's a little Hogwart's is what it is, if you know all about the
false bottoms, trick panels, and salted queens of hearts. I'm Harry
Potter. The wand's in hock.

I parked at a thirty-degree angle with two wheels perched on a
snow pile and approached the fifteen-watt twilight of the foyer.
The frail illumination made a mirror of the plate glass with the
night behind me as thick and dark as molasses. My overcoat
sagged open like a pair of shattered wings, traces of mud and clay

from Paul Starzek's grave still clung to my pants, and I was leaning heavily on the cane. I looked as old as the old fraud of a painter and not nearly as well turned out. I reached for the buzzer. I didn't have the energy to dig for my keys.

Swift movement in the mirror then, and I turned and lifted the cane just in time to deflect a blow meant to cave in the side of my head. It glanced off the bone in front of my temple, striking a chime. I followed through with the cane, gripping the crook tight in my palm like a roll of quarters or the bar of a set of brass knuckles, and collided with the slope of a jaw that shut with a snap and crunching teeth. A hand the size of a rack of ribs snatched at the lapel of my coat. I inserted my free arm into the tight space between us, pushed, sliced down the cane, and used it as a lever between a scissoring pair of legs, bracing it against the shin of one and twisting so it caught the other behind the calf and lifted that foot high off the sidewalk. I was still pushing, and the solid mass of muscle and bone and hard fat fell away from me and hit the sidewalk with a slap and a whoosh like a hot-air balloon collapsing on impact. It wore a dark snowsuit or coveralls with some sort of emblem on the breast pocket.

He wasn't through. I hadn't expected him to be; his work involved a lot of climbing and I assumed he'd taken his share of falls and learned to absorb the blow. He threw one leg across the other, trying to trip me with my ankle caught in the pincers, and although I saw it coming he succeeded; I was exhausted and in pain and my reflexes were slow. It was like fighting in a dream or in deep water. I struck the door hard with my shoulder, but the plate glass held, rattling like a thunder sheet in its steel frame. I pushed off, leaning all my weight onto the ankle still pinned between his and hurling a red-hot bolt all the way to the top of my skull—it was my injured leg. Black shutters closed over my eyes.

He made a little noise then, a pep-talk of a grunt as he tried to roll over and snatch my feet out from under me by sheer momentum. It held me from going under. I clamped my teeth down on my last ray of consciousness. Light returned in microseconds, not the minutes it seemed, and I twirled the cane, sliding my hand down toward the tip, and swung my arm across my body, connecting the heavy crook with the side of his head with a crack like an iceberg splitting. All of him sank then, as if the concrete and polar ice had turned to quicksand.

I kicked free of his slack grip, almost fell again, and braced myself with a hand against the door, panting while I waited for the man on the sidewalk to show some sign of life, or a gossamer copy of him to separate itself from his corpse and float to heaven, as in a cartoon. The principles of stick fighting were mired in the slag of decades that had slid down on top of my tour with the military police, but the object was to kill, not just neutralize.

He shuddered, groaned, stirred. I was definitely out of practice. I straightened up and tapped his shoulder with the cane. "Get up, Oral. I've done enough heavy lifting today."

FIFTEEN

osecranz didn't answer the buzzer. He never slept, so I assumed he was going through one of his periods of selective inertia. I disinterred my key and Oral Canon and I tracked dirty meringue onto the indestructible linoleum of the Perry Como era.

We stood for a full minute at the base of the stairs, I with my cane strumming under all my weight, the lineman holding his big bald head with one hand and looking as if all his air had escaped through the rip in the side of his slush-heavy Detroit Edison coveralls. The steps ascended steeply to base camp somewhere up in the shadows. Finally Canon spoke for both of us.

"Fuck it. There a place down here we can sit?"

I swayed over to the superintendent's door, two square panels of pebbled glass in an oak frame painted in fifteen coats of peeling green. The brass letter flap was sealed with verdigris. I banged with the cane until the door opened on Rosecranz and the little Czech automatic he kept in his hip pocket with his blue bandanna handkerchief. It wasn't that late; he'd heard the commotion outside. His eyes were wet circles of gray felt in the crumple of his face and he'd pinned up the broken strap of his bib-front overalls with a button that read WIN WITH WILLKIE.

"He lost," I said.

The wet gray circles floated past me to plop on Canon.

"Him, too," I said. "I meant Willkie. FDR went on to two more terms and got to be played by Jon Voigt."

His lips undulated a little before parting. "Ralph Bellamy."

"No, that was before. When was the last time you went out to see a movie?"

He thought—I thought. His face had only two moving parts. "Esther Williams. At the Broadway-Capitol." He brushed up on his Russian accent by listening to recordings of Khrushchev's speeches.

"Both gone. Maybe not her, but she hasn't had on a bathing suit in years. I need to borrow your place for an hour."

"What is wrong with yours?"

"Yours is more homey."

"Where will I go?"

"The bulb on the second-floor landing needs changing. I can see the floor." I thrust a wad of bills at him.

He put up the pistol, took the money, and stuck it under his bib. Then he sidled around the door without opening it any farther and passed between us heading for the stairs.

His office had been a cigar stand. It still smelled like a moldy humidor. Behind it, a bedroom and bath shared space with a forced-air gas furnace in place of the mammoth old coal burner of earlier days. Under the original stale tobacco the place smelled of pipe dope, half-washed laundry, and the shag he burned in his charred briar, scented with apple and bug repellent. On rent day Rosecranz squeaked his swivel up to a service-station desk with rings on it made by cans of Valvoline and scribbled his sums on the paper blotter, a palimpsest of old figures, doodles, and spilled

Mogen David. The rest of the time he sat in a fistulated armchair to watch television and teach himself English from his crumbling stack of pulp magazines. The colonial TV set muttered in a scratched walnut cabinet, its picture flipping like a window shade with its cord caught in an electric fan.

There wasn't room for anything else. In fact, there wasn't room for what was in it; the door traveled twenty inches and stopped against a cardboard carton piled with decrepit copies of *Airborne Ace* and *Ranch Romances*.

I left the perpetual flame burning. Turning it off and on after all those years might have blown the picture tube. Canon dropped his heap into the armchair. I sat down at the desk and started opening and closing drawers.

"What are you looking for?"

"The wine cellar." I twisted the cap off a bottle with Cyrillic characters on the label and sniffed. Pure grain alcohol lifted my hair off my scalp. I swigged, rubbed off the germs with the heel of my hand, and passed the bottle over to Canon while the heat blossomed in my belly.

He looked doubtful, but he wrapped his paw around it and poured an ounce down his throat. He coughed. "Holy shit. What is it, charcoal starter?"

"I don't think the fire marshal would approve pouring this on a grill." I held out my hand. He took another short pull, gagged again, and slapped it into my palm. A drop spilled on my pants, dissolving the dried Lake Huron clay on contact.

I drank. "How's your head?"

"I fell four feet once and cracked it on a cement block. This is a little worse. How's yours?"

"Mostly scar tissue. Your beef's with Jeff Starzek, not me. But I wouldn't choose him. He's got the reflexes of a jumping spider."

"Rose don't sleep around." He started to get out of the chair.

I pushed him back into it with the tip of my cane. It didn't take much pushing. God knew how long he'd stood outside in the shadows, stamping his feet and pounding his chest to keep his toes and fingers from freezing. January in Michigan had done half my job.

"I didn't say she did," I said. "I started out doing divorce work. You get so you can spot a cheater from across the street. She loves you, you big pile of compost. A woman like her can love two men and her baby without breaking training. Jeffie's yours, if you were worried about that. The great tragedy of the human genome is boys take after their fathers more than their mothers."

"I know that. You don't have to tell me that. I said what I said and I stand by it."

"In that case, what are we doing healing our bumps and bruises with Russian rotgut?"

"You and me had a business arrangement. It didn't have nothing to do with Rose. Well, it did, but it didn't. When a guy lets a guy he hired run around asking questions behind his back and getting answers the guy's wife wouldn't tell the guy himself, what's a guy supposed to do, I ask you?"

I took another hit. I was still too sober to sort that one out. I still had some White Castle in my stomach. It floated. "The husband's always the last to know."

"Fuckin' A."

I handed back the bottle without rubbing it. Any bacteria that could survive those fumes could arm-wrestle an octopus. I watched him tilt it.

"If you didn't know Rose wasn't Starzek's sister, how'd you find out he had a brother in Port Huron?"

My timing worked. He sprayed, gagged. Pellets of alcohol crackled on the TV screen. I watched him jackknife and claw for air. I wondered if I ought to get up and smack him on the back. It seemed like a lot of trouble when I'd just gotten my leg into a position that didn't hurt.

After a while he stopped barking. He mopped his face on his sleeve, elevated the bottle again, and bit the dog. He sat back cradling the bottle in his lap. His face was redder than usual. It would stop a train.

I said, "I was pretty sure Rose hadn't told you I found out about your trip to church. You wouldn't have given her the chance."

"You went up there too, I guess." His vocal cords twanged. "How'd *you* find out?"

"I'm a detective, not a splicing technician."

"What's that supposed to mean?"

"It means I don't make any money answering questions."

"For a minute there I forgot it was a business arrangement. What was that song upstairs about doing it for your old buddy Jeff?"

"Most of your fifteen hundred's in the bank. You can have it as soon as I can climb up and get my checkbook."

"Who'd I spend it on? Rose's left me by now." He looked at a set of scraped and oozing knuckles.

"Did you hit her?"

"No! God, no. I smacked my hand on the sidewalk out front. But she ain't the type to hang around after I said what I said." He started to lift the bottle to his lips, then leaned forward and banged it down on the corner of the desk. "Starzek or someone tacked a church flyer to a pole I climbed," he said, sinking back. "That's a no-no, so I tore it off and stuck it in my pocket to throw out later. I forgot about it till I got home and read it. There aren't that many Starzeks; I only knew of one. Anyway a storm hit that night and they sent me north with a crew to repair the lines. That put me only twenty minutes from Starzek's church, so I got somebody to cover for me and borrowed a truck. I guess I should be docked for the time I spent with the Bible-thumping old coot. What's five minutes out of twenty an hour?"

"Could be worse. Pay scale in Jackson's a lot lower."

"Edison can be a bitch to work for, but so far playing hookey don't qualify as a prison offense." A sad smile cracked his big face.

"Murder does. So far."

He blinked. "Jeff? Why the hell—"

"Not Jeff. I spent the afternoon with a sheriff's sergeant named Finlander, a real cupcake. Someone buried Paul Starzek under a pile of firewood next to his church. I'm not sure it counts as consecrated ground."

"Jesus. You don't think it was me."

"No, but sooner or later the cops will come around asking. You got directions to his place from the old lady who sells gas and groceries around the corner, and you may have been seen by someone else. You don't exactly blend into the scenery. I only spoke to Paul once, but I'm pretty sure he's the one who answered his telephone yesterday morning. If you can account for your movements between then and when I dug him up, the cops will let you alone. Chances are he was dead the first time I went up there. His truck hadn't been moved in a while and the old lady doesn't think he's the kind to go out for a stroll in the cold."

"I was out with a crew most of yesterday. This morning I had an overloaded circuit in a power station in Flatrock till just before noon. A dozen guys saw me. Paul was easy not to like, and I guess if I knew him better I'd hate his guts, but if I went around killing everybody I didn't get along with I'd be on the road all the time."

"What did you and Paul talk about?"

"I said I was looking for Jeff and asked him if he was any relation. At first he said no, but he wasn't much of a liar. Those people who went to his church must've been easy to fool; only not so much maybe, because the place didn't look any too prosperous. I kept on. He blew his top, said he hadn't seen his brother since he was a kid and didn't want to if he turned out anything like their godless hippie parents. That's what he said, 'godless hippies.' I bet he read the Bible every night till his lips got tired."

"What else?"

"He said he was fed up with people coming around asking about him. Then he threw me off his doorstep."

I looked at him. The sad grin crawled back up onto his face.

"Not really. I guess if he tried I'd've flipped him into a snowbank. He wasn't built nearly as stout as Jeff and he was a lot older. He told me to get out and I got."

"Did you happen to mention Jeff's a smuggler?"

"I don't know. I don't think so. We didn't get that far. What makes it important?"

"If you didn't, he was a better liar than you gave him credit for. He told the feds the same thing about not having had anything to do with Jeff in years and years, and they believed him, too. He knew Jeff was a smuggler. I think he knew because he was involved himself."

"You think that's how he got killed. Jesus, you think Jeff—?"

"No. Given the right circumstances anyone's capable of murder, but whoever killed Paul buried the corpse. Jeff might run from the law—that was his special skill—but he wouldn't scratch dirt over his leavings like a cat in a sandbox. No one knows him, not you or Rose or me, but I know him well enough to be sure of that. He took valuable time off a narrow head start to bring me to the hospital with law all around."

"That's him all over. Nobody ever saw him run scared. He's the original Roadrunner." He heard himself then. His face got dark behind the red. "That don't mean I admire him or anything he did. I saw Rose cry over him too many times. I guess I always knew why, I mean deep down. I wasn't so awful surprised to find out the truth as you might think."

"Still want me to find him?"

"Hell, yeah. Maybe I didn't, but just for a little while. I might have a chance against him with Rose, but the best man in the world can't go toe to toe with no ghost. I guess I proved I'm not the best man in the world." He seemed to sink deeper into the chair.

"The net's not too high, if you've seen the field."

He wasn't listening. He turned up his thick palms. "If it turns out he's what she wants, they won't have no trouble from me. If he makes her cry again—" He closed the palms into fists. Then he shook himself like a horse and looked at me. "Where you figure to start this time?"

"He told me in Grayling he was headed down the Lake Huron shoreline. I don't know for sure if he got as far as Port Huron, though the feds think different. Anyway I'm going to start from there and work my way north, run his route backwards. When I know where he was most recently, I'll be a month closer to where he is now."

"Month. Guy that drives like him could've circled the world twice."

"I had a tune-up last fall. I've been waiting for the chance to open up."

"I shouldn't've jumped you. I ain't thinking any too straight these days. Last week I almost fried myself running a high-tension line straight into a transformer."

"I hate it when that happens." I drank. It seemed to be intermission. Then I remembered something. "Still have that church flyer?"

He sat up, slapped his chest and his hips, then drew a sodden twist of paper from a slash pocket. The slush on the sidewalk had soaked through his coveralls. I spread it carefully, recognizing the soured older version of Jeff Starzek's face on Paul Starzek's body and the smudged letterpress advertising the Church of the Freshwater Sea. It came apart in my hands. It was printed on regular paper. He wasn't dumb enough to make the same mistake twice.

Just then the hall door opened, Rosecranz leaned in, spotted the bottle on the desk, and asked what we were doing with his cleaning solvent.

SIXTEEN

North again. I'd become the needle on the compass.

The cleaning-solvent crisis turned out to be a false alarm. Oral Canon had the emergency operator on the telephone when Rosecranz confessed we'd been drinking from a bottle of vodka smuggled through U.S. Customs from Kiev. He only drank from it on Jewish holidays and used it to scrub the grime from the stair rail the rest of the year. Oral went back to Oak Park to recover what he could of the fragments of his marriage and I went home to sleep. I didn't know how he came out, but I got up only once during the night to swallow a pill and flush the cotton off my tongue with water.

I got the jump on the morning rush. The sun broke red as an angry boil over Lake Huron, dyeing the lake-effect snow across the roadway a shade of pink that did nothing for my hangover. The stuff had swept across both lanes with a feral will of its own, obliterating the centerline and aprons. Avoiding drifts, I drove over virgin countryside broken only by mule-drawn harrows and the curses of German farmers. I got stuck seven times and rocked my way out, abusing the clutch and my good leg as well as my bad. I crawled for an hour behind a snowplow and made five miles. I grew to hate Currier & Ives.

Then the push started for the eight o'clock whistle and a steady desperate stream of Tauruses, Infinities, buzzy little Civics, and a continuous iron girder of armored SUVs blew the powder off the road and tamped the heavy wet foundation into a footing of solid glass, sixteen inches deep and as hard as Old Man Winter's mean little heart. Up around Fargo—a city I'd thought was stored safely away in North Dakota—an idiot at the wheel of a twenty-ton Freightliner boomed past me doing eighty on a gentle curve. The volume of air spun me into a 360, shaving steel off a guardrail and my left front fender.

I sat there a minute with the motor running and my heart in my lap, then exited and drank a quart of black coffee at a Burger King. I eavesdropped on a party of old men telling Paul Bunyan stories in the window.

"You heard Lyle Mundy died."

"Who's Lyle Mundy?"

"Lyle Mundy! You remember Lyle."

"I don't remember any Lyle Mundy."

"Sure you do. He got his foot cut off by a brush hog."

"Oh, Lyle *Mundy!* How'd he die?"

"Brain aneurysm. Went like that."

"That cocksucker always did have all the luck."

Up around Lexington, in Sanilac County, I cut my speed and started paying attention to hotel and motel signs. If Jeff Starzek had run his last route directly from Grayling, that would be as far as he got when he stopped to rest. Contrary to popular folklore, smugglers are almost never in a hurry, smashing through road-blocks and careering down mountain roads with the police in hot pursuit. When they have a deadline to meet, they adjust their schedule so they can make it without tipping over the speed limit and risking a pullover, and when they do attract red flashers they generally stop and take their medicine, fleeing and eluding being the one rap that sticks when all the others fall away. They can cross three large states in a day when they want, but the best of them make regular stops to eat, fuel up, stretch their legs, and sleep. They're the safest and most law-abiding drivers on the road.

Jeff usually ran by night, when the troopers had their hands full with drunks and overweight trucks dodging the scales that are open only during the day. He bailed out of morning rush hour into someplace quiet, parking his muscle machine out back near a window where he could keep an eye on it or hear the grumble of the engine starting. The cargo was more valuable than the carrier. I was looking for a place that was likely to offer vacancies on the ground floor, off the beaten track but not far enough off to make the regular roust sheet, with separate outside entrances to the rooms. That let out most of the national chains, where any officer with a partner could seal off both exits. I wanted a Bide-a-Wee, an Alpine, a Hiawatha Motor Lodge. Someplace where Ma and Pa Kettle rubbed fenders with Bonnie and Clyde.

I spent twenty minutes following the directions on a pitted sign half-hidden behind shaggy hollyhocks ("FORTY WINKS INN for the Weary Traveler - Ice - Color TV") and found a burned-out shell on a two-lane blacktop. I turned around and went back to the main highway. There is no mountain in Mt. Clemens, or anywhere else in Michigan, Mounts Brighton and Pleasant and Peach Mountain to the contrary. The Great Lakes had planed the northern two-thirds of the state as flat as a cookie sheet before the first Indian. I passed a gaunt grain elevator I saw for a mile, read three plain signs welcoming me to my own cottage at the Edelweiss Chalet, and turned onto a freshly plowed gravel road between farms lying fallow under three feet of snow. In a little while I was in pickup city, where a plywood cutout of a jolly fat man in lederhosen and a Tyrolean hat beckoned me into a faux-Tudor office with half-timbered bungalows behind it, lined up under a common roof.

The office was a plasterboard box, overheated, with a Coke machine, a waist-high woodgrain-printed counter, and behind it a man who'd never been nearer Switzerland than Atlantic City. He'd STPed his muddy brown hair into a ducktail and carried his shoulders up around his ears in the classic convict's cringe. He didn't recognize Jeff from the picture and couldn't remember anyone specifically requesting ground-floor accommodations within recent weeks. I didn't ask to see his registration cards or try to sneak a look. Jeff would disguise his handwriting and write in a phony automobile make and model and plate number; he couldn't be sure it would be me looking. Out back I caught a teenage housekeeper shaking out a bath mat. The photo didn't ring any bells. I gave them each a couple of bucks and got back on the road.

The story this time out was there'd been a death in the family and I was working for the estate lawyer to round up all the heirs. It was old enough to be respectable, even if nobody believed it, and implied there was money to be made in return for reliable information. I'd dressed down for the natives, in a green parka, worn Dockers, and work boots, and the cane was good for sympathy. The new year was only a few days old but was starting to look pretty much like all the others, give or take a crippling injury.

No major expressways have carved up the Huron shoreline yet, dropping trails of Taco Bells, Wal-Marts, and Uncle Ed's Oil Shops. Of course the fast-food chains are represented—they travel on the wind like parachute seeds—but in singles only, not acres of plastic and steel and overflowing trash cans. The local steak-and-egg cafes operate inside the survival margin. The state highway is one long Main Street running past Woolworth's, small navigable hardware stores, and the one-screen movie theater. The parks have cannons, the VFWs hold bingo tournaments. When you slow down, the pedestrians either wave at you or put their hands in their pockets and glower; strangers are a big deal. The dogs are all named Duke.

I ate several bowls of chili in several Sugar Bowl Diners and bought a roll of Tums in each of a half-dozen pump-and-pantries, just to cover the bases. All the conversations I overheard had to do with some variation of Lyle Mundy and his fortunate fate. The counter help and regulars shook their heads when I showed them Jeff Starzek's picture. I didn't really think they'd tell me they bought merchandise from a smuggler, but their faces were easier to read than the urban kind. The trick was not to expect a break, but not to miss it when it broke. Complacency had gotten me shot once.

Just to be thorough I tried a bed-and-breakfast, in an old brick farmhouse; the barn, a massive relic from the golden age of European immigration, was an antiques mall in warm weather. It was one of those places with big poofy beds and two rooms to a bath, with plenty of oak and flocked paper in the foyer and a guestbook on a stand. A funeral director could have moved in without redecorating. A sweet-faced old lady doused in lavender told me she rented to couples only, lifted the glasses on the chain around her neck to stare at Jeff's picture, and apologized for not being able to place him. She offered me ribbon candy from an oval dish.

Wherever you go, there is someone willing to take your money and give you a roof for the night. I drove past three or four likely places because I was tired of talking to strangers and absolving them of their ignorance.

In Port Sanilac, just below the nail of the Thumb, a squall blanked out the windshield, lifted the Cutlass off its wheels, and set it down on a Y branching off to the left. At least it felt that way.

Probably it was nothing less prosaic than the gust blowing me off course when I couldn't distinguish between road and country. Anyway when the white dust settled and the wipers gouged out eyeholes in the mask I found myself on a snowmobile track with nothing but DeKalb signs on either side, and up ahead, like a lighthouse beacon, a rectangular sign on aluminum poles sunk deep in snow, illuminated by sickly yellow beams from a row of cup lights on top:

THE SPORTSMEN'S REST
Rooms by day or week
Your journey ends in 1500 feet

I shifted into first to beat the drifts and powered on. I had no illusions. Fate whispers in your ear. It hardly ever screams in your face.

SEVENTEEN

The road—some kind of access that had had its day as a major artery before the state bulldozers came through—bent to the right around an old-growth oak hoary with vines and sprung birds' nests to parallel the newer blacktop and the lake. I passed a deserted glazed-brick filling station sprayed all over with graffiti, the boarded-up remains of a frontier false-front souvenir shop, ropy also with garlands of black and green acetate, and a half-collapsed sign in a snowfield advertising a roadside zoo. It was all reminiscent of an extinct civilization that hadn't progressed far beyond cliff-dwelling.

I saw a leaping fish, then descended a gentle grade and saw the angler on the other end of the line, dwarfed by perspective in water almost up to his vulcanized waist, gripping his bent rod with both hands; an *Outdoor Life* cover blown up to Cinemascope. A timber framework supported the sign on the curved slope of the roof belonging to a railroad caboose, painted schoolhouse red and parked on a forty-foot section of track. It was as if car and rails had been lifted in one piece from the Oregon Short Line and deposited in the middle of four scraped acres. Around it, broadcast as if by the same great hand, were six smaller structures, four of which had been trucked in and plopped down on concrete blocks, the other two assembled on-site from boxes of giant Lincoln Logs. White aluminum sided the modular units and someone had painted the log cabins the muted orange of Campbell's tomato soup.

Behind this prefab fairyland, trucks and passenger cars hummed along the charcoal line of the state highway, and fishermen's shanties dotted the white apron of the lake like houses on Baltic Avenue. It was as surreal as the Thumb area gets, and just the kind of place for the traveler who likes to avoid the main track and blend in at the same time. I had no hope of tracing Jeff Starzek to it. It was too on the nose.

It was a weekday, and I shared the freshly cleared parking area with a snowmobile chained to a railroad tie and an old station wagon with woodgrain sides and a bumper sticker on the rear hatch reading FISHERMEN DO IT WITH A LURE. A gargantuan CXT pickup, nine feet tall, eight feet wide, twenty feet long, squatted on tractor tires next to the farthest bungalow with a snowplow blade mounted in front.

I walked around a parked snowmobile, climbed gridded metal steps to the caboose's door, and opened it to the smell of old wood and generations of cigarettes. Someone had varnished the walls to slow down dry rot, sparing only a knotty-pine partition in back, which presumably sealed off the office from a living area. It looked yellow against the dark shellac of the walls, but did nothing to lift the gloom. Even the four-paned window looking out on the white-on-white landscape looked like a decoration intended to brighten the interior. There was an Indian rug woven by the Taiwan tribe on the floor, some overstuffed chairs no one ever sat in, a display of antique fishing lures locked behind dusty glass, and a yellow-oak sauropod of a teacher's desk, complete with a crank pencil sharpener mounted on one corner, holding up a small wooden file box, a perpetual calendar and message pad set in matching pebbled brass, and a lethal projectile of a ceramic ash-tray the size of a platter, heaped high with squashed butts, some of which continued to smolder sullenly. A side-by-side shotgun with curled brass hammers hung on pegs on a wall behind the desk.

"Welcome to the Rest! You here for Tip-up Town?"

The woman seated under the shotgun, with a hand-rolled cigarette gushing smoke in one hand and a wedge of lime bobbing in a bottle of Corona in the other, was the roundest thing I'd seen on feet. Her face, nearly as red as Oral Canon's, was a mass of bunched globes anchored by a tiny nose that curled like an endive at the tip. Bosom and belly heaved at the buttons of her XXXL flannel shirt. Her hair was an improbable shade of yellow, brighter than the pine partition, flipping up at the sides and mashed flat to her head. Hat hair; I blamed the ear-flapped woolen cap hanging on an antler next to the wall telephone.

All that bulk, and all those cigarettes, should have given her the voice of a factory whistle, but it was as small and bright as a bird's. Her eyes stuck out like blue marbles.

"What's Tip-up Town?" I asked.

The eyes started out another sixteenth of an inch. I nearly lunged to catch them.

"Mister, don't *tell* me you haven't heard about the ice-fishing festival. It's the biggest thing to happen here since the French landed."

"The knob came off my radio. I didn't even know the French landed."

"Don't be fresh. Come Saturday you won't be able to steer a bike between the shanties. They pretend they're fishing, but what they're really doing is drinking beer and peppermint Schnapps. Their little spring-loaded rods do all the work."

"Oh, tip-ups. I tried it once. I'm still thawing out."

"Drying out, you mean. If those boys put as much antifreeze in their radiators as they put in themselves, I wouldn't spend half the weekend giving them jumps to start them back home." She took a puff and chased the smoke with two ounces from the bottle.

"You charge for that?"

"It's a service of the establishment. I make enough off them in three days to shut down the rest of the winter."

"I believe you. That truck outside retails at ninety thousand."

"Oh, that. I'm keeping it for a friend. His ex-wife's on the warpath." She paled to a brick shade. "I sure hope you're not her lawyer."

"I've got an ex-wife of my own. Your sign says you're extended stay."

"I've been meaning to take that down. I don't get much business by the week now that divorce is so easy. Hiding out from the wife used to be a bigger deal. I'm Miss Maebelle." She thought for a second, then decided to park the cigarette in a notch among the old butts and stuck out a hand.

I shifted the cane to my left and took it. It was like shaking hands with pizza dough. "A woman who does as well as you must be able to afford a husband."

"I buried two. Well, one, if you want to be technical; they never did find Jim after he took his Subaru out on the ice five years ago April. I was Miss Maebelle when I taught school. I never did get used to Mrs."

"You gave up teaching for innkeeping?"

The globes rearranged themselves into a scowl. "The school seems to be getting along fine without me. They just don't have an art or a music program. Don't let anyone ever tell you the arts have any importance in our society. They're the first thing the boards find they can do without when money gets tight."

"Which one did you teach, art or music?"

"Art, and the timing was a dirty shame. We were just getting into the expanding world of computer graphics. Another semester or two and I might have turned out the first Picasso to compose all his work on a keyboard. Don't forget, all the great twentieth-century artists came out of rural America."

"I think Picasso was Spanish."

"I should have said Pollock. Not the point." She put the cigarette back between her lips. "At least I had the Rest to fall back on, thanks to Jim. Poor old Arthur Weeks gave thirty years to the district. Thirty nails in his coffin when it came to finding someone who'd employ a sixty-two-year-old academic with an MA in Renaissance music. He moved in with his daughter and son-in-law and just faded off at the end like an old song. All because someone in Lansing couldn't balance his own checkbook, let alone the budget." She squirted out bitter gray jets as she spoke, the cigarette bobbing on her lower lip.

"I'm not here to fish," I said. "Not with a pole."

She stiffened. The globes that made up her face jiggled for a few seconds after she went motionless. Maybe she thought I represented CXT truck's ex-wife after all.

I showed her my license and the deputy's badge I got in a box of Cocoa Puffs. "I'm working an inheritance job." I traded the folder for the picture of Jeff Starzek and Rose Canon.

She put down her beer bottle to take it. "I don't get many couples."

"The woman's the client. It's her brother I'm looking for. The family can't settle the estate without him present."

"How big is the estate?"

"It isn't the Illitches, but there's a consideration in it for anyone who shortens the search."

"How much?"

"I'm not at liberty to say."

"Horse trader. Is he a fisherman?"

"He's in sales, spends most of his time on the road. This is part of his territory. He likes the quiet, out-of-the-way places."

"It won't be so quiet come the weekend. Those anglers can drink, and then there's the snowmobiles, waking people up at all hours and scaring away the fish."

"I see you've got one of those, too. Unless it belongs to CXT Truck."

"A woman in my condition needs a little help getting around the cabins. I never take it out on the ice. One of these years someone's going to say something at the Air Horn and it'll be bloody as all get out. I haven't seen him, mister." She gave me back the picture.

"What's the Air Horn?"

"Truck stop up the highway, only you won't find room to park a Peterbilt between the pickups and snowbuggies this weekend. I don't mean to say the place is a bucket of blood. Fifty-one weeks out of the year you can take your kids there, buy 'em a Coke and a bag of chips while you drink suds with your friends. Mix the snowmobilers with the fishermen and anything goes."

"Would it be okay if I talked to your staff?"

"You already are. You might have noticed this isn't the Trump Tower."

I wrapped a five-dollar bill around a card and slid them under the edge of the mammoth ashtray. "This will cover long distance if you see him. There'll be more if you do. You can get a new sign painted. The one you have could use touching up."

"I painted it myself. I was a magazine illustrator before I got the call to teach. No work there now. You have to be half my age and know how to use a camera."

"Norman Rockwell's spinning in his grave."

She brightened. She looked exactly like a cartoon sun.

"I met him once, showed him my portfolio. I wanted to study with him."

"What'd he say?"

"He told me to paint signs."

"What'd he know?"

"Those who can't, teach," she said. "Only those who can can't teach. Try telling that to the governor."

I zipped up my coat. "Okay if I walk around outside and smoke? My doctor says I have to exercise my leg. I fell on some ice."

"Don't sue me if you fall on mine. I can give you a key if you want to check out one of the cabins. All but Twelve. Furnace broke down and I had to drain the pipes and turn off the water to keep 'em from freezing. All the repairmen are busy till next week. Biggest weekend of the year and I'm taking a beating because I can't sell out the shebang."

"I counted only six cabins."

"I started at seven. Makes it sound like a bigger place."

"Thanks. I'll just walk around."

"Too bad. You look as if you could use a little peace and quiet."

"Except for the snowmobiles."

The globes parted in a sweet smile with the cigarette growing out of it. "Jim always said you have to take a little snake with your Eden."

"A wise man."

The smile went behind a cloud. "Not so wise he didn't take his car out on the ice during the thaw." She picked up her beer.

Something caught my eye on the way out, a wall rack with display pockets containing pamphlets and flyers advertising area attractions. I pulled out one. "What's the Church of the Freshwater Sea?"

"You got me. People are always sticking things in there without asking. I ought to charge for the space."

"Can I keep it?"

"Knock yourself out. You don't look the born-again type."

"You never know. I almost died last November."

Outside I lit a cigarette and let the smoke warm my ears as I stumped around the grounds. The ache in my leg eased a little after being in one position so long, and I'd put together a happy meal of painkillers and a fish sandwich near Lexington. Far out on the ice, the angry spitting sound of one of the promised snowmobiles rose and fell above the constant whirring of wheels on the state highway. I stood in watered-down sunshine and watched a full-scale blizzard slap up against the sides of the fishermen's shanties, flexing them like animated Disney houses. It was over in seconds, leaving behind a crystal carpet that sparkled like shattered windshields in a sudden break through the overcast. The Great Lakes is a region like no other, brutal and beautiful.

The paper in my pocket didn't have to mean anything. It was printed on regular stock, and such things do circulate, hence the name. Still, I was forty miles north of Port Huron, and if what the old woman there had told me was true, most of Paul Starzek's congregation could barely make it to morning services from down the street. It seemed a long way to go to proselytize.

The wind reached me in a delayed effect, stiffening my cheeks and striking matches off the tips of my ears. I stood my collar on end, stuck my free hand in my coat pocket, and got my circulation moving. The snow squeaked underfoot, a sure sign the thermometer was brushing bottom.

The cabins and bungalows, identified by curlicue brass numerals tacked to the doors, were heated independently, but fueled by a common propane tank as big as a whale, beached on a concrete slab down from the caboose-office. The thermostats would be cranked down in the unoccupied buildings to conserve energy, which explained the heavier than usual frost on the windows. I went down to Twelve, one of the modulars brought in on flatbeds, next to which the leviathan CXT was parked. You needed to carry a lot of cargo or push a lot of snow to justify the payments.

This was the building Miss Maebelle said she couldn't rent because it was without heat. In that lake climate, the hoarfrost on the windows should have been as thick as plaster of paris inside and out. It wasn't. I looked up at the chimney vent that pierced the roof just below the center ridge and stared at it a long time before I decided I could see a shimmer of escaping heat.

I turned my back on it and gazed out across the lake, dragging smoke deep into my lungs to slow down frostbite. I wanted to look through a window, but I didn't want to be seen paying the place too much attention.

My instincts were sound. When I snapped away the butt and turned back toward my car, a broad shadow that could only be Miss Maebelle's face slid away from the window in the caboose.

EIGHTEEN

You never know what kind of music will greet you when you enter a bar up north. The closer you get to the Arctic Circle, the evener the mix of bluegrass, reggae, heavy metal, and polka. It all depends on whose quarter is in the slot.

Chet Baker sobbed at me as I opened the door of the Air Horn on a puff of overheated atmosphere and rubber galoshes. The place was an island built on the truss principle in a sea of diesels, clearing their throats in puffs of blue smoke that hesitated from time to time but never quite stopped; in that latitude, you burn less fuel letting the engine run than trying to start it back up. A row of refrigerated cases separated the bar and grill from a convenience store stacked high with canned soup, windshield-washer fluid, prepackaged sandwiches, pinetree-shaped air fresheners, cases of Bud Lite, and blunt instruments designed to test tire pressure and stave in skulls. There were showers and lockers in back. "My Funny Valentine" followed me to a booth made of molded plastic, where an exposed port in the wall had accommodated a telephone until recently, for the convenience of homesick truckers; the cellular revolution had made it redundant. I was either going to have to break down and get one of my own or brush up on my semaphore.

The place took the long-haul theme as far as it would go. Antiqued tin signs advertising Mack Bulldogs and heroic watercolors of Freightliners climbing icy mountain passes decorated the walls under a continuous shelf of oilcans, toy trucks, and wooden battery crates, and the juke was shaped like the front end of a 1930 International; an engine revved quaintly between selections. A bullet-headed bruiser and a lean coyote with a cigarette stuck to his lower lip clacked balls around a green felt table to no apparent purpose and the owners of a row of exposed butt cracks seated at the bar were watching *Duel* on video and rooting for the truck. There were still six hours of daylight and the place was more than half full.

Ambience seemed to be the chief sell. I waited five minutes for service, then got up and took a stool at the bar, far enough away from the truckers to spare me most of the cheering when the demon tanker obliterated Dennis Weaver's telephone booth.

The bartender was a fresh-faced kid with freckles and an ancient soul peering out through windows as blue as dime-store sapphires. I ordered a beer and asked him if the owner was present.

"Present." He stood a bottle on a paper mat with a square grille bearing down on the viewer.

"What'd you do, run the trifecta?" I drank ice-cold beer and waited for the heat. The British had the opposite theory about hot tea in India.

"Pluck and luck—and a trust fund that'd choke an elephant. Go ahead, call me a rich little snot. I'm used to it."

"Everything's relative. You probably had to fight your way out of dance class. This whole part of the country seems to be run by one-man shops. You know the Sportsmen's Rest?"

"Miss Maebelle." He grinned a flinty little grin. Whoever straightened his teeth had used a plumb line. "I went to her husband's funeral, not that there was anything to put in the ground.

Everyone's related here, or friends, or enemies of long standing. How is the old tub?"

"Healthy as a hippo. Drinks her weight in fresh lime every day."

"I guess that makes you a friend." He swept a drop off the bar with his thumb and sucked it clean. "What's the beef? You with Triple-A, checking up on her star-and-a-half?" He looked as suspicious as Opie Taylor.

I gave him a card. Proprietors of saloons don't like it when you flash a folder in front of the clientele. "A guy came into money. I'm trying to find him for the family. She hasn't seen him, she says."

He read the card. A lot of people just make a show of it, but he seemed to be looking for a watermark. "I get you guys from time to time," he said. "It's always a guy came into money. What'd he do, duck out on child support?"

"I do that kind of work too. This is legit. The family wants to find him."

"No inheritance, though." He slid the card back my way with a fingertip.

"I've got an expense sheet." I showed him the picture.

"Hey, Buzz! This a business or a hobby?"

"Excuse it, please." He snapped a finger at the photo and went over to the bunch watching *Duel*. He hadn't given it more than a glance. He filled two fresh glasses from the same bottle of Old Setter, parked it under the bar, and came back my way, mopping the top with a cheesecloth as he came. "How big's your sheet?"

I smoothed out a five on the bar. "That's to start. I haven't paid for the beer."

He left it there. No contempt on his face. I was starting to like him, but my judgment was suspect since the shooting. "He play piano?"

"He's pretty good. I like tin tack myself, so don't go by me." I left it there, the way he had the bill. It wasn't easy. I was starting to feel warm all over, and it wasn't the alcohol. I got out a ten and laid it on top, squaring the edges even.

"Me neither. I got a bum ear. First Gulf War."

I nodded. He was older than he looked.

"Ordered Old Milwaukee," he said. "Clydesdale piss, with a water chaser. I've got a policy. I sell alcohol, not bench space. He drank maybe a quarter of the bottle, never touched the water. What do you make of that?"

"What do you?"

"He set the glass on the piano and never moved it. A glass of water makes a pretty good mirror."

I rotated a quarter turn. A spinet, fairly new and inexpensive, with a plastic veneer, stood near the short hall leading to the restrooms and lockers. It was just something to take up space instead of a potted fern. I nodded again and turned back. "When?"

"Christmas Eve."

I drank from the bottle and pinned the two bills under it. "If you don't know, say so. I don't pay by the word. Next time, hesitate a little. You might put it over."

He straightened his spine.

"The beer's a buck six bits. Thanks for coming and don't call again." He turned his back and started wiping his taps.

I drank up. I was still sitting there two minutes later when he turned back. I pushed the bills his way. "That was a test. The job's a little like surfing the Net. You have to sort out the genuine screed from stories about alligators in the sewer."

He leaned on his hands with the bar rag still in one. He didn't touch the money or look at it. "You don't forget Christmas Eve in the saloon business. Half the place is celebrating and the other half is drinking to drown out the jingle bells. Either way they drink just as much and they don't go home before two o'clock.

Sometimes not even then, and ten minutes later the cops come around and threaten to call liquor control. You can set your watch by them.

"Meanwhile you got a wife at home who's three months along and she won't see you for another hour because you've got to balance out the register and put the cash in the safe and see out the help and swamp the sick out of the stalls in the bathrooms and look under all the tables for stowaways. You can't rush home because you might hit a deer, and all the time you're opening your presents next day you're listening for the telephone and the call that tells you you're being sued by the survivors of some smashed-up drunk because you sold him a perfectly legal beverage without giving him a Breathalyzer test first. I don't need a calendar to remember what happened last Christmas Eve, or the one before that, going back to when I bought the place."

I lit a cigarette. "Work's tough. I got shot outside a bar a lot like this one a few weeks ago."

"I thought maybe you were Bat Masterson."

I laughed. He laughed. It wasn't that funny. We were letting out the bad air.

"Buzz. That your name?"

"Also Mac, Ace, and Slim. At home I'm Ronald. My folks were Reagan Democrats in California."

"Mine named me after half a radio show." I shook his hand.

"I don't know what that means."

I showed him the picture. He nodded and made a circular motion with the rag. The bills vanished.

"Yeah," he said. "Solid little guy. I broke my hand on one of those in high school. They're as easy to knock down as a fireplug."

"Talk to him?"

"I asked him if that was his Hurst Olds parked outside, a cherry heap. He said yeah and I said I was all set to make a guy an offer on a Shelby Mustang when my wife peed on a stick. He said he'd trade places with me anyway."

"What'd he mean?"

"I guessed he meant he'd rather have a head on the next pillow than a car in the garage. You hear a lot of maudlin shit that time of year, but the way he said it was like saying he had to stop for gas before he left town. I liked him saying it. Most of the guys think it's a tragedy of our time I had to settle for a minivan. I offered him another beer on the house. He said no thanks."

"What else?"

"Nothing. The next wave came in and I got busy. I didn't know he'd left until Hap Hansen started playing and singing 'Grandma Got Run Over by a Reindeer.' The little guy was pretty good. Next to Hap he was Chopin."

"I think it's *show-pan*," I said.

He grinned tightly. "I know. That was a test."

I thumbed out another five-spot. He took it and opened the register to make change. I didn't take it. "How well you know Miss Maebelle?"

"Better than some, not as well as others. I wasn't one of her students. I'm not as young as I look. She buys her beer to take out." He jiggled the bills and coins in his hand, waiting.

"The owner of a truck stop must have noticed that CXT she's got parked out at her place. International doesn't sell more than a hundred of those a year."

"It's a lot of truck, even for a woman her size. Tip-up Town won't pay it off in ten years."

"She says she's holding it for a friend."

He found a place for the cash and put the rag to use. A fly would starve to death in that bar. "I hope for her sake she's charging storage. It's been parked in that spot for a month."

"It hasn't moved? Maybe in the last couple of days?"

"I couldn't swear to it. I don't look that way every day."

"She says she's got heating problems in one of the buildings."

"No shit?" He looked unimpressed. "I had to shut down for a week last February on account of burst pipes."

I showed him Paul Starzek's church flyer. "See anyone passing these out?"

"Not that one. I get Witnesses, Adventists, Church of Christ, Scientists. One raggedy-ass Buddhist with a bad case of the shakes; I don't think he's committed. No Freshwater Sea."

I put it away and got my wallet out one more time. He held up a palm.

"It's not a good idea to flash too much cash here. Truckers are as honest as anybody, but the pilot fish that swim around them are as bad as bad gets. The hookers bang on cab doors before they come to a stop. What's the racket, hijacking?"

I put the cigarette out in a tray shaped like a truck tire. "Seen any queer bills lately?"

He made a move for his apron pocket, checked himself.

"The ones I gave you are good, so far as I know," I said.

"I found a bad twenty Christmas morning. I reported it."

"How'd you spot it?"

"Cheap paper. What's counterfeiting got to do with inheritance work?"

"Not a damn thing, brother."

"My brother's a dispatcher with Roadway. I only hear from him when the Lions don't cover the spread."

"How well do you know Miss Maebelle?"

"I tend bar. I know everybody and nobody at all."

I thanked him and left. On TV, the evil truck was plunging into the canyon. The gang at that end of the bar had lost interest and started arguing about the bill.

NINETEEN

B ack on the highway, I got out of the path of a Sanilac County cruiser with its lights and siren going and watched its square rear end sproing into the distance, slush flying from all its tires. That settled the point. As hunches went, the one that had led me to the Sportsmen's Rest wouldn't hold up to cross-examination by a six-year-old. An experienced lammister like Jeff Starzek wouldn't have put up there for an hour, let alone overnight. If he broke for it, his low-slung bucket wouldn't make six hundred yards on the snow track that ran past the place with a four-wheeler in hot pursuit. Ditto a dash across country to make the blacktop. I'd been pushed that direction by nothing more substantial than a divine wind: *Kamikaze* is the Japanese term. It fit me so well it sent cold splinters up my back with the heater blowing full blast.

He'd stopped to play piano at the Air Horn Christmas Eve. It seemed to be the only rest he knew. That was nearly a month fresher than any other news about him, but it was ten days old, and it didn't put him any closer to Miss Maebelle than two miles. I wouldn't have found the place on my own. The only evidence the cheerful fat woman had told me a fish story was a monster truck that retailed higher than her four acres lakeview and the fact she'd lied to me about Cabin Twelve, and daylight was no time for me to make that long a cast. I needed a place to curl up until nightfall.

In Thumb terms, Port Sanilac is San Francisco. It has a harbor, an airport just large enough to accommodate commuter planes, and a number of motels belonging to the smaller chains. Lake freighters steam right past on their way down to Detroit and Toledo, but in summer the pleasure boats stack the slips six deep. They were in mothballs now; the marinas were shuttered tight and the harbor itself looked as bleak as Little America. The clerk at the place I checked into, a compact redhead in a green vest, French cuffs, and from the amount of makeup on her face an Avon rep on call day and night, glanced at my cane and said she had a handicap room available on the ground floor. I said I needed quiet and took a smoker on the second floor back. It had a radiator, a bathroom with a chute for throwing away used safety blades, a telephone, a TV with a dial and no remote, and a mattress made from old refrigerator boxes. I sat up in bed with my leg propped on pillows, smoking and watching real people discussing their infidelities with an interviewer, waiting for more real people to come on and practice their infidelities before a coast-to-coast audience. That would be the evening lineup, and time to go to work.

When I got tired of smoking I napped. Fifteen minutes later I got up, took the .38 Smith & Wesson Chief's Special out of my overnight bag, and sat down on the bed to check the chambers and test the action. I hoped it wouldn't throw off my balance.

TWENTY

The curtain dropped square on six with a nearly audible thud, pierced only by the security lights in the motel parking lot and the tiny yellow glow of the odd Coleman lamp out on the lake, the other side of the universe. I snapped on the bedside lamp and got into warrior mode.

I stripped and put on a thermal suit I'd packed. It clung to my skin, all loose-woven cotton and space-age elastic, and felt like chain mail. Over it I pulled on wool slacks, a flannel shirt, and heavy ribbed socks that reached almost to my knees. With my feet in the lace-up boots I'd worn all day—which I'd parked next to the radiator to evaporate clammy sweat—my coat, and a navy watch cap that molded itself to my skull and covered my ears, I felt impregnable, a sensation that would last for about two minutes in the cold. I left my snap holster in the overnight bag and slipped the revolver into the deep patch pocket on the side of the coat. Last I tugged a brown jersey glove onto my left hand, leaving my shooting hand bare. The material was too bulky to fit easily through the trigger guard; I could keep the hand in the gun pocket until I needed it.

In the full-length mirror on the closet door, I was a study in

muted earth tones, which blended into the shadows far better than
cat-burglar black. They'd be of no help at all when it came to
crossing two or three acres of snow. I looked around the room,
picked up the bag, and went out, but I kept the key. I didn't know
how late I'd be and if I'd have the energy to drive all the way
home that night.

I left by a back entrance at the base of a rubber-runnered flight
of stairs and walked through a vapor of spent breath to my car.
The crystals lit on my face like scampering spiders. The overcast
had vanished, opening the earth to the cruel constellations that
come out in winter and a cold that came straight from outer space.
The moon was a tattered semicircle and gave little light, a break.

The 455 ground, groaned mortally close to extinction, and
caught with a smoker's cough that settled into a smooth four-
barreled rumble. I'd left the blower on, and switched it off when
the first icy blast shot straight through three layers of material to
my feet and ankles. A shudder racked me shoulder to sole. I got
out with the scraper to clear the windshield, pausing several times
to tuck my bare hand under my arm and wait for the sensation to
return to the fingers. It had been a mistake to throw the other glove
back into the bag. When I got back behind the wheel the heater
had warmed up and I thawed the hand out the rest of the way in
front of the vent. Now it burned and throbbed as if I'd scalded it.
That was okay; it took my attention off my leg. I'd forgotten to
take Vicodin before leaving the room. I thought about the bottle in
the bag, but I didn't reach for it. Pain keeps you alert.

The little burglar kit I keep in the glove compartment got the
once-over in the dome light and went into the pocket on my left
side. In its vinyl snap container it looks at a glance like a portable
assortment of miniature mechanic's tools, appropriate to the owner
of a car thirty years old. At a second glance the wire picks and penlight are probable cause for arrest. In detective school they tell you

you need a steady hand, an analytical mind, and a gift for gab. They don't mention second-story work.

I took the side road to the Sportsmen's Rest in first gear, but just below the speed where I'd have to shift into second to prevent stalling. I needed it in order to churn through some new drifts courtesy of the lake. Even then I got stuck once and had to rock my way out.

At night the caboose and low bungalows set at picturesque angles looked like the aftermath of a train wreck. The only light visible came through the window of the caboose and the floods on top of the sign, another break. Apparently the fishermen on the lake were locals and the place was vacant until the weekend, with only Miss Maebelle present, drinking her beer and smoking her handmades.

I drove on past without slowing and went another half mile before I found a place to park, in an angular cut on the side of the road where the most recent snowplow had turned in to shove aside its load. The Cutlass' left rear fender stuck out a couple of inches into the roadway. I hoped it remained as untraveled as it looked. Outside the car I hesitated with the door open, then threw the cane into the passenger's side. From here on in it would hamper more than it helped.

South of Greenland and north of the Elephant Latitudes, there is no cold like the cold on the shore of a Great Lake after the sun's gone down in early January. It closes on you like the hinged halves of an iron maiden, exerting pressure like the weight of a great ocean. You can't get your breath, and what you manage to suck in sears your lungs like the air in a burning building. When the gusts come, pushing snow like clouds of volcanic ash, you can only turn your shoulder into them and wait for them to pass; otherwise you'll lose your sense of direction and they'll find you in the spring.

I trudged through my own wheel tracks with my chin on my chest and both hands stuck deep in my pockets, the cold touch of the revolver like a pump handle against my bare palm. In some stretches the loose snow had caved in to fill the tracks and I had to wade through it, soaking my trousers, but not for long. It refroze in the near-zero air, stiffening the wool and turning it into aluminum siding. The walking kept my feet from freezing, but I lost all feeling in my lower legs. Unfortunately, that wasn't where I'd been shot. I felt that part fine. Trying to keep my weight on my good leg made me wobble like a rickshaw with a broken wheel.

At last I made the driveway of the Sportsmen's Rest. I leaned against a tree trunk as hard as *Pilgrim's Progress* to wipe my runny nose on the heel of my glove and blow steam. The sweat of exertion froze on my face. I rubbed feeling back into my cheeks with my bare hand, put it back in my pocket, and shoved off.

A row of tall white pines flanked the driveway like giant pickets. I kept close to them for cover, and when I came to the last one I took a deep breath and sprinted jerkily across a broad clearing to a huge juniper spread nearly flat to the ground beneath the weight of snow, spreading myself flat alongside it. If she was looking through her window, I hoped Miss Maebelle would think I was a gimpy deer. I hoped she didn't need the venison. Folks up there don't decorate their walls with shotguns for *House and Home*.

I was lying on my belly on the earth's iron core, and it wasn't nearly as warm as advertised. A minute grunted past, also on its belly. The snowmobile parked near the caboose blocked my view of the door, but I was between gusts and didn't hear anything. I rose into a crouch and made for the big salami shape of the propane tank on its slab. This was slower going, because the way led across a shallow dell filled with drifted snow. I wallowed through it hip-deep, the slowest-moving target since the great woolly dodo and as hard to spot in reflected starlight as an eight ball on white linen, but I had the caboose's blind corner between me and the window now and I could concentrate on my destination. I was wheezing when I reached the tank and sat down in the snow with my back against the slab's hard edge. My pulse ping-ponged between my ears. This was no work for an aging PI with a disability.

The thermal underwear had been a mistake. Cotton is absorbent, and the longer I sat the clammier I felt. My leg had given up throbbing and sent a clear unbroken signal to my brain like a needle through my eye. I got up again, and even though there was another window on the side of the caboose that was now facing me I trudged a straight line through snow over my boot caps to the prefab bungalow with the Incredible Hulk's truck parked outside it. I needed all the physical resources I had left just to finish the job.

Luck and inertia—Miss Maebelle's inertia, not mine—were on my side. A middle-aged woman of her girth didn't push herself up out of her chair just to look at the scenery, and so far the blanket of snow had been insulation enough to muffle whatever noise I'd made, mostly of the panting variety. Nobody shot at me as I passed around the end of the truck, placing it comfortingly between me and the caboose. The snowmobile stayed silent. I laid my naked hand on the truck's hood. The engine was cold, and from the snow tented around the tires it hadn't moved since my visit in the afternoon. Standing close to it for the first time, I felt like half a dwarf. The cab stuck up a yard above my head, a giant straight out of Norse mythology, and I could stretch out across the front seat with almost a foot to spare on either end. The extension behind the seat was bigger than my kitchen. The bed, lined with stainless steel, ran only a third of the total length, but you could have parked a spare pickup inside it if you didn't mind dropping the tailgate. The vehicle was what Goliath drove to the field of battle. Later, David pulled the wheels and made it his palace. Next to it, a Hummer was a Shriner's car. Telephones installed front and rear would have different area codes. You needed a rope ladder to climb inside and a parachute to get back down. It was taller than the Flatiron Building, wider than Hadrian's Wall, longer than the first flight at Kitty Hawk, and burned more gasoline than Saddam Hussein. It was a very big truck.

I hoisted myself up on the step plate, rubbed a hole in the frost with the heel of my hand, and peered inside. The key was in the ignition with a nickel-plated CXT tag dangling from it. I worked the door handle and pulled. It snicked open. I pushed it gently until it clicked shut. That was carelessness, or arrogance. It made you want to drive it around the corner and park it, just to teach a rich motorist a lesson. I stepped back down and turned my attention to the bungalow.

I laughed a short laugh, a cone of smoke in the sharp air. The scale was all wrong. It was HO, and the truck was O. Hyperbole aside, the porch roof was lower than the roof of the cab. To exit the truck and enter the house was instant claustrophobia.

As phobias went, that didn't make my top five. With the truck for cover, I got out my Acme Little Giant housebreaker's kit, knelt, and inspected the lock on the front door. It was a standard cylinder on a spring latch, not a deadbolt, but the frame curled around the edge of the door, making the celluloid strip in the kit useless. I went through the inventory, snapping the light on each pick a tenth of a second, then selected one bent into a question mark at the end to move the tumblers and another shaped like a flathead screwdriver, but much thinner, to hold back the shield while I probed. Then I laid the penlight and kit on the doorstep and worked by touch and starlight.

I'm no Jimmy Valentine. With a pick in my hand I'm barely Jiminy Cricket. When it comes to breaking and entering, I'm more comfortable with a pry bar or an elbow to a pane of glass. It didn't help that I had to work with one ear cocked for the creak of a hinge in the direction of the caboose, footsteps in the snow, not knowing how far the little clinks and tinkles carried in the icy stillness. After fifteen minutes I had to put down my tools and blow on fingers with no more feeling in them than wooden dowels. When they started tingling I went back to work.

They were growing numb again when something gave with a tiny sliding sigh, ending in a click I felt in my testicles. I turned the knob as gently as possible and pushed, just enough to make sure there was no resistance. I didn't know what might be on the other side, waiting, listening, breathing in shallow gusts.

I put away the picks, keeping out the penlight, snapped shut the case, and returned it to its pocket. I took the glove off my left hand, put the light in it and the glove in the same pocket, rose to my feet, and drew the revolver with my right. I stood there for a moment waiting for my feet to feel like feet again and not flagstones. I'd as soon have fired three shots in the air as stamp them on the boards of that hollow porch. I swung the door open, stepped around it quickly, bumped it shut with my elbow, and sidestepped wide along the windowless wall to the right. Shooters in dark rooms always aim at the door first.

I stood hunched over, more out of alertness than self-preservation, listening to the language of the house. Each is a living organism, with its own vocabulary of squeaks, snaps, and moans of contentment and pain. Wind, the weight of snow on the roof, and timbers contracting in the cold kept my ears busy for a full minute. Something thumped, like a cloth-wrapped cudgel striking a human skull, and I nearly jumped out of my thermals. I twisted right and left on the balls of my feet, swinging the gun. Then the building shuddered and a forced-air furnace whooshed and rattled, exhaling warmth at my feet. The fan needed new bearings. Apart from that, there was nothing wrong with the heating in Cabin Twelve. And I was pretty sure the fan was the only other thing moving in the place.

Directing the penlight at the floor, I slid the switch to On and poked the thin beam here and there, never higher than the baseboards. The little house seemed to be all one room without partitions, kitchen, parlor, and bedroom sharing the same open space, with only a pair of louvered doors separating it from what was probably a bathroom. It had no furniture except an old-fashioned white enamel stove and refrigerator on the kitchen end. The compressor made no noise; the refrigerator would be unplugged to lower the electric bill. The warm air came from baseboard registers, placing the furnace in a crawl space under the house. It shut off after thirty seconds. The thermostat seemed to be set well below sixty, just enough to keep the pipes from freezing and dampness from the walls.

When the blower stopped, something flapped one last time and drifted to a stop like a falling leaf. My beam was on it, a white triangle that glittered a little, as if it were shot through with silver threads. It was the corner of a protective cover shielding something large and bulky from dust and the elements. I slid the little circle of light along its base. It took up the center of the floor, extending from kitchen to what would have been the bedroom if it had had a bed. It was shaped like a bed, but larger than king size. It would just fit in the back of the big truck parked outside.

I wanted to see more. The penlight could show me only a piece at a time. I groped for a light switch and found it, but couldn't risk using it. I turned off the flash and waited for my eyes to adjust to the gloom. In a little while I could make out the object's size and shape—rectangular, as guessed—but it wasn't enough. I made my way into the kitchen and felt above the sink until I encountered cloth. I pushed aside a pair of coarse curtains on a rod and let the accumulated light of stars and snow into the house. The window wasn't in line with the caboose. Even if Miss Maebelle was looking out, she wouldn't have seen the movement.

With my pupils opened all the way I owned the place. I could almost have read a newspaper, if my eyes were ten years younger and I had one.

The cover was white plastic, reinforced with fiberglass to keep it from tearing in the wind. That connected with what I'd guessed about how the cargo had been brought there. It would have been tied down during transport, but it was loose now. I bent, took hold of the corner flap, and peeled it up and back, like turning down a bed. The block of paper underneath stood high enough to use as a workbench. It was actually four stacks of table-size sheets, the stacks pressed so tightly together they might have been sliced in place, like a cake. I separated a corner of one sheet and stroked it between index finger and the ball of my thumb, just to be thorough. I'd known what it would feel like.

I realized I was still holding the revolver, and put it away to turn back the cover the rest of the way; the stack was uneven at the other end. A waist-high table stood there, supporting a paper cutter two feet square with a chopping blade the size of a machete, and next to that a rounded rectangle made mostly of black PCV plastic that looked like a model spaceship. I was just computer savvy enough to recognize a laser printer when I saw one, but this one looked like the prototype of something that wouldn't be on the market for another year or two; something that hadn't been invented yet. There were no buttons on what looked like the control panel, just a row of tiny portholes. I figured you could operate the machine just by passing your hand in front of them. State of the art times ten.

I took a calculated risk. I got rid of the glove on my left hand, which was making the palm sweat, positioned myself with my back to the windows facing the caboose, and lifted the plastic-and-fiberglass cover, pinning one corner to my chest with my chin to free one hand—holding it up like a harem keeper protecting the modesty of a concubine stepping from the tub. I hesitated, snaring my breath, and passed the hand along the portholes.

They lit up, illuminating only themselves. The few moving parts inside—rollers, conveyers, whatever—made no more noise than falling snow. I wasn't sure at first if I heard anything, or if the thing worked. Then a long sheet of printed paper slid out of a nearly invisible slot under the control panel, licked out like an enormous tongue. The lip of a plastic tray slanting down ten degrees from the edge of the printer stopped it from sliding to the floor. As soon as it was clear the lights went out and the machine went silent, trailing off in a dying whir.

Pale as they were, the lights had spoiled my night vision. It was at least a minute before I could pick up the sheet by the edges, to avoid smearing the ink, and study it on both sides. I was holding four hundred dollars in old-style twenty-dollar bills, all squared off like a sheet of stamps, back and front, altogether about ten inches wide and a little over legal length. Ironic term. Three minutes with the cutter and they would be ready to spend.

Just then I heard the tenor thunder of a snowmobile starting up near the caboose. I hadn't been as discreet as I'd hoped.

TWENTY-ONE

The snowmobile engine barked and chortled, warming up. It was a feral sound; in imperial Russia it would have been a pack of wolves clearing their throats for a good howl, followed by an old-fashioned feeding frenzy.

I folded the sheet of bills into a square, then a rectangle, and stuck it in my pocket. It felt like the world's biggest banknote. I pulled the cover back over the stack of treasury stock and the cutter and printer and looked for a back door. I didn't know for sure if it was Miss Maebelle aboard the snowmobile, but even a fat motorist with a shotgun trumps a lame pedestrian with a short-barreled revolver.

There was no back door. As I'd thought, the louvered doors belonged to a narrow bathroom, with a shaggy throw rug on the floor and a ventilator fan installed in a tiny window. The windows in the rest of the house were also out of the question. After thrashing through the snow on a leg and a half, I hadn't the strength to hoist myself over any sills in under five minutes. One foot dragged. I had a cocker spaniel attached to the ankle. The snowmobile settled into a steady angry whine and sounded closer than before.

Just then the furnace thumped on. I remembered the crawl space under the house.

I made a quick turn around the long open room, poking the penlight toward the floor and looking for a seam. I saw none. I didn't think whoever had delivered the merchandise that stood in the center would knowingly block access to the furnace, risking an extended breakdown and destructive mildew, but you can't always find good criminal help. I definitely had no time to try to shove it all aside by main might, even if I'd had the might.

A powerful beam raked the front windows. I hunched from instinct. The snowmobile was turning in the direction of the house.

I went back into the bathroom and kicked aside the throw rug. There it was, a rectangle two feet wide and three feet long, cut directly out of the floorboards and set back in, the classic trapdoor.

I put away the light, pulled the trap out all of a piece by its recessed handle, and lowered myself through the black opening; one leg hung like a Christmas ham. The space was only four feet deep. The tricky part was arranging the throw rug into a sort of sandwich with the trap and drawing it back into place as I sank to my knees on the cold bare earth below. I had no way of knowing how it looked from above. Whatever time it bought was to the good.

A glimmer of yellow came through slots in the sheet metal of a squat square furnace propped up on bricks. The attached ductwork reduced the headspace another eight inches. There was no other sign the unit was firing. The snowmobile's engine was so close now it drowned out the fan.

The light faded as I was looking at it. The blower had shut off. I fumbled out my penlight and snapped it on. The beam penetrated only a few feet through the dank gloom, which smelled of potatoes. It was failing. It's always a good idea, before embarking on an act of burglary, to replace the batteries. You should also have a good detonation man, hired muscle, and Julia Roberts, for romantic interest. I'd have traded all three for fresh batteries.

I was looking for the way out. Modern building codes require a second exit, in case fire breaks out or the ceiling falls in, trapping someone underneath the house. I hoped the place was up to code. I felt along the nearest wall and found only cinderblock. I started crawling on hands and knees, training the light along the unbroken surface to the corner of the house, then made a perpendicular turn. The earth was loose and slightly pulverized, prevented from freezing by ambient heat from the furnace and ducts, but still it was cold, and littered with sharp rocks that stabbed at my palms and tore a hole in one knee of my trousers. The combustive noise from outside filled the space and scraped at my eardrums. Then it stopped, and the silence was more painful yet.

The ground was an excellent conductor of sound. A set of springs released, sounding like a screen door opening. A woman of Miss Maebelle's substance was hard on springs. Snow creaked beneath the tread of heavy feet. Then something pounded the porch boards. A sudden, sharp report made me cringe: the door flying open and striking the wall on the other side.

"Who's here?"

Miss Maebelle's voice didn't sound nearly as friendly coming from eight feet above my head. The sibilant was blurry, but I didn't take any comfort from that. Beer and shotguns go together like cigarettes and gasoline. I knew she had the shotgun with her as surely as I knew I'd put myself in a hole with no promise of a way out.

A switch snapped. Thin blades of light sliced the darkness through the spaces between the floorboards.

"Who's here?" she said again. The second time they ask that question, they always know the answer.

I put away the penlight, drew the Smith & Wesson, and resumed crawling, tilting the barrel upward to keep dirt out of the
muzzle. All the way at the other end of the house, a small section
of wall looked different from the rest. It might have been a trick of
shadow, but it was someplace to go. I tried to keep my breath from
sobbing in my throat. I was close to played out.

Feet thudded the floor, releasing thin streams of dirt and saw-
dust onto my head and back and down under my collar. A merry
tinkling accompanied each thunderous step: loose galosh buckles,
a sound remembered from childhood. It's funny what comes back
to you when you have five minutes to live.

Something swished. She'd torn the cover from the Treasury
stock and laser printer. I didn't know if she could tell if it had been
operated recently. I didn't think it had been on long enough to
warm up noticeably, but she might discover there was a sheet
missing from inside.

For a long time she stood without moving, the boards straining
a little beneath her weight concentrated in one spot.

Suddenly she broke into a stride. It was like someone skipping
a bowling ball across three lanes. Hinges squeaked: She'd thrown
open the twin doors to the bathroom.

Then nothing. I could almost hear her blue-marble eyes swivel-
ing from side to side and up and down. Down last, to my blind job
of covering the trap with the rug. I had no confidence in that.

I crawled faster, raking the knee of my bad leg across another
sharp stone; pain from old wound and new connected with a blue
spark that burned a long time and never went all the way out. I was
pretty sure she couldn't fit through the opening, but—

The house exploded.

I jumped and looked back over my shoulder at what was left of
the trapdoor fell into the crawl space, towing a rectangle of bright
light from a ceiling fixture and a cloud of dust and splinters and

curling blue smoke. She'd blown a hole through it as big as my head with both barrels of the shotgun.

My ears rang from the blast. Beneath the ringing, something went *tunk* twice, like two corks being drawn from bottles, and two small objects slapped the floor and rolled a little distance like ball bearings. She replaced the spent shells, *plunk, plunk,* slammed shut the breech, and strode back across the long open room.

Wham! More dirt and smoke, and a ragged disk of light opened in the floor in the corner diagonally opposite mine. Dirt jumped up from the bottom, forming a shallow crater. The antique piece had to be ten-gauge, a mammoth caliber that went out with robbing stagecoaches. I don't know where she found the ammunition.

She cleared the barrels, reloaded, and struck off the length of the house, a rolling gait. The place swayed like an offshore oil derrick. Halfway down she stopped.

Panicking, I rose into a jackknife crouch and made for the anomalous patch of wall and possibly freedom. My head struck ductwork, but the reverberating boom was lost in another explosion from above. I covered my mouth to avoid breathing pure earth. The low ceiling was beginning to look like a whack-a-mole game, from the point of view of the mole. I was in a bit of a tight.

Tunk, tunk. Plunk, plunk. Slam. The minor chords were almost as bad as the major.

I braced myself on one hand, my head still echoing from contact with the duct, and took aim at the spot where she'd stopped, but I held off. At that angle I couldn't be sure if the bullet would penetrate the floor, and the report would place her target. I put the gun back in its pocket and made like a bug.

I reached the wall and spread my palm against a network of coarse wood. The diamond pattern, visible in the light gushing down now from above, belonged to a three-foot section of lattice set into a space between blocks. I felt cold air from the other side. My fingers curled around the slats. Quarter-inch pine.

Floorboards creaked. Through the hole nearest me I saw a pair of spread galoshes with thick ankles clad in blue jersey growing out of the tops. A pair of shining tubes bound side by side poked through the hole, angling in my general direction. Smoke drifted out of the muzzles.

I wished I hadn't put away my gun; but I wouldn't have had the time anyway. My left palm was resting on yet another tiny pyramid of stone. I closed my fingers around it, leaned my shoulder against a cinder block for leverage, and flung the stone with a snap of the wrist that propelled it toward the long wall to my right; a girl's throw, emasculated by exhaustion and the world's worst position for throwing. The stone made a hollow click bouncing off the concrete.

Before it fell to the ground, the air compressed all around me, boxing both ears, and a fireworks of red-and-yellow flame sprayed the crawl space with blinding light, knocking a chunk out of the porous concrete where the stone had struck. A bee stung my right cheek at the top of the bone. An inch and a half to the left and the ricocheting pellet would have taken out my eye.

I only thought about that later, and felt the sting itself only in a delayed reaction. Just as she'd pulled the trigger I rammed my right fist in a haymaker beginning at the shoulder straight through the lattice, routing deep gouges along my forearm to the elbow, and then along both cheeks as I stuck my head through the hole, and without giving up momentum launched the upper half of my body behind it, snaring the splintered wooden edges on all four sides and bringing the whole patched-in piece with me as I shoved off with the balls of my feet and wriggled the bottom half of my body through the space I'd made. Meanwhile she got off another shot with the one barrel she'd reloaded, hurrying; a hot wind smacked my right hip and pellets rattled off cinderblock like seeds in a gourd.

It was lakeside. Snow had pushed up above the foundation. I was in darkness, darkness with texture and cold that filled my eyes, nose, and mouth and tunneled under my collar all the way to the waistband of my trousers, which were soaked through with snow and sweat. Possibly blood; you never know in a situation like that how many times you've been hit.

I burrowed desperately, flailing my arms and angling upward, swimming through surf as coarse as sand, and popped out suddenly into the beautiful freezing air, wearing the rectangular section of lattice around my hips like a tutu. I stumbled upright, pushed it down and off, scraping an ankle in the process, and turned right, toward the front of the house and away from the vast expanse of white separating me from the state highway, where cars and trucks followed their pencil beams along the shore of the lake. That was a shooting range, and even if I could flounder out of shotgun reach, Miss Maebelle had ample time to retreat to the snowmobile, fire it up, and hunt me down with all the ease and safety of a kid playing a video game.

A revolver is scant protection against a vehicle that can turn on a pin and a street sweeper in the hands of a woman who isn't afraid to use it. I didn't want to die out there in the snow like a deer and spend the rest of forever on the bottom of Lake Huron with Maebelle's dead beloved Jim.

That gave me an idea, but before I could think it through I ran straight into the shotgun.

TWENTY-TWO

We surprised each other. I'd expected her to try for a shot from the windows, and she hadn't expected me to double back. When I came around the corner she had one foot on the porch, the other on the ground next to the snowmobile, a yeti in a man's faded red-and-black-checked Mackinaw and the ear-flapped woolen cap I'd seen in the office. She looked even bigger than she had there, and the way she held the shotgun cradled along her forearm said it hadn't spent all its time hanging on the wall.

Before she could swing it up, I ducked around the bed of the huge pickup. I was still dragging one foot; the gun bellowed and snow sprayed the back of my pants leg halfway up the calf.

Fat people often move fast when motivated. Once they overcome the problem of inertia they're mostly momentum, like a barrel rolling downhill, and this one knew how to get around in deep snow. She cleared the end of the bed just as I reached the door on the driver's seat, slamming shut the breech as she ran, stopped, spread her feet, and swiveled the shotgun to her hip. The twin bores were as big around as beer cans.

I had a foot on the step plate. I worked the door handle, pushed off, and swung around with the door, hanging on with one hand

and using the door as a shield. That part was illusion. Steel side rails or not, a car door is no guarantee against buckshot fired at close range. But she seemed unwilling to damage a hundred thousand dollars' worth of heavy equipment. She hesitated.

I was less picky. Hanging on tight, I clawed the revolver out with my free hand and fired through the window in the door.

I didn't aim. I'd closed my eyes tight to keep out pulverized glass and didn't see where I hit. When I opened them, Miss Maebelle was nowhere in sight.

I didn't look for her. I pivoted around the edge of the door, pebbles of shattered glass showering off me, swung into the driver's seat, and twisted the key in the ignition. The leather seat was slick and cold, but not as cold as the engine. It turned over sluggishly, like a fat bear stirring. I didn't know how long it had been hibernating in those temperatures.

Maebelle had overcome her first timid impulse. I saw a flash of movement through the window on the passenger's side and ducked just as the window flew apart.

I stayed down, shoulders jammed between the seat and the curved underside of the dash, turning the key and pressing the accelerator pedal with the hand holding the revolver. Above me, the cab's headliner hung in ribbons; she'd fired at an upward angle from the ground. The engine muttered, chuckled, muttered again. Diesels are as slow to wake up as teenage boys.

The cab listed slightly toward the passenger's side. Miss Maebelle had climbed onto the step plate.

The engine caught, rumbling through my spine where it pressed against the hump over the drive shaft. I forced the pedal to the floor. The truck pounced forward three feet and stalled.

But the motion had been enough to jar loose the fat woman's grip. There was no sign of her in the vacant window as I propelled myself back into the seat and ground the starter to life again. A glittering blanket of broken glass covered both seats and crunched under my hip pockets.

I found Drive and spun the wheel left, away from the house and toward the country road that ran past the Sportsmen's Rest. The tires alone were taller than the drifts that had stopped the Cutlass.

The top of Maebelle's cap nudged above the sill on the passenger's side. She'd managed to grab hold again. I fired at it and it vanished.

Meanwhile the truck was still turning. It had come all the way around the end of the house, putting the road behind me.

That didn't upset me. On the dash, an illuminated simulation of the chassis told me all four wheels were in drive. I groped for the switch and shifted from high to low. The gears grumbled, hunkering down. If I wanted to, I could make my own road.

I wanted to. A handful of rubble nattered off the window behind my head. The pulse of the shotgun came after. I pressed the pedal to the fire wall, putting the truck the rest of the way out of range. White fantails spread away on both sides of the cab.

The nose dipped, plunging into a drift as high as the windshield, then shot skyward. I floated above the seat and slammed back down, jarring my tailbone and snapping my jaw shut. My organs scrambled to adjust.

I couldn't see through the windshield. I groped for a smart stick, found it on the left side of the steering column, and skidded my fingers past the sliding switch that operated the cruise control, bringing them to rest finally on the barrel cylinder that activated the wipers. I twisted it all the way forward. The blades cracked loose and scooped away two pounds of thick powder. A sea of snow opened in front of the headlamps, bisected three hundred yards ahead by the shining black belt of the state highway, polished by the friction of many tires. Past there I couldn't tell earth from ice, right up until the empty dark maw where open water met sky.

The ludicrous Brobdingnagian truck kept rolling as if it were on the Autobahn. I was a convert. I could sit next to the gear jammers in the Air Horn, watching *Duel* and rooting against the hero in his silly little car.

A spitting whine stood my skin on end, an angry hornet trapped in a dice cup. In the rearview mirror I saw the cyclops eye of a snowmobile's headlamp closing fast. The truck had more horsepower, but most of it went into plowing through snow. The snowmobile rode on top of it. I'd be back inside shotgun range in less than a minute.

Maebelle ran a test. Orange flame blossomed in the mirror, followed closely by thunder. I hunched my shoulders out of instinct. Nothing hit the truck. I leaned forward, as if that would make it go faster.

Now I was climbing the long grade toward the highway. It was dinnertime, and traffic had thinned, but there was always another pair of headlamps coming from upstate and down. I didn't think she'd risk another shot in full view of other motorists, but I didn't know her. She might welcome the challenge.

Twenty-five feet of steel guardrail prevented spinouts from plummeting down the steepest part of the bank. The near end bent down into the earth, a feature devised to avoid impaling those vehicles that ran off the road and struck it head-on. I'd once lost a close friend that way, and nearly my own life. I still had flashbacks.

Climbing, I turned to go around the end. If my timing worked I could swing into the outside lane in the gap between an approaching house trailer and the tanker downshifting behind it to take the next hill.

Something struck a spark off the side-view mirror mounted outside my window, crazing the glass. The snowmobile's light reflected back at me in disjointed quarters. She was almost on my rear bumper, and didn't care who saw what from the highway. That rugged individual pioneer spirit was a pain in the ass. I slumped down in the seat and punched the transmission back into four high, for the speed. That was a risk. If I got stuck now they'd be sponging me off the upholstery. The frame shuddered, but the truck leaped forward, putting on another ten miles per hour.

In the same instant I changed plans. I couldn't turn left without bringing my head into her line of fire, and I couldn't turn right without hitting the tanker head-on. When the house trailer passed, I straightened my leg against the pedal and shot across both lanes.

The tanker blasted its horn. I felt it in the roots of my teeth. Then it was behind me and I heard its air brakes hiss; I knew without looking that Maebelle was still on my bumper. I braved one glance at the rearview and saw sparks flying from her skis on bare asphalt. That bought me some space, but she had the scent. Nothing would stop her except a broadside, and a yellow fastback accelerating to pass the slowing tanker on the inside lane spun 180 degrees on its brakes as the snowmobile flamed in front of it. When the fastback collided with a vehicle following the tanker I felt the impact pulse in the soles of my feet.

Another guardrail came up, too fast to avoid. My plow blade made a hole through it without slowing down. A two-foot section of broken four-by-four bounded up over the hood and cartwheeled away into the night.

I almost stood the truck on its nose coming off the built-up highway onto the apron of snow-covered earth that separated it from the lake. The snow was over my hubs. My tires spun for a heart-stopping instant. I switched back to four-wheel low and stumbled out of the hole. Snow spouted out both sides of my prow.

I may have taken out a road sign. Something dragged beneath the undercarriage, growling, snagged in the frozen earth, and scraped the bottom of the fuel tank as I passed over it. I hoped the tank hadn't torn through.

Something struck the tailgate like a deck chair in a hurricane. Whatever Miss Maebelle's opinions about snowmobilers in general, she knew how to steer with one hand while reloading with the other. She might have spent her summer breaks from school hunting rhinoceroses from a Land Rover. I sunk my head between my shoulders and charted a course straight for the lake.

My tires told me when I'd left dry land for ice. The surface was smoother than fresh pavement and as slick as talcum on glass. The rear tires slewed right. I rode the skid, hands off the wheel, then gently coaxed the front end the other way. The rear end fishtailed and locked back into line. That put a fisherman's shanty square in my path. It was built of black Cellotex, invisible until the owner's name and address lettered in white paint sprang up in my lights. I corrected right, not in time. My left front bumper clipped a corner, sending me into a spin that swept the left side of the truck around like a sickle, broadsiding the structure and folding it like origami. It wasn't lighted. I hoped the fisherman had gone home for the night. I straightened out coming out of a wide arc. In the mirror, I saw the snowmobile's light veer sharp left, then right, then straight, threading a hasty path through the wreckage.

After that she continued to close. The surface wasn't built for tires.

I had other things to worry about. Drowning was number one. The Great Lakes freeze over only once in generations. A current runs through their centers, too swift most years for a good frost to take hold. Every winter the Coast Guard rescues a party of hapless fishermen or hikers from a broken floe. I didn't figure to make Canada without getting my feet wet.

Just as the thought occurred to me, the truck went into a dip on a perfectly flat section of ice. It was growing rotten, and would get rottener still the closer I came to open water.

Then, of course, there was the open water. I wondered if any of this had dawned on dead Jim before he and his Subaru went under. I throttled down.

His widow was still behind me, as inexhaustible as her supply of shotgun shells. She let fly with another in an orange starburst, missing but letting me know she wasn't turning back.

I looked at the speedometer for the first time. I was doing thirty-five; it felt like eighty. I set the cruise control at the going speed, adjusted the wheel right to block Miss Maebelle's view of the driver's side, opened the door, and bailed out.

Subzero air burned my face and whistled past my ears. I tucked myself into a tight ball and hit the hardest surface I'd hit since the Grayling parking lot, emptying my lungs in a series of gusts as I rolled. I seemed to be picking up speed. I might have kept rolling until I ran out of ice, where the water would seize my heavy clothes and drag me down among the broken French barques and bootleggers' Cadillacs and lovestruck Indians like in the song.

I stopped abruptly, spread-eagled on my back with my heart trying to punch a hole through my chest. I couldn't blame it; I'd violated its trust. I couldn't get my breath. I may have been unconscious for a few seconds. Anyway I didn't hear a thing when the ice collapsed beneath fifteen thousand pounds of truck and eight hundred pounds of Arctic Cat and Miss Maebelle.

TWENTY-THREE

flagged down a fresh-fish delivery truck with my last twenty-dollar bill and gave it to the driver to go four miles out of his way and drop me at my car, which was where I'd left it in the little cleared spot past the Sportsmen's Rest. The driver, a weathered-looking old salt with scales in his beard, watched me engineering the climb down from the seat.

"I don't get why a guy with a bum leg'd ankle it all the way to the highway just for a ride back to where he started," he said. "There's a motel just down the road."

"Nobody home." I shut the door on his next question.

For a few minutes after he left I just sat behind the wheel. My leg burned, my cheek was sore where a shotgun pellet had torn out a divot on its way past, the eye on that side swollen. I had my keys in my hand but they were too heavy to lift. I ached in more places than Paul Starzek's St. Sebastian and my ears still rang from shotguns and snowmobiles. I was shivering and sweating at the same time. I felt under the seat, found the pint I kept there for emergencies, and took a long pull. Not surprisingly, it was lighter than my keys. It had no taste and left no traces. I wondered if liquor could go stale. I'd never had a bottle around long enough to find out. I capped it and put it back.

I missed the ignition twice, speared it on the third try. It took two hands to turn it. The motor started eventually and I backed the Cutlass around in the tracks left by the fish truck and followed them back to the state highway. Nothing seemed to be happening at the Rest. Lights burned on the sign and in the caboose and bungalow, where the officers who came to investigate could draw whatever conclusions they liked from the counterfeiting setup and a floor full of holes. I wasn't in any condition to help out. I had a case of shock and walking pneumonia, to start.

On the highway, blue and red lights strobed where the yellow hatchback had turned to avoid hitting Miss Maebelle and smacked into a minivan, bending sheet metal and locking bumpers. There was a big hammered-steel box of an ambulance along with two or three police cruisers, but I couldn't see if there were any injuries. I hoped there weren't. I had a retired schoolteacher heavy on my conscience, and she'd tried her best to kill me. A state trooper in a fur hat directed traffic around the guttering flares with a flashlight. Out on the ice, more flashlights probed at the spot where the truck had fallen through with the snowmobile hard behind it. It was a pretty story, if you liked them that way: husband and wife reunited.

I don't remember most of the drive back into Port Sanilac. I found myself sitting in the car with the motor running in the parking lot of the motel where I'd booked a room to rest and wait for the sun to go down. I switched off and put the keys in my pocket, but I couldn't find the key to my room; my pockets were full of gun and gloves and burglar tools and four hundred dollars printed on one sheet, hastily folded. I hadn't the energy to dig deeper.

I picked up my cane, but when I bent over the backseat to grab my overnight bag, I began to black out. I drew my head out into the fresh air to clear, then swung the door shut. There was nothing in the bag I'd need soon. I thought about the bottle then, but that required more bending over. Anyway I prefer to get drunk when I'm alert enough to enjoy it.

The redhead was still on duty at the desk. I thought at first she must be on a twenty-hour shift, but the clock behind her read just past nine. I couldn't fathom it. But then three hours had made all the difference between the World Trade Center and Ground Zero.

She was on the telephone. Her mouth parted a little when she saw me. She brought an end to the conversation and hung up. "May I help you?"

I hadn't looked at myself in a mirror. I probably had dried blood on my cheek, and in my watch cap and skulking clothes, streaked with dirt, trousers torn and soaked through, I must have looked like America's Most Wanted.

"Amos Walker. I registered this afternoon. I lost my key."

She recognized me then. Some of the color returned under the heavy cosmetics. "Were you in an accident?"

"A little one. I went snowmobiling with a friend."

"Do you need a doctor?" She handed me a key.

"Just a good night's sleep." I coughed, a lung rattler that alarmed even me. "Could I trouble you for an envelope and a piece of paper?"

The telephone rang. She handed me an envelope with the motel's return address printed on it and a sheet of stationery and answered. While she was busy talking, I turned my back, refolded the sheet of twenties to fit into the envelope, folded the paper around it, dropped in one of my cards, and sealed it. I got Agent Clemson's card from my wallet and scribbled his name and office address on the outside with a pen reserved for check-ins. When she hung up, I asked for a stamp, and when she tore one off a sheet I opened an empty wallet. Irony.

"I'll put it on your bill," she said.

I gave her the envelope to send out with the morning mail and turned away. Turned too soon; but then I hadn't thought I'd make it up the stairs without passing out.

TWENTY-FOUR

The lake was a living thing made of ice and fire, with a broad cherubic face under an Elmer Fudd cap whose flaps curled up at the ends to form devil's horns. It opened its mouth to laugh and sucked me in like a moth. I spiraled downward as if someone had pulled the plug out of a drain, debris swirling around me in the form of faces: Oral Canon's, huge and red and hairless; Rose Canon's, a pale oval with a delicate upper lip and jet-stream eyebrows like Kim Novak's; Herbert Clemson's, chilly-eyed, fashionably stubbled; Jeff Starzek's, round and calm and watching. I think I saw the Michelin tire man, too. Even delirium has to pause now and then for a word from the sponsor.

The deeper I plunged, the hotter it got, until I was swimming through flaming oil. I smelled alcohol and iodine, which as everyone knows are the principal ingredients of brimstone. From the black depths a monstrous truck came toward me, turning and rising on a collision course; I paddled like mad to get around it and almost made it, but a fender clipped me and sent me cartwheeling toward the surface and back into the cold. Up there, someone was blasting big holes through the murk from above. Fragments of shrapnel skidded past me like tiny torpedoes, plucking at my clothes and slicing peels of skin off my cheeks. I tried to reverse directions, but my limbs were getting stiff. I was freezing to the bone, and all the time I was drifting up, straight toward the source of the blasts.

I had four days of that, they told me, and when I finally broke through to the surface, my bedsheets were soaked. It was like one of those "Was it a dream?" episodes of *The Twilight Zone*. Rod Serling came in a number of shapes, all of them female, including the doctor, a traffic-stopping blonde with ambitions beyond residency in a small hospital in a port town. Her name was Immelman, like the old flying maneuver, and for a couple of minutes I was in love; but then I'd have fallen in love with the bed rail after being rescued from the lake.

She was more concerned with the condition of my leg than the fever, which had broken, and with the three shotgun pellets that had fallen out of my trousers when I was undressed, pressed between the layers of clothing like flowers in a book. I remembered feeling the heat from the blast against my hip as I dived out of the crawl space beneath the bungalow at the Sportsmen's Rest. I'd never make a joke about long underwear again.

"Jealous husband?" she asked.

"Hunting accident," I said. "I got a little ahead of my party."

"It was buckshot. Firearms deer season is over. And you weren't wearing hunting clothes. You were dressed like a gas-station bandit."

"Who are you, Mr. Black?" I resisted the impulse to touch the gauze taped to my right cheek.

She scowled at my chart in her hands. She wasn't reading. "The details are none of my business, except we have to report this kind of thing to the police. I'd brush up on my answers before they come back."

"Back?"

"They've been here every day, state *and* county, waiting for you to come around. They think you may know something about an incident on the lake."

"What incident?"

"Some fools went joyriding on the ice the night we checked you in. There were two vehicles involved, and someone reported shooting. One body's been recovered, a woman's. They're looking for others. We get that a lot, and there's always alcohol involved." She flipped a page. "Your blood-alcohol was three-point-oh when you came in."

"What about my leg?"

She flipped the page back, pursed her lips. "GSW, several weeks healed. I guess you left your thermals behind that time, not that it would have stopped the bullet that made that wound. Can I assume the authorities were notified?"

"They were all over it. What about the leg?" It wasn't hurting, but I was hooked up to an IV and whatever was dripping into it wasn't apple juice. First thing I'd done when I woke up was to check and see if the leg was there.

"You strained a ligament. At first we thought it was ruptured. Half the staff wanted to amputate. Another couple of hours stumping around on it and the vote would have been unanimous. I never saw anyone abuse a major injury so completely."

"Can I get a second opinion?"

"Not in this facility. You can't afford it. I just found out this morning you don't have insurance."

"Were you surprised?"

"No. Just from what I've seen, you couldn't get a group rate with the bullfighters' union. What are you, a crash dummy for Smith and Wesson?"

"Only on the side. The rest of the time I'm a detective."

"I thought detectives were stealthy."

"I didn't say I was any good at it. Are you kicking me out?"

"Not right this minute, but you might want to make arrangements for a change of clothes before the end of the day. We had to cut you out of what you came in with."

"What about my wallet and gun?"

"You'll get your personal effects when you sign the release."

"Only dead people have personal effects."

She pointed to an aluminum walker standing at the foot of the bed. "There's your ride for the next couple of weeks. It'll appear on your bill."

I was alone with my thoughts for two minutes before the cops came. The first one wore a county uniform, trimmed like a Christmas tree in Baghdad, with weapons of small destruction and electronic equipment that muttered and peeped throughout his visit. He was a large black man with a round jolly face and eyes as hard as hammers. When he started asking questions I pretended to be asleep. I actually did fall asleep before he gave up; I hadn't felt so tired since basic training, or so weak since I forgot and drank the water in Cambodia. Getting shot was easy compared to a night of blind fear followed by four days of fever.

I found out from his questions that Miss Maebelle's body hadn't been identified, or maybe I didn't. It might have been a snare, but I was too full of morphine to step into it. He left.

For a while between visits I lay in the twilight between boredom and sleep I didn't need, listening to the sounds of a hospital at work. It was a pretty noisy place, all things considered: Rubber casters squeaked on waxed linoleum, monitors bleeped, the nurses at the station down the hall spoke into telephones and among themselves, a maintenance worker strode past my door jingling his keys and humming. Outside the double-paned windows a turboprop took off from the harbor airport, whooshing its after-burners and fluttering its pistons in what sounded too much like a death rattle for comfort, but then I don't fly well. The flutes and ricochets of a spaghetti western drifted out of one of those rooms where the TV was never turned off. I'd seen the four walls of my room only but knew what the rest of the place would look like, the way a microbiologist reconstructs a lake from a single drop of water. I was becoming a reluctant expert on hospitals.

I elevated the head of the bed, took a lidded cup off the rolling bed tray, and sucked water through an old-fashioned glass straw. The jointed plastic kind hadn't yet made its way up the two-lane blacktop on that side of the state. The water seemed colder and wetter that way, and it gave me an idea.

A nurse came in to disconnect the IV and drop off the lunch menu. When she left carrying the empty water cup, she didn't seem to notice the straw wasn't in it. I was grateful for that, but I hoped she paid more attention to such things in surgery.

The next visit was from the State of Michigan. It was a two-man invasion, a tall trooper in uniform and a bearish skinhead in a black trench coat over a suit with a wild check; I figured he used the pattern to hypnotize suspects into confessing. There was nothing jolly about either of them. They'd come in straight from outdoors and brought with them a chill I felt through the thin sponge-rubber blanket that covered me to the chest.

"Mr. Walker. Glad to see you're awake. I'm Lieutenant Kunkel." The plainclothesman tipped open a folder. "We have some questions to ask."

"Who's your friend?"

"That's not important."

"Doesn't know your name," I said to the trooper.

"I said never mind." Kunkel's face darkened under the flush from the cold. "A man answering your description was seen getting into a delivery truck on the state highway Wednesday night. We got a partial plate number and traced it to the driver. He said he gave you a ride to your car."

I looked at the trooper. "Even if he just borrowed you from the local post, he could've asked you your name on the way here."

"Evans." The trooper opened his mouth just wide enough to let out both syllables.

Kunkel ground on. "That was the night you collapsed in the lobby of a motel here in town and were taken by ambulance to the emergency room of this hospital and checked in for treatment and observation. That same night, two vehicles, a snowmobile and an International CXT diesel pickup truck, this year's model, drove out onto Lake Huron and fell through the ice. The Sanilac County Sheriff's Department pulled the truck out yesterday morning. Divers are still looking for the snowmobile, but they recovered a body.

"Those same two vehicles caused an accident on the highway," he said. "We've got a good description of the operator of the snowmobile. It matches the corpse. No description yet of the truck driver. Someone saw shooting. You came here with buckshot in your clothes. Maybe you'd care to connect the dots, save us trouble and expense, help out the deficit in Lansing."

The nurse came in. I took my thumb off the call button I had under the blanket and asked her to check my blood pressure.

"Are you experiencing anxiety?"

I looked from one cop face to the other and back to hers. She cleared her throat and unslung the equipment from around her neck.

"Later, please," Kunkel said. "We're busy here."

"So am I." She tugged down the blanket and slid the cuff up over my right bicep. The arm was bandaged from wrist to elbow. I'd gouged it punching through lattice.

"Nurse—"

"Van Ash." She pumped the rubber bulb.

"Nurse Van Ash, you're interfering with the police in the performance of their duty."

"Who's stopping you?"

"What about it, Walker?" Kunkel said.

I'd broken two inches off the end of the glass straw, stashed the rest of it in a Kleenex box on the rolling tray, and was holding the jagged piece in my left hand under the blanket. As the cuff filled and tightened, I made a fist. I gasped a little, coughed to cover it.

Nurse Van Ash's face didn't change during the reading. It wouldn't. She was a short-haired brunette of forty with old campaign lines drawing down the corners of her mouth. She let out the pressure and slipped the cuff down and off.

"You gentlemen will have to come back later. Mr. Walker is in no condition for visitors."

"We're conducting an interview," Kunkel said.

"Sorry."

"Who's your supervisor?"

"I'm in charge of the station on this floor. You can talk to Mr. Baird, the administrator."

"Where is he?"

"Out on the lake. He's the official mayor of Tip-up Town this year."

The lieutenant spun on his heel and clomped out into the hall. Evans hung back.

"You, too," said Nurse Van Ash. "Shoo."

He slouched on out as if it were his idea. The nurse stayed. "Show me your left hand, please."

I brought it out full of blood. She seized it, picked out the glass, stuffed a wad of Kleenex into my palm, and closed my hand tight. Her fingers were strung with steel cable. "That's going to take a couple of stitches to close," she said. "Your timing was off. The spike came in the middle of the reading."

"Where'd you work before this, Jackson Prison?"

"Port Sanilac High. Some of those kids would do anything to get out of gym. What are you going to do when they come back?"

"What kind of cultures you got in the lab?"

The lines in her face didn't stir. "The police put in more time here than the residents. Most are okay, but you've got to take the Kunkels with the rest. Did I do the right thing keeping my mouth shut?"

"You weren't the only one. The lieutenant didn't mention the buckshot holes in the truck."

"You'll have to do better than that," she said. "Miss Maebelle's a beloved local character."

"Who said anything about Miss Maebelle?"

"The description's all over the news. There's only one fat woman around here who drives a snowmobile."

"Do the police know?"

"If they don't, they'll put it together when she doesn't answer the telephone. One of the buildings at the Sportsmen's Rest burned to the ground last night."

TWENTY-FIVE

Nurse Van Ash helped me into the bathroom the first time. After that, I took the walker for a spin around the room. It took a little longer than the Rose Bowl Parade and all I got for my efforts was a fresh case of the shakes and a view of a maintenance man blowing snow off the walk outside the window. My leg was a little swollen, the foot dragged. Mostly I needed the support because my body had used up all its strength fighting fever, but I didn't like the way my foot felt as if it weighed fifteen pounds. Dr. Immelman might not just have been trying to throw a scare into me after all. Hauling a cane around for the rest of my life would throw a crimp into climbing through windows and dodging buckshot.

I hated to do it because I owed him already, but I put a call in to Barry Stackpole. I couldn't think of anyone else who would drive all the way up there to bring me a change of clothes. Nurse Van Ash may have been the original immovable object, but Lieutenant Kunkel was an irresistible force with a bald head and a loud suit. He wouldn't waste time poking his face into a couple of hundred ice shanties looking for Administrator Baird; he'd go straight to the nearest district judge and come back with a warrant for my arrest. That could take hours or minutes, depending upon whether court was in session.

Barry didn't answer, and the cheerful nasal voice of the new Ma Bell told me I couldn't keep ringing. I hung up just as Herbert Clemson entered.

"Nice legs. You ought to wear Bermuda shorts."

I was sitting on the edge of the bed in a paper gown and slippers with a bandage on my scraped ankle. The Homeland Security agent was better turned out. He'd traded his gray coat for an insulated parka, boots with felt liners that stuck up above the tops, heavy woolen trousers, and a cable-knit turtleneck. With his cool eyes, clean features, and cultivated blue chin, he looked like a ski instructor. I asked him if he'd been downhill racing.

"I've just come from a long walk along your beautiful Lake Huron shoreline. It reminded me all over again how many thousands of miles of border I have to protect. I can't get enough staff to sharpen pencils." He was carrying a briefcase, the bulky old-fashioned kind with straps. He set it down, took off the coat, and flung it across the visitor's chair.

"What's it pay? I'm looking for a desk job."

"I don't blame you. I saw your chart."

"I thought that information was confidential."

We laughed.

He picked up the briefcase and started unbuckling. "I like you, Walker. I'd put you in for it if I didn't have a conflict."

I watched him draw out an envelope I'd seen before.

"Three days from Port Sanilac to the Federal Building in Detroit," he said. "That's a couple of hours by automobile. Seems to me the post office was more efficient when it didn't have any competition, but that's someone else's department. You should know it isn't a good idea to send cash through the mail."

"I didn't, technically."

"Let's not split hairs. We have people who do that. They're testing the sheet now." He took out the piece of folded motel stationery, tipped my business card out of the end, looked at it as if he hadn't seen it before. Then he put both items back in the envelope. "I went to the motel first. That's the reason you sent it. Were you really planning to wait for me?"

"I don't know. I wasn't exactly hitting on all cylinders."

"They told me you were here. I got the rest from the local authorities. For a man with one good leg you manage to get around."

"The good leg isn't that good. I tricked out the knee in basic. I don't guess you brought cigarettes."

"I don't use them. You never know when they've been smuggled."

"Company man." I ran my fingers through my hair. Gray hair feels more brittle than brown. I felt a lot of brittle. "What now?"

He spread the briefcase, tucked the envelope in a pocket, and drew out a bundle wrapped in a paper Marshall Field's bag. The mattress bounced when he tossed it at the foot. "I had to guess at the sizes: sixteen-and-a-half neck, thirty-four waist, eleven double-E's."

"Ten and a half. My toes won't mind the extra room. What about a coat?"

"Listen to the man. I could've come with a couple of beefy marshals and marched you out with your bare ass flapping in the breeze."

"I figured you'd bill me later."

"Consider it recompense. You just became a paid government informant."

I shook my head. "Not even for Armani."

"Well, put them on. You can always return them."

I pulled the bag over and looked inside. I saw plaid. "This how you recruited Jeff Starzek?"

"There was no haberdashery involved, but the situation was similar. The old patriotic pep talk doesn't go as far as it used to."

I got up, supporting myself on the bed rail, took off the flimsy gown, stood naked while he watched, memorizing scars and moles, broke new underwear out of cellophane, and began the long drawn-out business of dressing. I sat down a couple of times to rest. He didn't offer to help. The shirt, a black-and-white buffalo plaid, was a little short in the sleeves, but the flannel gave comfortably in the shoulders. The socks were heavy and warm, and the slacks, a sage-green cotton-and-polyester blend, broke just right at the insteps of the stiff new oxfords.

"Where's the letter sweater?"

He said, "They were running an overstock sale on back-to-school. I have to look out for the taxpayers. Hang on a minute."

He went out, shutting the door behind him. He was back in less than a minute, pushing a wheelchair. "Hospital regs. We cooperate where we can."

My cane hung over the back. He must have parked it outside the room.

"I haven't been released."

He took a pregnant manila envelope out of his briefcase and dumped it out on the bed. "I took care of the red tape. We invented it, don't forget."

I braced a knee against the bed frame, inspected the cylinder of my .38, stuck it in my hip pocket. I put away my ID folder and opened my wallet. There was a twenty-dollar bill inside. I held it out. "I was down to bare leather when I got back to the motel."

"Personal loan. You can't get back home without gas. I took care of your motel bill, too. You'll have to make your own arrangements with the hospital. I'm only a poor civil servant. Pay me soon."

I put the twenty back in the wallet. "How do I know it's genuine?"

"How does anyone? Anyway, there's not so much Treasury paper floating around as there was last week."

He'd heard about the fire.

"You're under arrest, Walker. Suspicion of homicide."

This was a fresh voice, or as fresh as it got coming out of Lieutenant Kunkel of the Michigan State Police. He stood in the doorway holding a fold of official-looking paper. Trooper Evans stood behind him and a little to the side. His right hand rested on the walnut handle sticking out of his holster.

Kunkel aimed his face at Clemson. "Who are you?"

Clemson asked him the same question. General flapping of leather as the two compared ID folders. I sat down on the bed to wait.

"This man's in federal custody, Lieutenant. You can have him when we're through."

"Where's your warrant?"

The agent put away his folder, took out a long flat wallet, and handed him a folded sheet from the collection inside.

"This is a John Doe."

"For now, so is Mr. Walker. My agency would consider it a favor if you didn't spread that around outside your division."

"What's Homeland Security got to do with what happened out on the lake?"

"I can't discuss that."

"Where are you taking him?"

"I can't discuss that either."

"It's always the same old shit with the G, isn't it?"

"It's war, Lieutenant. We're all in it together."

"Yeah. I didn't see you out there bobbing for bodies. I have to call my commander." He took a step toward the telephone on the bedside table.

I put my hand on it. "Not on my bill."

He stopped, patted his pockets. The trooper drew a cell from a flap pocket and held it out. Kunkel snatched it.

While he was talking, I looked at Clemson. "The Age of Communication."

"I could do with less of it. You can tap a wire. There are just too many voices in the air."

"I never got one."

"Good God! How do you manage?"

"I seem to."

The lieutenant thrust the cell at Clemson. "My commander wants to talk to you."

"What's his name?" He took it.

"*Her* name is Villanueva."

The agent began talking. I pointed my chin at Evans. "Did he ever get around to calling you by your name?"

"Shut up," said Kunkel, to both of us.

Clemson held out the cell. "She wants to talk to you again."

This conversation was more brief. "Yes, ma'am." He snapped shut the little telephone and threw it at Evans, who caught it against his chest. "Let's go, Trooper."

"Evans," I reminded him.

"Go fuck yourself." They left.

"You didn't even try," I told Clemson.

"It would've been a waste of diplomacy."

"Was it the shaved head?"

"Partly. We profile everyone, not just the enemy. Here." He took his coat off the chair and threw it on the bed. "I'm wearing Kevlar under the sweater, so I'm good to ten below. You should,

too, and not just because of what happened the other night. Your
file reads like Tom Swift at the Alamo."

"I'd probably get shot in the head." I shrugged into the parka,
which was Thinsulate and not as heavy as it looked, and let him
give me a hand up. I took the cane off the back of the wheelchair
and lowered myself into the seat. "Where we headed?"

"The airport. TSA maintains a room that stands empty most
days. It's a small airport. I've reserved it."

"Isn't that where they do strip searches?"

"Moot point."

"You've been busy. When did you find time to stroll out by the
lake?"

"I'm a multitasker." He tapped the telephone holster on his
belt. He'd have another one, for a slim semiautomatic, maybe
strapped to an ankle. He let his flippant mask slip. "These characters we're at war with may dress like the *Arabian Nights,* but
they're hip to technology and they've got deep pockets. I don't
want a gun mike picking up everything we say on a driving tour of
this picturesque stretch of Americana."

"Can I call a lawyer, or is that hopelessly old-fashioned under
the Patriot Act?"

"Call it a free exchange of information. The John Doe's just to
swat flies. When we're through I'll drive you back to your car. It's
still parked at the motel." He pulled my keys out of his pants
pocket, shook them, and put them back. "What about the walker?"

"I'll come back for it in about ten years."

"Walker on a walker. Kind of redundant, at that." He steered
me out into the hall.

TWENTY-SIX

Herbert Clemson's Chrysler was the same oyster color inside and out. When it came to the art of blending in, it stood out a mile.

There was no cloud cover that day. Sunlight butted in through the windshield, forcing me to unzip my borrowed coat and spread the flaps to keep from sweating. Meanwhile, merchants on both sides of the street bent over snow shovels on the sidewalks in front of their stores, their breath steaming thick as heavy cream.

Clemson drove the gray windswept streets a half mile below the limit with both hands on the wheel at nine and three o'clock and signaled all his turns. He had the radio tuned to a call-in talk show, just loud enough to discourage conversation. I was beginning to think he really suspected someone was following him around with surveillance equipment. Obsessive-compulsive disorder seemed to be the black lung of domestic espionage.

Iglooesque buildings, a squat control tower, and the tailfins of parked planes announced the little airport, fenced in with the usual chain link and razor wire. He parked in a red zone in front of the single terminal, and when security came to tell him to beat it, he flashed his credentials. Evidently the guard had heard from his superiors; he nodded and handed Clemson a permit to put on the dashboard.

Inside the building I had plenty of time to regret leaving the walker behind. I was unsteady on the cane and needed the agent's support on the opposite side just to cover the thirty yards to a brown steel fire door with AIRPORT PERSONNEL ONLY stenciled on it in yellow. It belonged to a perfect cube of a room with block walls originally painted a soothing aquamarine, but which time and the combined humidity of naked human bodies had begun to turn the bilious green of old-style public mailboxes and governments on both sides of the Eastern Bloc. Fluorescent tubes shed watered-down lemonade light through ceiling panels onto a folding trestle table and an orange plastic scoop chair, and a rectangular patch of unfaded wall indicated where the standard poster spelling out the rights of detainees had hung until recently. The U.S. Constitution hadn't been suspended, exactly; just placed out of sight.

I dropped onto the chair, sloughed off the coat, and sat with my hands folded on the crook of the cane like Clifton Webb. Cigarette burns scalloped the tabletop and the air was layered with nicotine. I hadn't smoked in days. I concentrated on the throbbing in my leg.

"Mary Bell Olinas." Clemson sat on a corner of the table, dangling one foot in its clunky boot. "Folks around here called her Miss Maebelle. A neighbor identified her in the morgue. That hasn't been released yet. She owned the Sportsmen's Rest, an old-fashioned motor court outside town. Stop me when I come to something that's news."

I said nothing. He'd put it cleverly, turning my own silence into evidence for the prosecution.

"She drove a lot of truck for someone who depended on the annual ice-fishing festival to stay off welfare," he said, "though she wasn't driving it that night. None of the witnesses saw who *was* driving well enough to identify him—if it was a man—but a woman her size piloting a snowmobile across two lanes of highway traffic is hard to forget, with or without the shotgun. The truck was registered in her name, bought from a dealership in Flint last November with a cashier's check for a hundred and fifteen thousand, with the options."

"Who was the bankroll?" I asked.

"So there *is* something you don't know."

"I'm learning more by the minute."

"You're a liar," he said cheerfully. "I'm not interested in you, just what you've managed to scratch up out of the rosebushes. The room's not wired."

When I made no response, he slid off the table and lifted one end to show me the underside, then set it back down and went up on tiptoe to push a ceiling panel out of its grid. An elaborate network of cobwebs quivered in the stirred air, woolly with dust. It might have been spun since the equipment was installed, but reliable listening devices require frequent maintenance. I was satisfied. He lowered the panel. "Get up and I'll turn over your chair."

I stayed put. "I'm tired enough to take your word for it."

He sat back down, swinging his leg. "We just started on the cashier's check. If they did it right—and they haven't done much wrong since the beginning—they laundered the money through enough corporations, legitimate and dummies, to implicate half the New York Stock Exchange. But we'll sniff out the source; the CPAs we've got on staff make the team that broke Al Capone look like Remedial Math. In eighteen months we'll have enough to prosecute. But I'm going to break this terrorist cell wide open before then."

"Still convinced it's terrorists?"

"It's too well-funded and organized for anyone else. The federal racketeering laws have the mob on the run, and the independents don't partner up; they're jobbers, nothing higher. We've known for some time the radical fundamentalists have been expanding their money-raising activities beyond Muslim church groups. Chaldeans are Christian Arabs; most of those who live in suburban Detroit have little sympathy for Islamists. But there's a lot of bad feeling in this country toward Arabs in general since nine-one-one, and Homeland Security and the Justice Department don't have the best track record when it comes to sorting them out. Mistakes were made. Toes were stepped on, and they limped over to the other side. Disgruntled Christians with Middle Eastern ties have opened the doors to other charities. Not so much the traditional sects, but in this country anyone with a philosophy and a gift for gab can start his own church. You'd be surprised how many of those there are just here on the east shore."

I had the idea that if I asked, he'd have the number handy. "The Church of the Freshwater Sea," I said.

He nodded with a tight smile, the professor pleased with his student's performance. "Terrorists make mistakes too. Paul Starzek was fanatic enough to offer his church for their printing plant, but unstable enough to forget himself and use stolen Treasury stock to print some of his flyers. The one you gave me is the only one of those we've found so far. I doubt there are many others. He probably stopped after one sheet."

"Someone stopped him."

"That was mop-up. I told you these people have brains. They fix their mistakes. They'd put him in the position of caretaker, and that was just a little bit outside his aptitude. Probably they put a tap on his phone after I interviewed him about his brother. When you called asking more or less the same questions, they decided that was too much interest and took him out of the rotation. FBI medical examiners dug a jacketed nine out of the base of his brain, assassin's work. That makes you indirectly responsible for his death, but I wouldn't let it affect my appetite. He sold them the use of his hall. If they told him where the money came from or where it was going, it didn't change his mind."

"He had a thing for martyrs. Look at the saint he picked out."

"I was raised atheist myself. Anyway they moved fast, figuring you or me or someone else would come poking around. The woodpile was handy, so they stuck him under it and fetched the truck and moved the merchandise out of the church. I hear Miss Maebelle wasn't any too pleased with the government in the state capital. People have turned their coats for less than that. What I can't figure out is how you traced the shipment here."

"That twenty you gave me doesn't buy detective lessons."

"No good. Not even clever. I'm not Lieutenant Kunkel. I print John Doe warrants the way these characters print twenties. Your friends won't know when to visit you, because as far as the paperwork goes, you won't exist."

"I've been waiting for you to put on the brass knuckles. The suspense was getting to me."

He smiled his disarming smile. He was good cop, bad cop all in one package. "I shouldn't have to. You've worked for lawyers, so you're a sometime officer of the court. You, me, the military, and the cop on the beat are all part of the first line of defense. If that doesn't work for you, don't forget you didn't stop being a citizen when they gave you that plastic badge. Just being born here comes with responsibilities."

I grinned. "Does that one work anymore?"

"Almost never. Too many Watergates. Too many White House sex scandals. Too many lies. Too many microwaves and plasma TVs and Game Boys and SUVs. Too many people watching cable, and all divided into tribes. What we need to bring them all together is an Attila the Hun. What we've got is the Constitution. So I threaten people and give pep talks. Anyway, I just gave you a lot more than I'd give my congressman, whoever the hell he may be, because you won't turn back and because of the week you've had. Free exchange, remember?"

"You should've said that first."

"I make mistakes. We all do. Every one of us was doing something else when the roof fell in. It's all on-the-job training. What tipped you to the Sportsmen's Rest?"

"Dumb blind luck."

"You're not dumb, you're not blind, and you're sure not lucky. Start again."

I straightened my leg. "Actually, I was snowblind. If I weren't the other things I wouldn't be here on several counts. I was working a reverse trace up the shoreline, looking for the place Jeff Starzek stopped last on his way down. There are hundreds of motels and comfort stations on his route, so it was hit-and-miss and hunchwork. A white squall blew me off the highway, that was the luck part. The rest was detective work like I said. Miss Maebelle lied about Cabin Twelve being out of service to keep me from snooping around it. If she lied half as well as she handled a snowmobile and shotgun, I might have moved on. Except she had one of Paul Starzek's church circulars in her tourist rack."

"Where is it?"

"If it wasn't with my clothes—"

"It wasn't. I went through the rags."

"Then I lost it crawling around under Cabin Twelve. It wasn't government paper."

I told him all of it then, from Miss Maebelle trying to pin the tail on the donkey with her scattergun through the black comedy out on the lake. The details weren't worth holding onto. His interest in manslaughter only ran toward terrorists on the dealing end, and if he wanted to shut me away he had a Christmas list of charges under the Patriot Act. He listened without expression. The

only sign he was paying me more than polite attention was his leg
had stopped swinging.

"I still don't like the element of chance," he said when I'd finished. "Every setup has at least one of those; legitimate information almost none."

"That was just a break. There's a truck stop called the Air Horn
a couple of miles north on the state highway. I'd have stopped
there to ask about Jeff, and found out what I did. Then I'd have
checked out all the local motels, including the Sportsmen's. The
barkeep, who says he owns the place, recognized him from his picture. He cooled his heels playing the piano there Christmas Eve."

He swung his leg twice, stopped. "You might have started with
that."

"You asked about the motel."

"He's sure it was Starzek?"

"He knew he was driving a Hurst Olds. I didn't prompt him on
that. Ask for Buzz." I got tired of leaning my hands on the cane
and laid it across my lap. "Tell me about the fire."

"Locals suspect arson, but then they always do when it involves
a vacant vacation stop. The fire-department investigators aren't
too happy with me. I've got them sitting on their hands until the
federal team arrives. Someone saw flames around eleven o'clock
last night. Firefighters managed to keep them from spreading to
the other buildings and more importantly a five-thousand-gallon
propane tank, but Cabin Twelve was a total loss."

"Think the mop-up squad got the Treasury paper out before
they torched the place?"

"Maybe not. The story about your little excursion didn't break
until yesterday, and the heavy equipment they used to deliver it in
the first place was out of service thanks to you. They might not
have had time to replace it. Anyway there was no sign in the snow
of any other big rigs. My thought is they set a match to the evi-

dence and cut their losses. We won't know for sure until we sift through the ashes."

"Jeff didn't deliver the paper," I said. "Not in his little muscle car, and probably not in the truck. He was overqualified for that. Any lug can drive a truck; look at me."

"Well, we won't know that either until we debrief him. Which means finding him."

"You think he's alive?"

"I think he's been a busy little bee." His mouth formed a straight line.

"Double agent?"

"Why not? We don't have the monopoly. And we sure can't match whatever the competition's offering."

"I don't see it. Jeff's an honest crook."

"Once you cross that first line, the others get harder to see."

"It isn't that. You don't change your lay in the middle of your career."

"Don't put too much store in his Albert Schweitzer act. Lots of times the people you can't buy or intimidate are surprisingly easy to back into owing you a favor."

"He isn't the one who shot me."

"True. I read the police report. But his reflexes were too good to let an opportunity pass." He hopped off the table, stretched. He looked a little worn around the edges. He'd been busy since he got my message: driving, violating the seal of the medical profession, making enemies for life of state and local authorities. "After we tossed Paul Starzek's place in Port Huron, the research librarians in Washington went to work on his church's boss martyr."

"I hope you don't pay them too much. A friend of mine got all that off his PC."

"I bet he didn't take it as far forward as they did. During the Crusades, the Knights Templar formed a sect called the Order of

St. Sebastian. His symbol's the arrow, so they took up the practice of forging and sending solid-gold arrows to suspected informers as a warning not to betray their secrets. The implication was the next one would be traveling much faster. It wasn't as extravagant as it sounds. They'd looted the gold by the ton from what was then called the Near East, and nine times out of ten they could reclaim the arrow, since its most recent owner wouldn't be using it anymore. After that I suppose it was just a matter of sending the same arrow to the next name on the list."

"Cheap sons of bitches."

"The order was wiped out during the Inquisition—executed, tortured to death, imprisoned for life. Seems the Catholic Church wasn't amused by the infidel ways they'd acquired while raping their way through Jerusalem. I suspect our little terrorist sympathizer in the woodpile had a pretty good founding in that area of medieval history."

"So why didn't his friends send him an arrow first? Too hard to wrap?"

"That's just it. They did. Only they sent it parcel post, and at holiday time, yet. It showed up at his place the day after you found him. One of my men signed for it. That's what put us on the trail of the order."

"Solid gold?"

"Painted. There's just no glamor left in the underworld."

"It still seems a little gaudy for your garden variety holy warrior. Why warn your victim in the first place? It just makes the job harder."

"Could be they intended for it to arrive late. It makes a nice object lesson for other screwups."

I lowered the tip of the cane to the floor. "We through here?"

"Can you drive?"

"I just can't walk." I levered myself to my feet. Blood slid from my face. I tightened my grip on the crook until the dizzy spell passed.

He watched me. "You headed straight home or over to your client's?"

"We've been through that. I'm working off a debt. Jeff didn't rig it."

"Your life hardly seems worth all the trouble."

"I've only got the one. I'm used to it." I dragged my foot toward the door. He didn't step forward to help.

"I took a look at your bank account yesterday."

I grasped the knob tight. It felt cold in my palm. "How's it doing?"

"Better than I would've thought based on your last tax return. You finished out the year with six hundred and change. On January second you deposited twelve hundred. That's just three hundred less than you soak your clients to start an investigation. I figure you needed the rest to walk around."

"What if I told you I tapped the blackjack table at Motor City?"

"Too easy to check. They withhold taxes and report to Uncle. There's a sizeable gap in Starzek's history between his parents' deaths and his first arrest. We found his school district, but they lost years of records when they converted from file cases to computers. We're requisitioning that equipment. You'd be surprised how much a geek with determination can get off a crashed hard drive."

"Like maybe Jeff's grade-point average?"

"Like maybe who signed his report cards. He had a family we haven't been able to track down because there was no official paperwork involved in the transfer of guardianship. You can save us some overtime and give up your client."

TWENTY-SEVEN

My Cutlass was where I'd left it, with my overnight bag in the backseat. The air in the motel lot stung, but it was clean and clear after the stifling heat in Herbert Clemson's Chrysler, and the sun felt good on my back. I left his overcoat on the passenger's seat and shook out my keys.

There was no outlet. The federal agent turned around at the end of the lot and crept past as I swung open the door. His window squeaked down.

"That's two you owe me," he said. "From now on I charge interest. Meter's running." His rear tires spun, caught hold, and catapulted him around the corner of the building.

I drove slowly, leaving plenty of room between me and the other cars in my lane. My legs had turned to lead and I needed a winch to lift my foot off the accelerator and press down the brake. My thoughts were slower still, from the lingering effects of morphine and the loss of adrenaline out on the lake. I hadn't taken Clemson's bait, but he'd find out about Rose and Oral Canon soon enough. They needed preparing. I turned north toward the Air Horn Truck Stop and a public telephone.

Overnight, a Hooverville had sprung up on the ice. Shanties occupied every square yard not left to the fanatics who sat on minnow buckets out in the open, dandling lines inside their chopped holes, and hundreds of spring-operated tip-up rods with no attendants in sight. When a fish struck at one, the rod would jerk upward, setting the hook and ringing a bell. The temporary shelters were commercially manufactured from canvas and nylon and homemade of plywood, Cellotex, and old metal roofing. Arranged in neat rows, with aisles running north and south and east and west like a street grid, they formed the world's most organized hobo jungle. Concession trucks sold pretzels, roast bratwurst, elephant ears, and hot and cold drinks from the side of the highway. A prefab gazebo made to look like a Swiss chalet spread its shelter over a brass band playing something buzzy and flatulent. A bullhorn squealed the score so far: Fishermen 62, Fish 11. It was the liveliest and most temporary of civilizations since Deadwood.

Highway traffic lock-stepped past cops directing the flow around several hundred vehicles parked bumper to bumper along the gravel apron. Some of those same polar-coated officers would have been with the crew diving for bodies and vehicles in the sub-zero waters beneath the ice only days before. One life more or less seemed to have had no effect on the festival atmosphere.

At the Air Horn I filled the tank, bought cigarettes, and poked my head into the bar, but Buzz wasn't on duty. A capable-looking Marine type with a brush cut and tattoos was busy rubbing the chrome off the fixtures with no customers to watch. They were all busy drowning worms. A canned-looking feature on bow hunting for bucks droned away on the TV monitor.

I got change from the clerk on the convenience-store side and dropped some of it into a telephone in the short hallway leading to the restrooms and showers. Rose Canon answered. The baby jabbered cheerfully in the background. I gave her a quick update on events, punctuated by sharp silences on her end, and told her Clemson was closing the gap in Jeff Starzek's history.

"You didn't tell him about me?"

"No, but he's got the scent. Expect a visit. When he makes it, tell him everything. You've got nothing to hold back now that Oral knows about you and Jeff."

"There is no me and Jeff. Jeff always saw to that." She paused. Little Jeffie gurgled. "Oral's left."

"Left for where?"

"Left me. I don't know where. We thought it was best we separated for a while until he can sort things out."

"We or he?"

"Mostly it was his idea. I've made such a mess of things. I should've told him years ago the way it was."

"He might have left you then. And you wouldn't have Jeffie."

"He asked me if Jeffie was his."

"He'd be an idiot not to wonder. Did you set him straight?"

"I told him he was. I don't know if he believed me. Do *you?*"

"I've seen the kid. A head like that can come from only one source. Anyway, there's no sense in lying to the hired help. Call if Clemson or his people give you any trouble. I'll check in regularly with my service."

"Just how much trouble am I in?"

"None. Not that it carries any weight with Gestapo Light. These cloak-and-dagger clowns will protect you at the cost of your life."

"Now I'm really afraid. What did I do wrong?"

"Right or wrong's an outmoded concept. These days it's all gray areas and nuance."

"Do you really believe that?"

"Nope. Someone told me just today once you cross that first line, the others get harder to see. You can hide a whole Holocaust behind mist and smoke. For the record, you haven't done a thing wrong from the start."

"I shouldn't have lied to Oral."

"He canceled that out when he went looking for Jeff on his own and lied about that. It's the truth that split you up. If you want him back, you need to put together a whole new set of lies."

"Are you married, Mr. Walker?"

"I've been divorced most of my life. The question is, do you want him back?"

"Yes. Yes, I do. I may be in love with Jeff, but it's Oral I love. I've only had a day or so to myself to think about it, but I know now what's important."

"Mazel tov."

"For what?" She sounded suspicious.

"It took you only twenty-four hours what it took me twenty-five years to figure out."

I said I'd be in touch and pegged the receiver. Her good-bye was tentative. The problem with having a reputation for irony is no one knows when you're sincere.

It hadn't snowed while I was in the hospital. What had fallen before lay white and polished-looking on either side of dry asphalt, with treacherous patches of black ice on bridges and underpasses. Traffic was heavy in the northbound lane as I approached Detroit, with helicopters whuppering above to tell the motorists with their radios on how heavy it was, but it thinned out before I crossed Eight Mile Road and entered the city limits; my lane was deserted for blocks. The sun was perched on the rooftops of the northern suburbs. I adjusted the mirror to keep the glare out of my eyes, throttled down, and let the gray tangle of overpasses weave their net overhead. The snow was shoved into clumps in the gutters, bleeding rust like iron ore, and a stray dog plugged along one of the broken sidewalks with head and tail hanging, misery dripping in icicles from its chin. It might have been a coyote. The city's ratio of buildings demolished to new buildings erected remained at two to one, and as unpopulated country reclaimed it block by block, various forms of wildlife had set up housekeeping among the thistles and Burger King cups. The place wasn't nearly as lively as Tip-up Town, and didn't look any more permanent.

I'd given up on Detroit's ever returning to what it had been before 1967. There'd been a brief flurry of construction and hope after the death of the old mayor, but then the casinos had come in with their on-site restaurants, ATMs, bars, and cabarets, each shrink-sealing its own self-contained community inside four walls, and the life they brought with them was strictly the shambling walk of the living dead. The next change of administrations had rebuilt the old party machine that had never worked well to begin with, not like the ones in Chicago and San Francisco, slick and silent, where the graft was spread evenly. Here it wasn't so much a political system as an evangelical clip joint, pumped up with sermons and fireworks and supported by the lowliest members of the congregation, with no hope of return this side of the ghostly pale. The money came in on the hips of the faithful and went out over the Net to Switzerland, and the dopes who opened the accounts didn't know how much richer they could be if they'd put some of it back in the collection plate. They were an insult to the fine old art of corruption.

But that was just my mood talking. I'd finished out the old year with a hole in my leg and started the new one with my pants full of buckshot. I'd been chased, shot at, pumped full of painkillers, and threatened with arrest by two counties, the State of Michigan, and Washington, which was my personal best; drowned Mrs. Butterworth, been jumped by my own client outside my place of business, told I'd enter my golden years with a limp I'd take to my grave, and broken up a marriage, and the year was still new. I wasn't just wallowing in self-pity. I was swimming around it in laps.

I put the car in the garage, left the overnight bag, and let myself into the kitchen with no small support from my life's companion of polished wood. The fluorescent ring in the ceiling took full eight seconds to respond to the switch, then flickered awake like a rheumatic old dog, the way it always does when there's snow on the roof. The insulation in the attic is as thick as a typewriter pad, and asbestos to boot. I can't replace it without involving three government agencies.

The house smelled as dank as the crawl space at the Sportsmen's Rest. It had been shut up for days and I'd cranked the thermostat down to sixty before I'd left. I ran it up to seventy-two. I was shivering, partly from cold, partly from my old friend shock. Fever and morphine had only bought me a reprieve. The furnace thumped on and then the fan kicked in with a rattle of bearings that needed replacing, had needed replacing for two winters, filling the place with the smell of dusty ductwork. I knew the smell, but something new had crept in. It had gone beyond the homely stink of bachelor living into the beginnings of a lonely old age. I was still swimming laps.

I got coffee going. The aroma when I took the lid off the can lightened my mood a notch. In the morning, after a full night's sleep in my own bed and my first cigarette, more coffee, eggs in my belly, I'd be as chipper as Dr. Kevorkian.

My body was as sore as my leg. I couldn't raise my hands above my head without crucifying pain across my shoulders and up the back of my neck, so I leaned on the stove and used the cane to open the cabinet and hook the kitchen bottle off the shelf, catching it against my chest with one arm. That hurt, too, but relief was in sight.

When I saw the label I decided against doctoring the coffee. I'd thought it was bourbon. Scotch and caffeine make carbolic. I propped my hips against the stove and took a long gurgling swig straight from the bottle. While I was waiting for the tingle to reach my toes I took another. The alcohol cauterized my throat, still scratchy from pneumonia, and made a cartoon kettle-drum sound in my ears when it hit my stomach. I stood the bottle on the range, left the pot percolating, and went to the back door to collect my mail.

It was in four bundles on the little covered porch, bound with rubber bands: catalogues, bills, an alumni newsletter from a college I hadn't attended in almost thirty years, several opportunities to dig myself a credit hole and pull the sod over my head, and a cardboard tube about two feet long, gaily emblazoned with the red, white, and blue of Priority Mail. I shook it. No sound. I used the knife on my key chain to cut the tape and pry the plastic plug out of one end. They'd packed it with crumples of blank newsprint. I pulled some out, got hold of something narrow and unfamiliar to the touch, and tugged out eighteen inches of hunting arrow, spray-painted gold from the feather fletching to the razor-sharp point.

There was no note, no return address. The postmark was generic. I didn't need any of that. I knew who'd sent it, and who had killed Paul Starzek. Now I needed to find Jeff more than ever. He was next.

TWENTY-EIGHT

O K."

The voice sounded real, and weirdly familiar. I sat up straight in bed with those two initials echoing in my skull. I'd spoken them into my own ear.

Outside, the moon stood on edge, pouring light onto the snow and splashing it through the window. The furniture in the bedroom made hand shadows on the walls. Even my cane looked sinister leaning against the chair where I'd flung my clothes. Wind whimpered around the edges of panes, the proverbial wolf at the door.

I was thinking more clearly asleep than awake. I got up, clambered into my robe and slippers, and hobbled out into the living room and the only comfortable chair I owned, next to a lamp and the metropolitan telephone directory on their little table. I hauled the big book onto my lap and lit a cigarette one-handed while I paged through Automobile Maintenance in the yellow section.

OK Towing & Auto Repair was the oldest continually operating professional garage in a city that had spent the last generation eradicating every link to its historical past. I brought my Cutlass there for tune-ups and repairs; had bought it there, in fact, after the owner of the shop had found it abandoned in a field in rural Washtenaw County and dropped in a new engine and transmission. He hated collectors for babying their machines instead of driving them as God and Henry Ford intended, but he did all their work for triple what he charged his other customers, and they shut their mouths and paid up, because as mechanics went he was a Picasso in a world of Sunday painters. He was German, of course; and of course he was working at three o'clock in the morning. For all I knew he lived there, against all the zoning ordinances in his neighborhood. But then the only laws that meant anything to him were the laws of bodies in motion. He refused to report cash expenditures in excess of ten thousand dollars, as required by Washington to discourage the cash-and-carry trade in illegal narcotics, which was another reason why his operation was popular. When a fugitive like Jeff Starzek needed work done on his classic transportation, OK was the only place he could go in the state of Michigan,

"OK." Ernst Dierdorf's High German accent cut through the animal wail of air wrenches in the background.

"Amos Walker, Ernst. Nineteen-seventy Cutlass? I've got a question."

"Lay off premium. It's a car, not a racehorse."

"It's not about the Cutlass. It's about someone else's car."

"We open at eight. Come in then."

I blew smoke at the dial tone. He was just old enough to have served with the Hitler Youth, and his bedside manner was in keeping. I started to call him back, then hung up. He changed his mind as often as the Vatican changed popes, and if you annoyed him sufficiently, you were dead to him for months. Half the races in the old Detroit Grand Prix had been lost by drivers who'd found that out firsthand.

I put out the cigarette, stumped back into the bedroom, checked the load in the .38 for the eighth time that night, and tucked it back under my pillow. In spite of the package I'd received, I had an idea that when they came for me it wouldn't be with a bow and arrow.

At six o'clock I was up again, microwaving last night's coffee while I got dressed. It tasted like boiled socks, but the caffeine chased the pixies out of my head. I swallowed two Vicodins and pounded the second half of the cup down on top of them. Then I went out into the granite cold of predawn.

Barry Stackpole was awake when I got to his condo. He slept about two hours in the afternoon, hanging upside down. He heard me out, woke up a couple of people on the telephone, hacked into a top-level database on the computer, and gave me a printout. In return I drank his coffee and told him everything that had happened since we'd seen each other last. He took no notes—he never did—and said he'd sit on it until I gave him the sign. The only way you could tell he was excited was his eyelids looked sleepier than usual.

It was a white glazed-brick building on the east side, with a Standard gasoline pump rusting out front and an electric fence in back to protect the rolling stock. Dead birds littered the ground around the fence, but that was just staging. Dierdorf had barely ducked a conviction for reckless endangerment after a prowler tried to climb the wire and lost the use of one kidney. The owner cut back on the current on the advice of his attorney, but he'd made his point. There had been no attempts since.

I passed a hundred thousand dollars' worth of Detroit muscle up on hydraulic lifts and what looked like a bathtub-gin Duesenberg rendered down to its basic molecules on the concrete floor on the way to the office. A half-dozen overgrown Oompa Loompas in greasy coveralls splattered sparks off cracked frames, balanced wheels, and puzzled over parts older than their grandfathers to the accompaniment of a raunchy roadhouse beat galloping out of loudspeakers mounted near the roof. Dierdorf, a German national who'd been registering as a resident alien for sixty years, held a deep fascination for homegrown American culture that didn't include Americans themselves, whom he'd never forgiven for *Hogan's Heroes.* A professionally painted mural of Larry, Moe, and Curly Joe trying to crank-start a Model T covered the back wall of the garage.

A three-by-five card with a black thumbprint in one corner commanded me to KNOCK, THEN ENTER. I rattled my knuckles against the opaque windowpane, purely out of courtesy, and opened the door. A gasoline-tank explosion couldn't have penetrated the din.

Dierdorf, seated at his Edwardian rolltop heaped with insurance forms, bills of lading, a two-year run of J.C. Whitney catalogues, and empty Beck's bottles, recognized me and threw the switch on a power strip, cutting off the stereo on its shelf. Now only the silken whisper of pneumatic hammers drifted into the cramped space.

"You're at least a thousand miles past due for an oil change," he said by way of greeting. He knew me by sight, and could dredge up my name with a little effort, but the calendar in his head was always turning, on every vehicle he maintained on a regular basis. He could detect a faulty timing gear by the sound and a loose piston ring by the smell, but he'd never mastered English subjunctive. "I sold you that four-fifty-five, and I can sell it out from under you if you don't treat it properly."

He had a dashboard clock of some Art Nouveau design in pieces on a cleared section of desk and was poking at the cogs and

wheels with a precision screwdriver. It might have belonged to the
Duesenberg, or he might have found it rooting around in a pile of
scrap iron. His hands, blue-black with grease, were coarse and
misshapen, like his body, with knuckles flattened and scarred, but
tapered into fingers with spatulated tips like a concert pianist's.
His head, although white-haired now and sagging under the chin,
belonged to a Nazi sculptor's idea of a Roman god. His coveralls
were Homerically filthy. Contact with them alone would soil
whatever he wore underneath. My theory was it was his own
naked skin. For all I knew he lived in the garage like the Phantom
of the Opera and never went out, except on midnight raids of all
the salvage yards in the area. I knew he never bothered to test-
drive the results of his skill. Once they left the floor he stopped
thinking about them until their next service period.

"I'll make an appointment next week," I said. "It's a Hurst Olds
I'm interested in. Sixty-nine, powder blue. Stripped for speed."

"If one comes in here painted blue I take it away on principle. I
told them fockers in the Woodward Dream Cruise I shit on their
mutant spawn." He blew metal shavings off a tiny part and began
reassembling the clock. His fingers seemed to work independently, each with its own brain. The muscles of his face were
locked in concentration.

"Well, it's blue. This is the owner. Maybe you've done business
with him in the past." I got out the picture of Jeff Starzek with
Rose Canon and laid it on top of a 1939 Chevrolet owner's man-
ual. I didn't hold out much hope he'd make the connection. I think
when he looked at his customers he saw headlights, grilles, and
manufacturers' insignia instead of faces. Just to tilt the odds I in-
cluded a folded fifty I'd broken out of the safe in my office on the
way there.

His gray eyes flicked toward the photo, then back to his work.
His hands never seemed to leave the project, but when I looked

again the fifty was gone. He'd snatched it away without disturbing the picture on top.

The clock was mechanical. He opened a tiny drawer next to the pigeonholes in the rolltop, rummaged among a pile of Dumbo-shaped brass keys, selected one apparently by feel, fitted it in place, and wound it three or four times. The clock ticked and the sweep hand went into orbit. He set the time against the MobilGas advertising clock on the wall and stood it on its pedestal on the desk. Then he pulled out a deep file drawer and handed me a rounded paper cup with an elastic band from an assortment inside. "Put it on."

I stuck my head through the band and adjusted the cup over my nose and mouth. "Bank or party store? I left my gun in the car."

He said nothing, which after abandoning German was the only language he spoke fluently. He got up and led the way out of the office, walking stooped over with his arms bent in the permanent crook they'd acquired lifting engines without benefit of a chain fall. I figured he'd gotten the rest of his physical complaints during the sorting-out process at Nuremberg.

In the garage he stopped to fit together two deformed-looking parts of the Duesenberg for a mechanic seated on the floor amidst the carnage, then continued to the airtight metal door of the paint room.

"Where's your mask?" I said.

He tugged open the door and went on through, no response.

This room, a former bay no longer used for maintenance, was windowless and displayed all the colors of the spectrum on walls, floor, and ceiling, along with a few others invented by the design departments of all the major automakers past and present. Notwithstanding an elaborate ventilation system, it reeked of ozone and acetate. Steel shelves encircling the room held spray guns, portable drying lamps, and cans and cans of paint labeled in every language. The air swam with fumes. I sucked what oxygen I could through the paper mesh in my mask and still felt woozy. Dierdorf must have had his lungs removed and gills installed.

"Is it ready?" he asked.

"I was just about to rip off the tape."

The reply came muffled through a Neoprene gas mask covering the features of the man who occupied the room. It covered his head as well. The shape of his body was invisible under a loose smock that hung to the tops of his shoes. He stripped off a pair of rubber gauntlets.

The car parked in the middle of the room was a 1966 Hurst/Oldsmobile, still futuristic in line after all those years. Silver vinyl draped all four tires and miles of masking tape secured scraps and patches of brown paper to windshield, windows, headlights, taillights, and chrome. The exposed sections gleamed warm white with twin gold stripes bisecting trunk and hood and limning the sides, the original factory color scheme. The paint man tore loose the tape alongside a stripe with a shrill zipping sound.

I heard thumping. I thought at first it was a worker in the garage pounding out a ding with a rubber mallet. It was my heart.

"Let me. For this I live." Dierdorf snatched the vinyl off the tire nearest him, threw it aside, and walked around the vehicle, stripping off tape and crumpling paper as he went. He almost whistled.

Jeff Starzek tore off his gas mask and ran his stubby fingers through his chestnut hair. He grinned at me. "How about a spin?"

TWENTY-NINE

J eff gave Dierdorf a tight roll of bills as big around as a soup can and we strapped ourselves in and took off through the bay door before they had it all the way up. I confirmed there was no backseat. "Speed or cargo space?"

"Speed. Since the last tax hike you can carry a couple hundred grand in the trunk easy."

"Are we?"

He smiled at the windshield. He wore wraparound shades that made his round face look like a well-fed Steve McQueen's. "Wouldn't you like to know."

"Where we going?"

"Around. I like to drive."

"You'd think you'd be sick of it."

"Didn't Seabiscuit like to run?" He swung right and let out the clutch. The big plant under the hood gulped air through its scoops and we lifted away from the pavement. Neither of us worried about cops. One thing they let you do in Detroit is drive.

"I guess you got tired of blue."

"I never liked it. It was my cloak of invisibility."

"Are you looking to get pinched?"

"They have to catch me first."

We rocketed through the East Side, scattering Sunday supplements and one cock pheasant, which took off with a white blur and turned into the sun, glistening russet and turquoise with an arrogant cackle that drowned out the rumble of the 455. Jeff's engine was the same size as mine, but he'd science-fictioned it into a barely earthbound Concorde. Squat brick titty bars and patches of weedy vacant real estate shot past in a smear.

"Oral moved out on Rose," I said. "He found out you're not related by blood."

"It had to happen sometime. There's a brain in that big bald head. You tell him?"

"He figured it out for himself. She told him the rest."

"Well, I'm sorry about that. I never saw her as anything but a sister. Mother, too. She raised me from a stray pup."

"She told me that. I found out the rest for myself. My head's smaller than Oral's, but I flush it out with alcohol now and then."

"How's the leg?"

"Follows me around like an old dog. I'm told I have to get used to that."

"Bullshit."

"That was my reaction. Where've you been keeping yourself?"

"I been everywhere, man. Hotels, motels, YMCAs, the long open road. Did you know the Michigan coastline's the longest in the United States, not excluding Hawaii and California?"

"I heard. And there's a hundred public telephones to every mile."

"An exaggeration. For every working instrument there's five bird's nests and one honking big nest of seriously pissed hornets."

"You don't look stung."

"I'm a fugitive, son. I don't own a cell, for damn good reasons, and every time I stop long enough to make a call, five branches of law enforcement are waiting with nets. You'd think I was Ted Kaczynski. All I ever did was feed the good old American craving for nicotine."

"True. Well, there was that counterfeiting thing."

"I didn't have anything to do with that. I never take delivery on cargo I can't carry in one trip. And I never took a flyer on a rap I couldn't beat. Uncle's one unforgiving son of a bitch."

"Your brother did. He's dead."

"I heard. We weren't close."

We climbed the ramp onto I-94, the Edsel Ford Expressway, downshifting behind a Saturn trying to enter at thirty. At the last second he gunned it, shifted again, and we slipped into the passing lane through a space no wider than a pantry door. A Greyhound bus let him know what it thought about that. I took my foot out of the floorboards. "What brought you into contact with him after all those years?"

"Herbert Clemson. I'm betting you've met."

"Why'd he turn you?"

"You mean how."

"Start there."

"Saginaw cops pulled me over in November, ran my sheet, and frisked the car. I was hauling three hundred cartons of Tareytons, a real dog of a brand, but I had a buyer lined up in Toledo. Turns out my source had kicked in a big-box store in Midland Halloween night. He told me he'd bought the cigs wholesale in Tennessee. I was looking at three felony counts, including an ADW on a security guard he'd bopped on the head. Clemson came in and just took me away from them."

"Him and his John Does. He tried the same thing with me. How far back do you figure he set you up?"

"Midland. Maybe as far back as Tennessee. He's one bad hat. I was supposed to be his mule. You can pass a lot of phony paper when all the people you work with deal strictly in cash."

"That's his signature. It's the same with small churches and roadside motels. You were part of his fleet. He has a territory the size of Brazil."

"He said it was an inside sting to crack a terrorist counterfeiting ring. I was to pick up my first shipment from Paul."

"Clemson was rigging you to take the fall for Paul's murder. He'd already decided he had to go."

"Something of the sort occurred to me. I went to Paul and warned him he was in over his head. He was a crackpot and a crank, but he was the only family I ever had except for Rose. He called me a foul trafficker and sent me on my way. I've been burning rubber ever since. I guess you got my note."

"You know I did." I moved my leg into a position that didn't make me want to scream. "Clemson isn't the type to let a good frame go to waste. After you dropped off his screen, he used your brother's corpse to set me up the way he did you. What was the something else you told me in Grayling you were carrying down the coast?"

"A big load of government bullshit."

I waited, but nothing else came. His concentration was fixed on a street with plenty of visibility and no other traffic.

"Normally I don't even have to pump you for the brands you're smuggling," I said.

"That was before I got on this lifesaving jag. This is second-hand smoke you don't want."

"Life meaning mine."

"Mine too, if I can work it." He exited at Grand and we cruised past the Fisher Building and the former corporate headquarters of

General Motors, already losing some of its Art Deco shine to an indifferent city government now in residence.

I waited until we stopped for a light, then took out the computer printout Barry had given me and snapped it open in front of his face. He took it and read it.

" 'Operation suspended pending review.' What's it mean?"

"It means Clemson's freelancing. No help from Washington. He's been recalled, and he's taking his own sweet time about answering."

"Where'd you get this?"

"A friend. He's busting up his hard drive as we speak. It's evidence to prosecute if the FBI traces the hack."

"Hell of a friend."

"We saved each other's life a couple of times."

"That's long coin with you."

"You should know." I watched the scenery pass in a white wipe. "Clemson told me himself this Treasury-paper thing was too big for anyone but a well-funded gang of terrorists. The Mafia's gone bust and the independent crooks don't have the organization. Setting aside terrorists, that leaves just Uncle Sam.

"He's poured billions into the war on terror," I went on. "Who's to notice if one of his own people diverts a few hundred thousand from the operating fund to open his own shop?"

"Someone did. They're calling him in." The light changed. He chirped his tires crossing the intersection.

"That action's recent. He's been recruiting his people—people like you and Paul and a woman named Miss Maebelle—out of his operation's budget. Maybe it was serendipity at the start. Maybe he stumbled on a genuine counterfeiting mill in the course of his smuggling investigation and saw his chance to cash in. Look at the code name he picked out."

He took his eyes off the road long enough to look again at the printout on the seat between us. "I see what you mean."

"Call it Paul Starzek's legacy. We may never know how your brother came by that Treasury stock. Could be someone in his congregation caught a strong case of guilt and picked the wrong clergyman to hear his confession. They're all getting close to judgment. Whatever you say about Paul, he was devoted to his do-it-yourself church. He bought himself a state-of-the-art printer and spent his first dividend on a new statue of St. Sebastian. Clemson saw it in less spiritual terms. He may not even be guilty of treason, just misappropriation of funds and a count or two of conspiracy to commit forgery. And murder, of course."

"You're sure he killed Paul?"

"Paul was a liability. Clemson said so himself, when he was putting the rap on terrorists. Paul mixed up the stock with the paper he used to print his advertising circulars. If he was that unreliable, he'd have shown it in other ways as well. Clemson neutralized him and moved the inventory to another safe house."

"The Sportsmen's Rest. I heard about that business on the lake. It sounded a little like you."

"It couldn't have come as much of a surprise. You stopped to play the piano in Miss Maebelle's neighborhood Christmas Eve."

He used a right-turn lane to beat a red light, swerving around a cautious driver in a hatchback. "Paul bragged a bit. He wanted to impress me with his missionary work. Anyway I wanted to see how deep Clemson was in. I thought it might come in handy."

"I got a good look at Miss Maebelle when I showed her your picture," I said. "She didn't know you from Andy Jackson."

"I didn't get that far. I'm as good as I am at what I do because when I'm driving, driving's all I think about. I get most of my thinking done about other things when I stop. I had a swallow of beer, I played a little Bach and Fats Waller. Then I reverted to instinct and ran like hell."

"Like hell is right."

We went a block in silence.

"Pull over a minute," I said. "I want to show you something else."

He frowned, but took his foot off the accelerator and let the drag carry us onto a patch of gravel by the Grand Trunk tracks. Low empty buildings dotted the landscape like an adobe village. He braked. A lump of humanity in tattered Carhartt and a backpack looked over at the car from fifty yards down the rails, then resumed scouring the cinderbed for jetsam.

I'd lied to Ernst Dierdorf about leaving the gun in my car. I hadn't taken two steps from it since leaving Port Sanilac. I took it out and pointed it across my lap at Jeff.

He smiled, but he didn't try to pass it off as a joke. The world amused him. He saw most of it blurring past at eighty-five. He let one hand dangle over the steering wheel and faced me. Two seasoned duelists watching each other over their choice of weapons.

"Let's revise," I said. "You knew I'd come looking for you in an obvious place like a truck stop on the route you told me you'd be taking. You stayed long enough to leave an impression with the bartender. You had a conversation with him. You never do that. Why didn't you just go ahead and leave a trail of bread crumbs?"

"The Rest isn't easy to find from the state highway. I couldn't be sure you wouldn't miss it."

"How long have you been in Detroit?"

"Just long enough to pick up a couple of things. Change of socks. A new paint job. Clemson was looking for a blue car. I've done a lot of business over the years with OK. Who do you think recommended you when he was looking for a buyer for that Cutlass?"

"Were you planning on dropping by my place?"

"No."

"A man in your tight needs all the friends he's got."

"Open the glove compartment," he said.

I didn't even look at it. "Turn off the motor."

He twisted the key in the ignition. When the rumbling stopped, the silence hurt my ears. He'd torn out all the carpeting and insulation that muffled the noise from under the hood. Heater, too; our breath curled.

"Key," I said.

"Gun."

After a second I laid the .38 on the dash. He took the key out then and put it next to the revolver. I popped open the glove compartment.

It didn't contain any of the usual junk, not even an insurance card or registration. All it held was a No. 10 envelope. I slid it out. It was blank. I lifted the flap, spread it open to look at the Michigan driver's license inside. His picture looked recent.

" 'Jason Argo,' " I read. "You better hope you don't get stopped by a classical scholar."

"What are the odds?" He smiled, waggled the hand hanging over the wheel. "I'm a romantic. It's always been about the driving. The money was just for gas and oil."

"There's always NASCAR."

"Too many rules. Too many logos. Too many yellow flags. My parents were hippies, don't forget. It's in the blood."

"Paul must have gotten a transfusion somewhere else."

"Not true. He didn't have to start his own church. He could've been a Baptist."

I flicked a finger at the license. "This is good work."

"It better be. It cost me five cases of Luckies."

"Where's the Social Security card?"

"You don't need one in Canada."

I put the license and envelope back and shut the compartment. "Take the tunnel. Trucks on the bridge back up for hours. If you'd asked me to keep Clemson and his people busy, I might have said yes. You didn't have to snag me in with a phony cry for help."

"It wasn't phony. Cops and hijackers I can handle. I know the playbook. The spooks change the rules as they go. I needed another guerrilla to split their concentration." He spread his fingers. "I didn't know you well enough to ask. You might have said no."

I leaned back and closed my eyes. I was tired, my leg hurt.

"I didn't mind so much," I said. "Not even screwing up the leg. You pulled me out of that parking lot. I might have, if I knew I was just there to drag a dead skunk across Clemson's path. I'm not saying I wouldn't have done all the same things. It just would have been different."

"Does he know about Rose?"

I looked at him. I felt lonely suddenly. Whistling in the wind will do that.

"Not yet, but he knows where you went to school. He knows I have a client, from a bank deposit I made. He's closing in."

"How do you figure he got all that without help from Washington?"

I sat up. "He's got a mole. Probably the same one who forwarded all his calls and mail from the Detroit office. He said it took three days for a note I sent from Port Sanilac to reach him. He'd have found Rose long before this if he could go through regular channels. He can't pay for the service much longer. He put a match to his working capital."

"He's folding his tent."

I lit the cigarette I found between my lips. I didn't remember

240 LOREN D. ESTLEMAN

putting it there. "His cards, maybe. He doesn't usually overplay his hand."

"He doesn't have to. He owns the deck."

I shook out the match. While I was doing that he snatched the key off the dash. The Hurst's engine grumbled to life. I made a move for the gun. Then I saw the blue-and-red flashers in his mirror.

"Hang on to your teeth." He threw the car into gear. Gravel sprayed.

THIRTY

J eff Starzek laughed. "God, I love this."

His enthusiasm seemed inappropriate. We were flying down a long grade with a flat section at the bottom where streetcar tracks had been torn up decades ago, with a sharper grade rising from that. The topography presented a distinct advantage to the heavier Detroit cruiser on our tail, which gobbled up yards out of the gap with each second; its momentum would match the Hurst's acceleration on the climb. I hung on to the door handle and felt the siren yelping in my leg.

"City cops don't know Clemson's gone rogue," I said through my teeth. "You should've ditched the car, not repainted it."

"I broke the first rule: Don't fall in love with your machine." He didn't sound contrite. We struck sparks off the frame at the base of the hill, straining our seat belts tight. He put his foot through the fire wall. The carburetor gulped air and we headed for open sky. Behind us the cruiser hit the flat with a bang and bore down on our rear bumper.

I expected Jeff to swing left onto Joseph Campau, splitting the enclosed suburb of Hamtramck and gaining ground on the straightaway. He shot past it and took the square corner onto East Grand on two patches of tire no bigger than the palm of my hand.

"You know Detroit?" I asked.

"Does a Jew know Jerusalem?"

"You can't lose him downtown."

He said nothing, baring his teeth at the windshield.

We were nearly across Harper when he took a left, cutting the corner off the curb on the right side but not touching it with his tires; the world tilted thirty degrees, then righted itself with a report I felt in my teeth when our wheels touched down. I turned my head in time to see the cruiser slew around 360 in the middle of the intersection and come out of it with rubber smoking. It was no rookie at the wheel.

Another left on Mt. Elliott, two inches shy of a white Escalade waddling across from the other direction, and we powered past old Dodge Main, now a GM assembly plant. Jeff knew its history.

"I'm thinking Chrysler next time," he said. "See how that new hemi handles dirt roads."

The Escalade had stopped in the middle of the intersection, but the cruiser had looped around it and was coming on hard.

I said, "In your position I'd consider a paper route."

When Mt. Elliott branched off to the right, we went straight on Conant, lefted again on Holbrook, and tore across Hamtramck. This was home territory to me, but when we left that major cross street for the neighborhoods I saw signs I'd never seen before. We slalomed among the drives and courts, avoiding the cul-de-sacs, for several minutes, losing ten miles an hour to the turns, but the cruiser was no longer in sight. I heard its siren, baying like a hound quartering a field.

"You live around here, don't you?" Jeff asked.

"The garage is empty." I directed him.

In my driveway I scrambled out to lift the door, forgetting my limp. He nearly clipped the bottom edge with his roof. The door thumped down and I heard the furious yelping pass by a street or two over.

Jeff got out, looking as if he'd just scored a good space in the lot at Ford Field.

"We can't stay here," I said. "Clemson knows where I live."

He glanced around the windowless garage. "Does that door lock?"

It didn't, but I took a screwdriver off the peg board near the side door and jammed it through a slot in the right track near the floor. I gave the door a test pull. It lifted two inches and stopped when the roller met the obstruction.

"I've got time for a drink," he said.

"I thought you didn't drink."

"Only when I'm driving."

We went into the kitchen. I filled two tumblers with ice, poured Scotch, and we sat facing each other in the breakfast nook.

"Nice house." Jeff drank. "Rotten liquor."

"It was a tough choice." I drank. The stuff kicked like a kitten. My heart was still jumping two hundred to the minute. "Where to from here?"

He wore a green twill shirt and jeans, no overcoat. He patted the breast pocket. Paper rustled. I hadn't seen him retrieve the envelope containing his fake driver's license.

"They'll be watching for you at Customs," I said.

"They'll be watching for the car. I know a guy has a heap he'll be tickled pink to get rid of. Get what you can for the Hurst, if they don't confiscate it; I'll mail you the title. That should pay your hospital bill."

"You know Windsor?"

"I know all the places where cigarettes are cheap. I've got some cash there in a locker. You'd be surprised how much you can put aside when you don't pay taxes or insurance. I can live a year there on the exchange rate. Longer, if there's anything over there the politicians in Ottawa don't want people to have. There's thousands of miles of back road in the western territories."

"You might not have to."

He shook his head.

"You can't take him, Amos. They won't let you. They'll just close ranks. With me out of reach, he'll lose interest. Call it a draw. Paul won't mind."

"He'll find Rose."

He said nothing. His face said the same. He'd spent his adult life bluffing his way through Customs and traffic stops and the muscles had set into a bland mask.

"He'll use her to get to you," I said. "Me, too. We're the only ones who can tie him to counterfeiting and murder."

"He already got to you." He drained his glass and rose. "Thanks for the company. I can't remember the last time I had a passenger. I won't thank you for the hospitality. I'll send you a case of Canadian. The good stuff, not the grizzly sweat they export."

"Don't. I'm going on the wagon. Need a cab?"

"No. Not even Clemson will think to look for me on foot."

After he left by the front door, I sat there and watched my ice cubes melt. I thought about Rose Canon, the woman who loved Jeff Starzek, and of all the women who loved the wrong men for the right reasons. One wrong was all it took to waste your time.

I emptied the glass, still without effect, and got up to wash it. I scooped Jeff's off the table and chucked it into the trash can, hard enough to break it. I didn't want to take the chance of drinking from it by mistake.

THIRTY-ONE

'd left without breakfast that morning, so I threw two eggs in a skillet, made toast, emptied and washed the coffeepot, and made a fresh batch, extra brawny. I wasn't hungry, but I needed something to sit on top of the Scotch. It really was rotten stuff.

I ate without tasting and carried my second cup into the living room. Rose Canon's telephone rang four times before she picked up. Little Jeffie was mad as hell about something, raising blisters on my ear. "Just a second," Rose yelled. "I'll put you on speaker."

Her end of the conversation echoed after that. She stopped to sing to the baby in snatches, make cooing noises, jiggle it while her voice wobbled in response to my questions. Jeffie went on screaming.

"Heard from Oral?" I asked.

"He called this morning. We had a long talk. He's coming to take me out to dinner Friday night, an honest-to-God date. He thinks we ought to go back and start over. Is that a good idea?"

"I'm way underqualified to answer that one. Maybe you should start by just enjoying the meal."

"Is there any news about Jeff?"

"He's okay. Still running."

She jumped on it. "How do you know? Did you see him?"

"Not over the telephone. Agent Clemson call you yet?"

"No. You have to tell me about Jeff."

"I'm on my way." The baby was coming in loud and clear over the speaker. I had an idea. "Is there someplace you can go for a couple of hours today?"

"Shopping, but we don't need anything. Why?"

"I want to set up a meeting with Clemson. I don't think he'll open up in my house or office, and I don't trust any place he'd suggest. I wouldn't ring you in, except if he doesn't know all about you by now he will soon anyway."

"Are you thinking of turning Jeff in?"

"No. Whatever he's done or hasn't done, I'm still carrying him on the books."

"You did see him, didn't you? Something happened between you. I raised Jeff. I know when someone isn't telling me the whole story."

"In person."

There was a little gulp of silence. The baby had paused for breath.

"I suppose it won't hurt to stock up," Rose said. "When?"

"I'll call back after I talk to Clemson." I worked the plunger and dialed the agent's cell number, which I knew now by heart. It rang three times and kicked me over to voice mail. I broke the connection again and tried his pager.

Two minutes later the telephone rang. "This better be good," Clemson said. "We just went on orange alert. Someone wants to blow a hole in the middle of Martin Luther King Day."

Something hummed in the background; tires on pavement. He was driving.

"Well, I can't touch that," I said. "I wanted to tell you I had a drink this morning with Jeff Starzek."

The line crackled. A hand gripped the receiver tight. "Where?"

"My place, but he left."

"You're there now?"

"I'm just leaving. I can meet you in Oak Park." I gave him the Canons' address.

"What's in Oak Park?"

"All the family Starzek has left."

It was dangerous bait, and I almost didn't use it. But he struck.

"Are you saying you're coming through with your client?"

"How long will it take you to get there?"

I felt him back away. I'd sounded too eager. I sipped coffee to flatten my nerves.

"Is it about Starzek?" he asked.

"Only indirectly. I owe you twenty bucks."

"Keep it. Be direct."

I hesitated, then set the hook. "Operation Sebastian."

Far away a bell rang. The humming slowed. I heard him pull over and coast to a stop. "Where'd you hear that name?"

"I want to give you back your arrow." I hung up.

Oak Park had enjoyed a brief thaw while I was north, just long enough to melt the snow on the Canons' hip roof before winter turned back and flash froze it into tyrannosaur fangs of icicle. A broad section broke loose when I slammed the taxi door and smashed the sleeping rosebushes flat. The only other vehicle on the street belonged to a plumber. Frozen and broken pipes are as much a part of the Michigan winter as hockey fights.

Rose was ready, dressed for the street in slacks, ankle boots, and a blue sweater that electrified her eyes and showed her collarbone, a feature I've always approved of in women's clothing. She was holding a tiny tomato-red snowsuit in one hand.

"You look terrible," she said.

"I put on a tie." I hung up my overcoat and pointed my cane toward one of the platform rockers in the living room. "That seat taken?"

"Take Oral's. It's the most comfortable in the house."

I hadn't come there to get comfortable. Aloud I said, "I don't want to jinx you with Oral." I wobbled over to the rocker and lowered myself into it. "I'll talk while you finish getting ready. We don't have much time."

Jeffie lay in a convertible stroller near the door to the kitchen, red-faced from crying but asleep. He barely stirred as his mother got him into the snowsuit, a complicated operation performed with efficiency. I told her what had happened with Jeff. I left out Herbert Clemson's connection with it all and Jeff's nonreaction in the kitchen when I'd said what I'd said about Rose still being in danger. I didn't know how she'd take it and I wanted her gone in time to make certain arrangements.

"How did he look? Has he been eating?" Her hands flew over snaps and zippers.

"You don't have to worry about that. He's the type that gets fat in the saddle, like Napoleon. He's leaving the country. You won't see him for a long time."

"Well, I'm used to that. What's going on, Mr. Walker? What kind of trouble is he in?"

"The murder kind. He's set to take the fall for what happened to his brother."

"He's no murderer. You must know that by now."

"I do. I know who killed Paul."

She pulled a knit cap over the baby's head and tucked him into his blue blanket. She straightened and faced me. "Not Oral." Her husky voice fell to a whisper.

"Not Oral. No one you've met."

"Who?"

"That's what the meeting with Clemson's about. I'll tell you when you get back from shopping."

"Why can't you tell me now?"

"No time."

She opened her mouth, then closed it with a will. She got a silver all-weather coat off the hall tree, put it on, took gloves and a matching wool scarf from a pocket. Then she steered the stroller into the kitchen. I heard a door slam, a garage door opening on a lifter. I got up, moved the chair closer to the brushed-black console telephone on its little stand, sat, made a quick call, and rested the receiver on its cradle. I took the .38 out of its belt clip and tucked it out of sight between the seat cushion and the arm of the chair on the right side. Then I straightened out my aching leg and rested the cane across it with the crook in my lap.

It wasn't until I focused my attention on the front door that I realized I hadn't heard the garage door closing.

A door opened, not the one I was watching. Rose Canon came in from the kitchen, pushing the stroller with Jeffie in it still asleep. Herbert Clemson followed two paces behind.

I slid my hand down to my side and closed it on the revolver.

"If you come up with anything more than a handful of lint, I'll blow a hole square through mother and child." He showed me the slim Beretta pointed at Rose's lower back.

I brought my hand up empty and laid it in my lap. Rose had stopped. Her gloved hands made tight fists on the stroller's padded handle. "He was waiting for me in front of the garage. He said he was with Homeland Security."

"He was."

The former agent looked as if he hadn't been out of his clothes since Port Sanilac. He had on the same turtleneck, felt-lined boots, and the parka he'd lent me to replace the overcoat I'd ruined crawling around under Cabin Twelve. His cultivated five o'clock shadow had begun to look like noon of the next day. Rose and I seemed to have come at the end of a long string of loose ends.

"Where'd you get Operation Sebastian?" he said. "That's a level-one secret."

"I started at level ten. I kept winning free games."

"What was that you said on the phone about an arrow?"

"I left in such a hurry I forgot it. I'll send it to you in the Milan pen, just the way you sent it to me. You got a little gaudy there. That story you made up about someone sending a golden arrow to Paul Starzek should have been enough. The Order of St. Sebastian. What a ham."

"It was sent. I sent it. Without Jeff Starzek, it had to look like terrorists. Where is he?"

"Flew the coop. You should take his example. Even if you kill us, he's a witness against you. You'll never run him down, even if you manage to talk yourself back into harness."

"I'll run him down. I did it once. What if I don't? He's a fugitive and a known felon. They're calling me in over irregularities in my operational budget, a bookkeeping snafu. Who do you think they'll believe at the finish?"

The baby woke with a shriek. Rose put a hand on him. "Jeffie."

"Jeffie." Clemson whispered. "I never thought he stopped anywhere long enough for that."

I drummed my fingers on my cane. "You didn't kill Paul just to frame Jeff. You can't always crook a man of God so he'll stay crooked."

He struck at the bait a second time. "That man of God black-mailed one of his own parishioners into giving him the stolen paper. He was a retired Treasury clerk with a sore conscience. I kept Paul out of jail and paid him as an informant. I knew he was a bad risk, but I needed the storage space until I set up shop. If I knew he was printing off twenties for himself, I'd have stopped him before he mixed up the stock."

"Meanwhile you made other storage arrangements with Miss Maebelle. Her price was a truck."

"Not just any truck. That's the item that got me in hot water. Sooner or later I'd have had to kill her, too. You saved me that chore. Don't move!" He dug the gun hard into Rose's back.

"I want to pick up my son."

"Let the bastard bawl."

I said, "I took Maebelle off your hands, but it cost you your operation. Burning it up was pure panic on your part."

He smiled his disarming, nongovernment-issue smile. "I've got a big territory. I split the stuff up after Port Huron. There were only a few sheets of the genuine on top of the pile. The rest was newsprint." He took a step back. "I got what I came for: You're an army of one. The buck stops here." The gun came up.

I raised my voice. "Did you get that?"

"Got it." Barry Stackpole's voice had an aluminum edge coming out of the telephone speaker. "Should I play it back?"

I looked at Clemson. "Your call."

The smile stayed on his face. The rest of him seemed to fade away from it like the Cheshire cat. He hesitated with his gun pointed at neither Rose nor me.

She shifted to shield the baby with her body. The movement drew the gun her way.

I threw the cane like a javelin. He ducked to the side, knocking it away with his free arm. The gun fired. Under the report, glass tinkled like bells far away. I scooped up the .38 and shot him in the chest.

The impact of the bullet hurled him into the wall. Baby pictures showered down. There was no blood on his sweater. I'd forgotten about his Kevlar vest.

He spun my way and snapped off another shot, but I was no longer in the rocking chair. I rolled onto my bad leg with all my weight and landed on my chest with the revolver extended in both hands. Barry was shouting all the way from his condo downtown. All he heard was gunshots and breaking glass.

Clemson flung his forearm across Rose's throat and back-pedaled toward the front door. His gun was out of sight behind her. She hung onto the stroller with both hands; it rolled with them, the baby screaming to bring down the ceiling. Clemson got the door open and tried to drag Rose through it, but the stroller jammed tight between the door and the frame. He gave up and ran.

I grabbed at the seat of Oral's big Naugahyde chair and pulled myself to my feet. I still owed Clemson twenty bucks.

A motor roared and climbed to a wail. Asphalt shredded tires in a long, tearing shriek. The shriek ended in a wet thud.

I manhandled Rose out of the way, stroller and all, and lunged out onto the porch holding the gun. Ten yards down the block, Jeff Starzek was stepping down from the driver's seat of the grimy plumber's van. The front end was caved in. The thing that had caved it in lay behind the van, a heap of rags in the street. I went over there.

"Put away the gun," Jeff said. "I hit where I aim."

THIRTY-TWO

The feds wanted to talk to Jeff Starzek, but the crafty little rats they pay to serve their subpoenas got no closer to him than the van he'd left in the middle of the street, which traced back to a small fleet belonging to a plumbing contractor who hadn't noticed it missing. Jeff's name is still on an FBI pickup list, but regional authorities scattered along the Huron shoreline stopped looking months ago. They've got their hands full with a new crop of smugglers since the tax on cigarettes went up again in March.

Rose and Oral Canon sent me a wallet-size studio shot of little Jeffie, a real porker at six months, with his father's big head. My physical therapist tells me I should be walking without the cane in time to attend his first birthday party. I bet him his fee, double or nothing, I'll be rid of the limp by next spring. He didn't take me up on it, but that was just a matter of ethics. I don't expect to get a birthday invitation either, because by then the Canons should have forgotten about me. That's my hope.

Jeff had two minutes with Rose before he fled the sirens on foot. I didn't ask her what they'd talked about.

I logged a lot of time in the Federal Building in Detroit. The investigators were convinced I knew where Herbert Clemson had hidden the rest of the missing Treasury paper, despite the evidence on the tape, and I'm pretty sure they know my current bank balance better than I do, in case I decide to make a large deposit in uncirculated twenties. Clemson's mole in the system, if he had one, never surfaced. A lot of press conferences in front of a lot of flags spent a lot of words talking about terrorist links, but all they really cared about was all that fake money floating around. They pretty much confirmed that when they let the terror alert fall back to yellow.

Barry Stackpole's story broke big in the *Detroit News. The New York Times* bid higher, but he went with his loyalties. Anyway the fee bought him a new hard drive to replace the one he'd destroyed to stay out of federal custody.

Not long ago an envelope came in the mail with the owner's title on the Hurst Olds, endorsed over to me. No note, and no return address, just a Charlottesville, Virginia, postmark, which was probably a blind, since Jeff has contacts in all the major tobacco-growing states. I'll miss the car when it sells, but the hospital's threatening to go to a collection agency, and I'll be glad to get the Cutlass back in the garage. The trunk was empty except for a single carton of Winston's—my brand—and a bottle of Scotch—Old Smuggler, if you want to know. I disposed of the evidence in a week.

ABOUT THE AUTHOR

Loren D. Estleman has written more than sixty novels. He has netted four Shamus Awards for detective fiction, five Spur Awards for Western fiction, and three Western Heritage Awards, among many professional honors. He has written more than twenty Amos Walker mysteries, *Nicotine Kiss* being the eighteenth. He lives with his wife, author Deborah Morgan, in Michigan. For more information visit www.lorenestleman.com.